THE
ICE CRADLE

Chapter One

SATURDAY

IT WASN'T AS warm as I'd hoped. In fact, we were freezing. Back in January, when the director of the Block Island Historical Society had been in touch with me, offering me a week's work in April, on an island I knew to be, well, somewhere vaguely *south* of us, drifts of snow three feet high had bordered the sidewalks and buried the gardens and yards of Cambridge, Massachusetts, where I live with my five-year-old son, Henry. Seven more inches had accumulated during the night, temporarily beautifying the filthy piles of ice, sand, and salt that lined the streets.

As I'd gazed out the window of our second-floor apartment and down at the fluffy white mounds I would soon be shoveling, I didn't go so far as to dream of tropical drinks with little umbrellas or sunblock scented like Polynesian fruit. But I sure didn't imagine that come the last week in April, identified on Henry's school calendar as "spring vacation," my son and I would be riding the Block Island ferry wearing mittens and scarves and three or four layers under our puffy down jackets.

School had been canceled that day in January, leaving me with a familiar dilemma: I could be a great mom or a not-so-great mom. A great mom would seize the moment and take her child sledding at Fresh Pond, then cheerfully agree to host whomever he wanted to ask back to the house for cocoa and popcorn and grilled cheeses, and a serenely supervised afternoon filled with board games and fort building and tent-tunnel making, using sheets and blankets and all the tables and chairs.

The trouble was, I had work to do, and as a freelance book-binder working from home, I couldn't call in sick or take a personal day. Sure, I could just *not work,* but our financial cushion, never plump in the flushest of times, had recently been getting flatter and flatter.

I wasn't sure why. I didn't feel like I was bleeding money, but I hadn't actually had time to sit down and go through all the bills and receipts. And what was the point of that, anyway? It wouldn't change the simple reality: I was obviously earning too little and spending too much.

Many single mothers wouldn't be happy with the agreement I have with Henry's father, but it suits me just fine. Declan is a Boston cop—a detective, to be precise—and by any measure, a first-class dad. He also happens to be married to someone else: Kelly, from whom he was separated when he and I had our little . . . thing. They ended up getting back together. I ended up having Henry. Then Dec and Kelly had two girls of their own, Delia and Nell, whom I adore, and with whom Henry now spends lots of time on weekends and vacations. It's not the simplest of family arrangements, but it's ours, and it works.

Dec and I had the talk about money before I even took Henry home from the hospital, when we were both over-whelmed and completely in shock. At that moment, he would probably have said yes to anything. But I have my pride. I'm healthy, hardheaded, and college educated. No way did I want to get a check every week. If he could just relieve me of the responsibility for our son's health insurance and his college education, I told him, I was sure I could handle everything else. And I have.

But the call from Block Island felt like manna from heaven. The man from the Historical Society, who identified himself as Caleb Wilder, had gotten my name from a bookbinder with whom I'd worked the previous fall, Sylvia Cremaldi. The Society had received a modest grant.

"What kind of grant?" I'd asked.

"To create a new collection, based on a set of historical papers."

"What kind of papers?"

"They have to do with something that happened here about a hundred years ago, a collision at sea."

"Oh!"

"Between a steamship and a schooner," he continued. "The *Larchmont,* the steamer, was making an overnight trip from Providence to New York City in February 1907. There's disagreement about how many people were aboard—the passenger manifest went down with the ship—but the number was somewhere around a hundred and fifty. She was hit by a schooner, the *Harry Knowlton,* and sank in fifteen minutes."

"Wow! What happened to all the people?"

"A lot of them went down with the ship. They were asleep in their berths when the crash happened. The ones who made it up to the deck weren't much better off: the boat was sinking, they were in the middle of a blizzard, and the seas were vicious. Most of the folks who got into the lifeboats were in their nightclothes, so even if their boats didn't capsize, they froze to death."

"That's terrible. Did anyone survive?"

"Nineteen people. Though many were never the same."

"And how does this—what does this have to do with Block Island?"

"The *Larchmont* sank just a few miles from here. A couple of the lifeboats reached us by morning, and the island became the center of the search-and-rescue mission. But there weren't many people to rescue. A few of the bodies washed up on shore the next day, and fishing boats picked up twenty or so more, but the tide carried most of the victims out to sea. All in all, it was a fairly big event for a fairly small island."

"I'll say."

Caleb went on to describe the nature and scale of the project and the salary they were able to offer me, a sum that struck me as more than fair. But he, or someone else, must have thought the pot needed sweetening, given that they were under a very tight deadline to get the work completed. For reasons he didn't explain, the money would not be available until April first, the volumes needed to be bound, and a new website, which someone else was going to design and launch, needed to be up and running by sometime this summer. So I was going to be housed free of charge at a Victorian inn that was under new ownership, a place right on the water called the Grand View Hotel. Meals were included. And all expenses.

"It sounds fabulous," I said. "I'd love to do it."

"Terrific!" cried Caleb. "Wonderful! Now if I could just get some—"

"But you see," I added, interrupting. "It's a little hard for me to travel. I have a son who's five. It's just the two of us."

"Could you bring him?" asked Caleb.

"Well, I could, but I wouldn't get much work done."

Caleb laughed. "I know the feeling. My daughters are eight and six. Does he have a spring vacation?"

"I think so," I said, "but I'm not sure which week."

"If he's on vacation the same week our kids are, the Block Island School runs a full-day drama camp—from nine to six."

"You're kidding."

"Nope. They do a musical every year. I hear this year it's *Grease*."

"He'd love it!"

So that's how, on a Saturday in April, Henry and I happened to be making a bone-chilling journey across Block Island Sound. We'd been warmer that day back in January, when, entirely pleased with myself for coming up with eight thousand dollars' worth of work (well, all right, *saying yes to* eight thousand dollars' worth of work), I blew off the day and took Henry sledding. We brought a pack of people home with us, kids and parents, ten or eleven in all. We got pizzas and movies and beer for the grown-ups, and it was great, even if it did take me three days to get the apartment back to normal.

So in the end, at least that day, I got to be a pretty fair mom. So much of it depends on luck.

———

It was just too cold to stay up on the deck, so we went inside to the snack bar. I was glad that the trip to the island only took an hour, because I couldn't stop thinking of all those people on a boat much like this one, turned out onto the seas in frigid weather. Inside, I tried to talk Henry into having a cup of chili, but he wanted an ice cream bar. I guess that's one of the differences between being five and being twenty-nine: at five, freezing temperatures don't keep you from wanting ice cream.

It being early in the season, there weren't many people on the ferry. There were several ghosts, though, and the one who caught my attention was the dim and faded spirit of an old man, dressed as though he'd spent his earthly days at sea. He wore hip-high waders and an oilskin jacket and cap, and he stood near the captain's booth, his eyes trained on the horizon. At one point, he glanced back at Henry and me, but I didn't make eye contact. I couldn't get through my day if I made myself and my abilities known to every ghost who crossed my path. It would be like stopping every stranger you met on the street and offering to help them with their personal problems—and having them accept. Shortly, the old spirit returned his gaze to the sea, assuming that I, like every other living person he'd come across since he'd passed out of this life, could neither see, nor hear, nor communicate with him.

How wrong he was.

I can see ghosts and talk to them, and I guess I always could. Earthbound spirits, the kind I can see and speak with, are the ghosts of people who have died, but who haven't been able to take their final leave of people, places, or objects they loved in life. Some spirits have special missions to which they're devoted that keep them here in the land of the living: victims of violent crime who want their attackers caught, or parents of young children who just can't bear to walk through that shining doorway and leave their babies behind.

Sometimes I try to think back to when I was really little, and to figure out which of the people in my earliest memories were ghosts rather than living human beings. Some of them certainly were, in those years before Nona, my grandmother, realized that I had inherited her ability to communicate with the departed.

I was four years old when she figured it out. It was an afternoon in June, and I was waiting for my father to come pick me up from my grandmother's house. My mother had died when I was a baby. Pushing me in a stroller, she'd stepped off a curb near my grandmother's house and a car had come out of nowhere, driven by a guy who'd just left a bar across town. In her last act on earth, she pushed me out of the path of the car, or I would probably have died with her.

My father raised me and my brothers, Joe and Jay. He was a champ, Dad was; born in Ireland, he believed in getting on with things. But I think he felt more comfortable hanging out with the boys, so I spent a lot of time with my mother's mother. Having a little girl around probably helped her, too. When my mother died, Nona lost her only child.

Anyway, I remember the afternoon perfectly. Nona was in the kitchen making sauce, and I had the contents of her button box spread out on the dining room table. I loved to play with that box. It was filled with hundreds of buttons: new leather ones still attached to cardboard; loose sets with lavender and pink rhinestones; light yellow buttons of real bone, which made me feel a little shivery and odd as I turned them over and over in my palm.

That was when the man appeared, when I was looking at the bone buttons and wondering what kind of animals they had come from.

"Hello, there," he said, in a language that was not English, but that I could understand perfectly anyway.

I looked up. Where had *he* come from? I hadn't heard the door open or close. I hadn't heard Nona talking to anyone. He looked gray and shadowy, so I knew that he was one of *those* people, that other category of being I had seen and spoken with all my life.

He and I didn't converse out loud. I could hear what he was thinking, and he could hear my thoughts, and it felt perfectly normal for us to communicate in silence. The way I understood it, there were people you spoke with and people you thought with. It was how the world worked, one of those crazy things a kid just had to accept, like daylight and darkness alternating, and the necessity of brushing your teeth before bed. As any child would, I assumed that everyone interacted with two categories of beings: regular people like me and Nona and Dad, and Joe and Jay, and those other ones, the ones you could almost see through.

Toward the end of our exchange, I must have spoken out loud. I remember him asking me if I knew how to play any songs on Nona's piano. I told him that I could play "Twinkle, Twinkle, Little Star" but that what I really wanted was a trumpet.

"What?" Nona called from the kitchen.

"A trumpet," I yelled back, sifting through the box to see if I could find the eighth bone button that would complete the set.

"What about a trumpet?" Nona responded.

"I want one," I hollered.

I heard one of Nona's little laughs, the one that meant, *Dream on.*

At this, the man smiled, but at the sound of her footsteps clicking across the kitchen floor, he faded into the air. When Nona appeared at the doorway, I did what the man had asked me to do: I told my grandmother that Vinny had come to say good-bye.

"Vinny?" Nona said. "What are you talking about?"

"*Vinny,*" I said. I was already annoyed with her about her attitude toward the trumpet, and now she was making me repeat myself. "From *Italy.*"

Nona wiped her hands on her apron and sat down.

"Vinny was here?" she whispered.

That seemed so obvious, I didn't respond right away. Where *was* that last button?

Nona pulled the box away.

"Hey!" I said, pulling it back.

"Anza!" she said sharply. "Look at me!"

She only used that tone of voice when she really meant business. I slumped down in my chair.

"What?" I said.

"What did Vinny say?" she asked me quietly.

"He said you were his favorite girl. He said—Lola made it to age sixteen. Who's Lola?"

"A puppy," whispered Nona, her eyes now looking the way they looked whenever we talked about my mother.

A little while later, when I was still watching out the window for Dad, a phone call came from her cousin in Palermo, confirming what Nona already knew: Vinny Sottosanto, the love of my grandmother's teenage life, whom she had not been allowed to marry, had died earlier that afternoon of a massive stroke.

I didn't know a lot about death, but I knew more than most four-year-olds. I knew for sure than when a person was gone, she was gone.

"But he was here," I said. "I talked to him."

"He was," my grandmother said. "You did."

Chapter Two

A THIN SWATH OF damp, russet sand lay to the right of the Old Harbor ferry landing, across the road and just up the boulevard from the Grand View Hotel. Henry couldn't wait to get across the parking lot and down onto the "beach," so he ran off ahead while I took a deep breath and gazed around at the quiet loveliness of the island. I felt as though we had not so much ridden a ferry to a vacation destination as transported ourselves back a few decades, if not a century. The streets were nearly empty; an old red pickup was the only vehicle on the road. I heard, far off, the low sounds of a radio playing some kind of dinnertime jazz, the sort that went along with Manhattans and taffeta dresses. I could well believe that here, people painting walls and building bookcases might listen to music like that, and not the sordid invective of AM talk-radio shock jocks.

The sky was the dim blue of a robin's egg. I looked back out across the expanse of churning indigo that we had just crossed and offered up a little whisper of gratitude to the Man, or Woman, upstairs. Clouds were scuttering across the line of the horizon as though chased by fierce and invisible breezes.

The sight brought to mind an illustration I remembered from childhood, from a book I had of Aesop's fables. The Wind—in that picture, locked in an epic battle with the Sun—looked just like Santa Claus, with white curls and a beard and huge cheeks puffed out like a tuba player's. Gales of blustery force curled out in swirls from his angry lips.

I heard a shrill squawk, and a nearby seagull hopped into flight. I glanced over.

"Henry?"

"What?" He looked guilty. I saw him drop a couple of pebbles onto the sand.

"Did you hit that bird?" I called.

"No," he said.

I set down our duffel bag and shifted the weight of my backpack. I said nothing.

"I didn't *mean* to," he finally conceded.

"So you *did* throw a stone at it."

"I just wanted to scare him," my son explained.

I sighed and shook my head. "He was only looking for food, honey. How would you like it if you had to fly around all day in the freezing cold trying to find old French fries and pizza crusts and—pieces of dead fish."

His face grew progressively glummer, but he didn't say anything. I persisted.

"Would you like that?"

Henry shook his head.

"Then leave them alone. They aren't hurting you."

Henry kicked at the sand, then turned and sprinted to the side of the road.

"Wait!" I called reflexively, though there wasn't a car in sight.

The Grand View wasn't the largest hotel on Water Street. That honor apparently belonged to the National, an enormous white edifice with a porch that could comfortably seat dozens of sunset-gazing cocktail sippers. The National didn't appear to be open for the season yet, but judging from the sound of power saws and the sight of sheer white curtains blowing out of open windows, the owners were getting it ready.

If the National was the diamond of Water Street, then the Grand View was its pearl. Perched back from the road, it was a quarter of the National's size, and so perfect in proportion and scale that it reminded me of a doll's house.

Some of its weathered shingles had recently been replaced and stood out like too-white teeth, but a few years of seasonal exposure would take care of that. Wide chimneys at either end of the house suggested fireplaces inside, and a cupola just big enough for a person or two rose above the parapet. In Cambridge, "widow's walks" topped plenty of landlocked mansions miles away from the sea. Here, I was sure, the structures were more than ornamental.

Henry flew up the Grand View's front steps and stood on tiptoe, pressed against the front door, straining to reach for the brass knocker. He looked up at me.

"Go ahead," I said.

He clacked it as hard as he could, three, four times. He was gearing up for a fifth when I grabbed his hand.

"Hold on!" I said. "Give them a chance to get here!" I would clearly have to take him for a long, long walk, or something inside was going to get broken.

The door was opened by a voluptuous woman with a cheerful look on her face. Just beyond her, I saw a creature far less full of life and good spirits: the ghost of a girl about six.

"Can I help you?" the woman inquired.

"I'm Anza O'Malley," I said. "Caleb Wilder said I should just—"

"Oh, yes, of course! Sorry! Come in!"

She stepped back to let Henry and me into the foyer, and I realized that she wasn't just curvy, she was pregnant. Seven months or so was my guess.

"I knew you were coming today," she said. "It just slipped my mind."

"That's okay. This is my son, Henry."

"I'm Lauren Riegler," said the woman, closing the door behind us. When she smiled, I noticed a prominent gap between her two front teeth, and for some reason, this made me like her immediately.

"Thanks for having us," I said.

She nodded, then looked down at Henry and smiled. "Hi, Henry. Nice to meet you."

Lately, I had been all over him about his manners, particularly his habit of mumbling and staring at the floor when an adult spoke to him. So you can imagine my happy surprise when he looked Lauren straight in the eye and quietly said, "Nice to meet you, too."

I barely had time to enjoy this little triumph, though, because I became aware of Henry's gaze wandering toward the stairs. I felt that swoopy feeling you get in your stomach when something catches you off guard, and for a moment or two, I could barely breathe.

From the time he was just a baby in my arms, I had wondered whether Henry would grow up to share my gift. Now, it seemed, I had my answer.

Henry could see the ghost.

—

When my child was three and a half, I realized that I could do something that really baffled me: I could read out loud to him, page after page, while my mind was thoroughly occupied with something else. This probably wouldn't surprise a neuroscientist, but it sure shocked me.

It wasn't just books that I knew by heart, either—the Babar chronicles, the rhyming tales of Madeline in that old house in Paris—but stories that were completely new to me. And I wasn't just idly drifting, mentally, while keeping most of my focus on the page. I would find myself three or four pages from the last words I remembered saying, while Henry sat perfectly happy beside me, having detected in my tone and manner no hint whatsoever that I was actually miles, or years, away. I suppose it's like driving on the highway at night and suddenly realizing that you are where you wanted to go, having been virtually unaware of the fact that you were getting there.

This was what the rest of Saturday felt like. To all the world, I must have appeared energetic and engaged, but inside, I was in shock. Something deep in my worldview had shifted, and yet I chatted with Lauren as she showed us to our room, an expansive double with a window overlooking the ocean. Then I took Henry exploring for close to three hours, to the Southeast Lighthouse and to the rocky cliffs I would later learn were called the Mohegan Bluffs. I watched Henry carefully in the area around the lighthouse, which was positively teeming with ghosts. If he saw them at all—and they were everywhere: on the rocks, on the wrought-iron balconies of the lighthouse it-self, on its deep, secluded porch—he paid no real attention. He seemed to care only about the dramatic bluff towering over the crashing waves; specifically, how close I would let him get to the edge.

Later, as I lay on my bed and gazed over at Henry's sleeping form, I turned my thoughts to what I had witnessed upon our arrival at the inn. It wasn't the first time Henry had seen a ghost. Like most children, he'd once had an "imaginary play-mate," an eight-year-old named Silas, the earthbound spirit of a child who had died after having been kicked in the head by a horse. This event took place in a barn that once stood where the house containing our apartment now stands.

Imaginary playmates are actually ghosts. Most kids can see and talk to them until they're six or seven. But eventually, chil-dren are taught the "truth" by adults: that ghosts don't exist. Once children come to believe this, they lose their easy access to the spirit world. Henry was only five, and I wasn't one of those nay-saying adults, but even so, I knew that just because he'd been pals with Silas, that didn't necessarily mean he would see ghosts all his life.

Earthbound spirits retain the personal qualities of the people they were in life, and Silas was a bully. I always figured that that was why he'd gotten kicked in the head in the first place. He'd probably been tormenting the horse. At a certain point, though, I decided that I'd had quite enough of his leading Henry around by the nose and teaching him rude tricks, like how to pull a chair out from under someone who was about to sit down. I cornered Silas one night just after Henry had fallen asleep and informed him that the fun and games were over, and it was high time for him to join his family on the other side. The poor young spirit burst into tears of relief.

I was able to create the white doorway for him, a skill I learned from my grandmother. As far as I can tell, this doorway, which I can imagine and then make real, leads to a shining tunnel to the other side. I can call it up through an act of will and imagination, closing my eyes and focusing on a pinprick of light, and then making the pinprick bigger and brighter. When I open my eyes, the light is burning in the real world, and not just in my imagination. I can project it onto a wall, as a doorway through which a willing spirit can actually walk, leaving our world for the next. I heard Silas joyfully calling out to his parents and sister just before he disappeared into the light.

Then there was an incident last fall. On Columbus Day weekend, Declan and Kelly had taken the kids up to a place Kelly's brother owns on Lake Sunapee. When Dec brought Henry back on Monday night, Henry mentioned something about having heard the crying of a ghost. The story was that a little girl had drowned in the lake long ago and supposedly, her cries could still be heard at night. Henry thought he had heard them.

At the time, Henry was going through a phase in which Declan basically walked on water, so when Henry asked Dec if he believed in ghosts, and Declan didn't respond with a quick and definite yes—explaining instead that he was open-minded on the subject—Henry backed down.

It was hard to tell, in that moment, whether a ghost story told around a flickering campfire had put ideas into Henry's head, or whether he'd actually heard the cries of a ghost. Of course, I could simply have asked him, or put him to a little test at any time in the past few years, but I hadn't. I just hadn't wanted to go there, not yet, not until I really had to.

I remember how I felt when I first came to understand that nobody else I knew, except Nona, could interact with the shadowy people I saw and talked to every day. Not Joe, not Jay, not Daddy. According to Nona, even my mother hadn't been able to communicate with spirits, and for years and years, I felt burdened by my ability. Then again, I would never do to Henry what Nona did to me—trotting me around to funerals and deathbeds, making me part of a sad adult world of loss, sickness, and conflict before I could even ride a two-wheeler. Why Dad let that happen I'll never understand. I suppose he felt that Nona and I were performing good deeds for our fellow beings, and if I wasn't complaining about the whole business, he wouldn't stand in the way. Sometimes I wish he had. It was a strange and lonely way to grow up.

On the subject of Henry's abilities, though, the jury was still out. Spying the little girl on the stairs was not really that different, after all, from having an imaginary playmate. And even if he did presently possess some supernatural ability, the kind that many children have, it still might fade in time.

Deep down, though, I didn't believe it would. The signs were all pointing in the same direction. So in the time between now and that moment when I knew for sure that my son shared my skills, I was just going to have to figure out how to help him make his way through the world without feeling scared or set apart. In that, I suppose, I was pretty much like every other parent on the planet, trying to help their kid navigate through life with whatever hand the child had been dealt.

In the short term, I decided I would handle it the way Henry's pediatrician recommended that I deal with questions about the birds and the bees. Don't offer information, she'd advised me. When they're ready to ask, she'd said, they will, and when they do, answer the question truthfully and simply, but *only* answer the question. If they're developmentally ready for more information, they'll ask for it.

"Really?" I'd said. "So I don't have to get a little speech ready? Check *The Joy of Sex* out of the library?"

"Not yet," she'd said.

The little ghost found us a few hours later. Henry was fast asleep in the bed by the window, and I had just begun to read a book I'd plucked from the bookcase in the hall, the title of which had caught my eye: *How to Cook a Wolf.* It turned out to be a collection of M. F. K. Fisher's musings on life, love, and food: specifically, how she had made the most of quite a bit less of it when the wolf of wartime poverty was at the door.

If I didn't have to make a living, I'd be reading all the time. That's all I did in college, basically, having purposely chosen a school that had few course requirements to stand in the way of my lounging around my dorm room seven days a week, often in my pajamas, reading at the clip of a novel a day. I still exhaust myself on weekends, when Henry goes to Declan's. I often stay up until three or four in the morning, finishing a book I just can't put down.

The little ghost was barefoot and wearing a flimsy nightdress when she drifted into the room. Ghosts are pure energy and can come and go at will, through doors, walls, and windows. They can't do much else, though, which is where Hollywood has gotten it wrong. They can't read minds. They only know about what they have actually seen and heard, so if ghosts aren't present when something is happening or being discussed, they won't know anything about it. They can move a light object, like a sheet of paper or a piece of jewelry, and they sometimes have enough energy to whip up a whirlwind that can scare the daylights out of a person. But that's pretty much where their powers end.

The little ghost didn't do any of those things. She drifted right over to Henry's bed and perched herself beside him, staring down at his sleeping form. I kept my eyes on the page, but since she had her back to me, I was able to steal glances without her realizing that I was doing it.

I caught my breath when she reached out and touched Henry's cheek. He didn't move. She leaned over and blew softly in his face, and he startled and drew away, as though a mosquito were humming around just above him. But he didn't wake up.

Then she came over to me and stood between the beds just staring at my face. I had an awful time keeping up the pretense that I couldn't see her, but I didn't want to talk to her yet. Even without scrutinizing her closely, though, I was aware that she was piteously thin, all knobby knees and elbows. Her hair hung down in two tangled braids, and it was all I could do not to reach out and fold her into my arms. She looked wretched, the poor little wraith. I *had* to do something to ease her suffering and loneliness as soon as I possibly could.

But not yet.

It was selfish, I knew, but the time had come for me to face up to the question of Henry's supernatural abilities—or lack thereof. Until this afternoon, I hadn't really needed, or wanted, to know. But now I did. And I couldn't just raise the subject with him in a casual conversation.

Well I *could*, but it's complicated. Henry doesn't know about my abilities with ghosts. I've been waiting for the perfect time to tell him, and it hasn't come. If it turns out that Henry has *not* inherited my abilities, I'd just as soon wait until he's a little older before I burden him with the awareness of what his mother can see and do, not to mention the prohibition against talking about it with anyone but me and his dad.

On the other hand, if I *have* passed down my abilities, and Henry is slowly growing into his own comfortable acceptance of them, I'd like to follow that doctorly advice and answer questions when, and only when, they're asked. I don't want to overwhelm the poor kid with a flood of information he may be way too young to handle.

What happened next made my heart thump wildly, and I was afraid that this involuntary burst of cardiac energy would somehow give me away to the little ghost, for she had stunned me by crawling into my lap! She was as light as a June breeze, making no impression at all on the blanket that covered my legs. If I hadn't been able to see her, I would have had no idea that she had curled herself in between my book and me, like a child being read to at bedtime.

I could feel the hairs on the back of my neck prickling up, fairly sizzling with the nearness of her energy, but I forced myself to relax back against the pillow. I slowly let out a long, deep breath, one I hadn't been aware I was holding.

I wanted to close the book, reach over, and switch out the light. But she was small, sad, and entirely alone in the world. I turned the page.

Chapter Three

THE BREAKFAST BUFFET was embarrassingly elaborate. There was granola that looked homemade, a bowl of fresh cantaloupe cut up with strawberries, three varieties of yogurt, three of bagels, two of English muffins (white and whole wheat), and a loaf of soda bread that still felt warm.

Lauren appeared at the dining room door, her cheeks even pinker than they were yesterday, probably from the heat and bustle of getting this feast together.

"Good morning!"

Henry was transfixed by the sight of the buffet table but managed a distracted "Hi."

"Coffee?" she asked me.

"Please."

She disappeared into the kitchen as Henry stood paralyzed by the choices before him. In a moment, she was back with a gleaming silver pitcher. She filled my cup with the rich, amber fluid as the aroma of freshly brewed French roast, my favorite, permeated the room.

"Now," she said, parking the pitcher beside my place setting.

"Would you like some eggs? An omelette? Or I could make pancakes, or homemade waffles."

"Waffles!" Henry shouted before I could impose restraint.

"That's way too much work," I said.

"Please?" he begged. "I love waffles!"

"Then waffles you shall have!" said Lauren. "I've got a brand-new waffle iron. I have to break it in sometime."

"All right," I said, "but *just* for today." I turned to Henry. "Only because it's our first day, *and* Sunday. Starting tomorrow, we'll be back to——"

"I know, I know," he interrupted impatiently.

I can lay it on too heavily sometimes, ruining, for example, the exceedingly rare and genuine pleasure of a stop at McDonald's with a lecture on chain restaurants' driving out mom-and-pop diners or on the evils of factory farming. Henry was warning me to zip it, before I managed to ruin this, and he was right.

In the end, I was glad he had lobbied for waffles. They were irresistible, even before I smeared a shocking amount of butter across their tops and watched it melt into little square pools. The maple syrup was real, too, sparing my poor child a lecture on the treachery inherent in corn syrup's being chemically flavored to taste like maple. We ate more than it was polite to eat, but in our defense, Lauren practically begged us to let her finish up the batter.

———

We had been sitting on the porch watching a two-sailed sloop glide gracefully along in the water, but the wind picked up suddenly and turned right toward us, driving us back inside.

Earlier, Henry had discovered a television and a collection of DVDs in one of the rooms off the main sitting area, and I was happy to hunker down with him for a couple of hours before dinner, assuming we could agree on a movie. We'd already had a long walk, followed by a short nap, followed by a shell-collecting expedition up the beach. On a Sunday in the off-season, on a quiet island in New England, there isn't much else to do.

"This one?" Henry asked, holding up *The Crying Game*. He was attracted, no doubt, to its dramatic black-and-white cover, which featured a smoking gun and a sultry femme fatale.

"No way."

"Why not?"

"That's for grown-ups." I reached instead for Hitchcock's *The Birds* and flipped it over to see if it had an MPAA rating. Personally, I'd never found the movie to be all that frightening, but most people obviously did. I didn't want to plant the seeds of any nightmares. Fortunately, a Three Stooges collection tumbled onto the rug, and Henry snatched it up.

"Perfect!" I said. "You'll love this!" He pried his feet out of his sneakers and climbed up onto the couch. I plopped down into the chair by the window.

Lauren came in about half an hour later, just as Moe, installed by a group of businessmen as the dictator of "Moronica," was pulling off an eerie parody of Hitler.

"Cup of tea?" she asked.

"That'd be great."

When five thirty came, she and I were sitting at the big oak table in her kitchen, and I was peeling carrots for our supper. From the laughter that still echoed through the empty downstairs rooms, Henry had neither lost interest in the shenanigans of Moe, Larry, and Curly nor budged from his spot on the couch.

Lauren and I had gotten several things out of the way. Henry and I weren't going to be served in the dining room anymore. I found it awkward to be sitting there like the grande dame while Lauren waited on us. I assured her that we'd be perfectly happy to have normal meals in the kitchen, and surprisingly, without too much protest, she agreed. She said she hated eating alone when Mark, her husband, who wrote articles on economic issues for the *Boston Globe* and the *Wall Street Journal*, had to leave the island on business, as he was going to have to do this week.

I didn't want her to clean our room every day, either. I told her we'd be glad for fresh towels on Tuesday or Wednesday, but we could make our own beds and pick up after ourselves. She agreed to that, too. She and Mark were trying to conserve energy and water, and daily washing of all the sheets was shamefully wasteful of both.

"How long have you lived here?" I asked.

"A little over a year."

"Are you from the island?"

"No, I grew up in Vermont, outside of Burlington. Mark and I met at Middlebury."

"How'd you come to be running an inn?"

"I was dragged, kicking and screaming. No, not really. I told him I'd give it five years."

"Fair enough," I said. "It's a beautiful place."

"The island or the house?"

"Both, but I meant the house."

"Thanks. We still have a lot of work to do, but we're getting there. Mark's aunt wasn't really able to keep it up."

"It's a family place?"

"Mark's great-grandparents built it in 1901. It was their summer home."

"Wow!"

"Yeah, I know. Alby—Mark's great-grandfather; his name was Albert Riegler—came from a family of Austrian bankers. He ran their New York office. He and his wife and kids lived on Park Avenue and spent their summers here on the island."

"When did it become an inn?"

"We got all the permits after we bought it. Eva, Mark's aunt, ran it for years as a kind of boardinghouse, after the family lost all their money in the stock market crash in 1929. Folks would stay for weeks at a time, even the whole summer. But it was always people they knew, extended family, friends of friends. You couldn't just call up and reserve a room.

"After Eva died, in the seventies, the house was passed down to Mark's parents and uncle. They used to come here a lot, especially when Mark and his sister were growing up, but now Mark's parents are retired and living down in Florida, and Uncle Pete's out in Santa Barbara. He rarely comes back East. The place was falling apart, but Mark had always dreamed of turning it into an inn."

"I wouldn't be able to do it," I said. "I don't have the temperament."

"Yeah, well, we'll see whether *I* do. It's been a lot harder than I expected."

"How so?" I asked. "The renovations?" *That* I could imagine. The floors had all been refinished, and the rooms freshly painted and papered with beautiful William Morris–style wallpapers. All the new hardware, from the bathroom fixtures to the hinges on the doors and cabinets, looked historically accurate.

"No, that was the fun part," Lauren said.

"Then what?" I asked.

She took the bowl of carrot peelings, stood up, and went over to the sink. She emptied the peels into a stainless-steel compost pail on the counter, then stood staring out the window overlooking the backyard.

"The reservations aren't exactly pouring in. The place has a—reputation," she finally said.

"Let me guess," I offered. "People think it's haunted."

She wheeled around. "How'd *you* know?"

"Just a hunch," I said. "A historic inn on an island? Come on, it's right out of Agatha Christie."

Lauren grinned. "I suppose it is. I can't believe I'm telling you this. You're not going to want to stay here."

"I don't have a problem with ghosts," I said.

"Really?"

"Really. My grandmother was kind of—psychic."

Lauren nodded but looked unconvinced. "It goes way, way back," she said. "There was a novelist who used to come here every summer, a guy named Antony Wicklow. This was back when Eva owned the place. He was a 'confirmed bachelor' who lived in New York during the winters and came here every summer. He always stayed in the same room, that back room on the second floor."

"The one with the green wallpaper?"

"Yeah. Anyway, he became convinced that the room was haunted."

"By whom?"

"Who convinced him?" Lauren asked.

"No," I answered. "Who was supposedly haunting it?"

"The ghost of a man in his fifties, who apparently looked

like Abraham Lincoln, and the spirit of a woman in her late thirties or early forties. Her hands were always pressed to her ears. Wicklow claimed to see them night after night, often at the foot of his bed. And he wrote a bestseller about it, a pretty spooky novel in which the ghosts end up smothering a couple of the boarders.

"People figured out that this was the place described in the book and nobody wanted to come here anymore. And at just about that time, a storm brought down one of the chimneys, which some people took as evidence."

"Of what?"

"I don't know, bad supernatural karma. Eva was hanging on by a thread, and some of her regulars, folks who usually came here for the full season, just up and cancelled. It really put the nails in the coffin."

"Of the boardinghouse."

"Yeah."

"What was the name of the book?" I asked.

"*Inn of Phantoms.*"

"Never heard of it."

"There's a copy around here somewhere. I'll find it for you."

I paused and took a deep breath. "And what do *you* think? Do you believe there are ghosts?"

"I really don't know. Some weird things have happened, in that room and one other. Mark thinks I'm off my rocker, or at least in a highly suggestible state, but I swear I can feel something in there. The air seems charged, like it's full of electricity, and when we were doing the work on those rooms, we kept having problems with the simplest things. I know it sounds crazy, but it was like someone—some*thing*—didn't want the room to change."

"You're not crazy," I said, trying to make her feel better. "They definitely exist."

"Ghosts? You think so?"

"I know so."

"On account of your grandmother?"

"Yeah." The time might come for me to level with Lauren about my own experiences and skills, but first I wanted to do a little private investigating. The ghosts that inspired the novel might be long gone by now. I certainly hadn't encountered them. The little ghost girl would be gone soon, too. I would see to that as soon as I learned a little more about Henry's relationship with the supernatural world.

"But that book was written so long ago," I said. "You'd think it would be forgotten by now."

"I wish. And we did something really stupid."

"What was that?"

Lauren let out a deep sigh and rolled her eyes. "Mark got a call from *The Ghost Detectives.*"

"The TV show? Oh, no!" The "ghost detectives" were two Australian guys who hosted a reality show on haunted buildings and spaces. They came in after dark with infrared cameras and never failed to "prove" the presence of spirits, usually "evil" spirits. I had seen the show a number of times—we don't have cable, but most of my friends do—and I'd read a lot about it. The ghost detectives never let a little matter like the truth get in the way of a gripping episode.

"They asked if they could do a show on us," Lauren went on. "We saw it as free publicity and thought it might be a way to lay all the old rumors to rest. Prove that there *aren't* any ghosts at the Grand View."

"Have you ever seen the show?"

"I have now. We should have done a little more research before we said yes."

"Can't you cancel?"

"We tried. They won't let us out of it."

"When are they coming?"

"Saturday."

"*Saturday*? This coming Saturday?"

"Mark has to go into Boston for some meetings. They're going to meet him there and come back with him Saturday morning. And if they find anything—"

"—which they always do," I interrupted. The show was completely formulaic. Not finding ghosts would be like the couples on *Wife Swap* getting along or Supernanny visiting a family with well-behaved children.

"I know, I know," said Lauren. "And they'll blast it all over the cable universe. Nobody will stay here but crackpots and kooks."

"It could be really great for business."

Lauren didn't smile. "Yeah, or it could scare it away." Her eyes looked tired and sad. She seemed like a different person than the one I had met yesterday.

"Maybe I can help you," I said.

"Thanks, but what can *you* do?"

"You might be surprised."

Chapter Four

MONDAY

THE BLOCK ISLAND school, a jaunty new brick and shingle edifice, served all the young scholars on the island, from age five to age eighteen. As Henry and I approached the building early on Monday morning, dozens of kids, some still small enough to be wearing OshKosh overalls and others sporting Goth-style makeup and downy upper lips, could be seen making their way to the island's only school—ambling in clumps of three or four, speeding on bikes, hopping out of the cars and trucks their parents had pulled in to the school's circular drop-off area.

The morning had gone smoothly enough, eased along by Henry's elation at the fact that he didn't to have to wear his school uniform: chinos, blue oxford shirt, navy blue clip-on tie.

"What?" I said, laughing. "You thought you'd have to wear your *uniform*?"

"You said it was school!"

"No, honey, I said it was *at* a school. You think I'd make you go to *school* on your vacation? Come on! It's more like—camp! It'll be really fun!"

"It will?" His hair was all cowlicky. He beamed up at me, prepared to believe just about anything I said.

I squashed the impulse to get all breathless and enthusiastic. I hoped he'd have more fun than I would have had doing this at his age, but things could go either way. I would have hated walking into a huge, strange school filled with as many big loud kids as with kindergarteners, having to be on my own all day long without a pal to eat lunch with, not daring to ask where the bathrooms were. I didn't want to promise Henry that he'd have fun, because he very well might not, not today at least, and maybe not at all. Fun, sadly, was not the primary purpose of this arrangement.

I could feel his apprehension kicking in as we approached the school. He started to lag behind me, eyeing the chummy clusters of kids, and beginning to bite his lower lip, a sure sign that he was getting the jitters. I paused on the steps, then took him by the hand and led him over to a bench at the edge of the playground.

I adjusted his scarf and attempted to subdue a stubborn cowlick.

"I don't want to go," he said.

"You have to, sweetie. Because I have to go to work."

"I can come with you," he announced, as though alerting me to this possibility for the very first time.

I shook my head.

"Listen," I said. "All these kids hang around together *all* the time. Every day, summer and winter. They are going to be *so* excited to meet somebody new—you!"

He looked up at me, then back at the kids streaming up the steps. A burly teenager wearing a Clash T-shirt chose just this moment to put one of his friends into a headlock.

"They're going to have so many questions for you," I said, trying to distract him.

"Like what?" he asked, eyes glued to the tussling teenagers.

"Like—about the T. They don't have subways here! I bet a lot of these kids have never, ever been on a subway! They might want to know all about it."

Henry made no response.

"And—the Freedom Trail! Paul Revere's house! Think of all the things you have in your hometown! Because even though we live in Cambridge, *you* were born in Boston!"

"And the Children's Museum," he mumbled.

"Right! And those gondolas down by the science museum! They won't believe we have gondolas in Boston. Gondolas aren't anywhere but Venice!"

"Yeah," he said quietly as I glanced at my watch. I had to go. Soon.

I stood up, but Henry didn't budge. When I looked down, I could tell he was about to cry.

I scooped him up, crossed the lawn, and walked firmly up the steps as he buried his face in the collar of my coat. There was only one way to do this—fast. That much I had learned, during what had felt like the endless nursery-school years. Long, bargaining good-byes might work for some kids, but they never worked for us. Sending the message that I was reluctant to depart made Henry wonder if there wasn't a very good reason for that, leaving him feeling even more worried and uncertain than he'd originally felt. The current situation might not improve if I continued to project confidence and excitement, but it would surely deteriorate if I didn't.

I checked Henry into his classroom, met his teacher, Michelle, who seemed barely out of her teens, made sure he was on the prepaid list for lunch and snacks, and verified my contact information. I hugged him, stood up, and left. I didn't turn around—I couldn't—but at least he didn't come after me, wailing and clinging to my leg.

I felt heartsick all the way to the Historical Society. You can console yourself with all kinds of platitudes about kids being resilient and able to adapt. You can remind yourself of how lucky your child is to be spending time like this, whether he realizes it right now or not. But it still feels awful to tear yourself away from an anxious little person who doesn't want to be left.

As I strode briskly toward the road, pretending to be a happy, well-adjusted mom looking forward to her day at the office, I wanted nothing more than to turn around, walk back, gather Henry into my arms, phone Caleb Wilder, and call this whole thing off. Instead, I sniffed, dabbed at my watery eyes, and kept on walking.

Caleb reminded me of a few guys I'd met since I moved to the East Coast, guys with Ivy League educations who'd decided to take a pass on finance and law and work in what were, at least formerly, genteel professions: teaching in prep schools, working in publishing and journalism; running discreet trusts and historical societies. I knew nothing about Caleb's background, but he wore horn-rimmed, literary-looking glasses, Top-Siders, a starched white shirt, and a now rumpled, though clearly expensive, sports jacket.

I imagined there was a very large sailboat in the picture.

The Historical Society was located on the first floor of a sprawling white farmhouse on Old Town Road. A plaque beside the main entrance informed me that the unassuming structure had been built in 1850, but the house seemed remarkably well maintained, right down to what looked like the original windows: four panes over four on the lower level, and six over six up above. Hydrangea bushes lined the long porch, which ended at an enormous Rose of Sharon hedge. I imagined it was stunning in summer.

"How'd the drop-off go?" Caleb asked, showing me into his office. "I saw you two there on the bench."

"Not so hot," I said.

"Yeah, I got that impression. Kara, my eight-year-old, she couldn't wait to get there. But not Louisa. It was a battle just getting her out the door."

"But you like the program," I prompted anxiously. "I mean, the people are good."

"Oh sure, yeah. You'll see. Kara went last year, which is why she was all revved up. They did *Guys and Dolls*, and she had a great time."

"*Guys and Dolls*? How'd they manage *that*, with all the little kids?"

"Well, the high school students get all the main roles, obviously, but anybody who wants to be onstage gets a part. Or they can make costumes or paint sets—they keep them busy, that's for sure. Your son—what's his name?"

"Henry."

"Henry. He probably won't want to leave when you go to pick him up."

"Let's hope so. Anyway . . . !"

"Anyway. So. You're all settled in at the Grand View?"

"It's a beautiful place. Thanks so much."

Caleb nodded. "They've done a great job on it. Nice couple."

"Very nice."

"I knew Mark from way back when. He's younger than me, but he was around every summer. Though I was surprised when he took the old place on. I really was."

"How so?"

"The house was a disaster, and not just cosmetically. The foundation was literally crumbling. A number of developers had scoped it out over the years, but they ended up walking away. It would have been cheaper to tear the whole thing down and start from scratch—in fact, that's what a couple of them wanted to do—but the family wouldn't agree to it."

"I'm glad they didn't."

"Everybody's glad. And they've really done it right, Mark and Lauren have."

"Have you been inside?"

"They had an open house about a month ago." Caleb shook his head. "Very impressive. You know, a lot of times people overdo it, take a simple, vernacular structure and gussy it up so much that it ends up looking like a Trump Tower."

I smiled.

"Anyway," he continued, "so here we are. I was thinking that you might want to spend today just reading and getting your head around all the materials we're going to work with. Then we could meet first thing tomorrow and make a plan."

"Okay," I said. "Do you have any ideas about how you want this done?"

"One or two," Caleb replied, "but I'd love to get your opinion. I was thinking it might be sort of interesting to formalize a timeline and bind the documents according to when they were important, to when they figured in the course of the week."

"That could work," I said. "So you mean, instead of keeping

all the similar items together, the—I don't know, what?—telegrams, search-and-rescue records?"

"Eyewitness statements, medical documents, all the reports from New Shoreham and Sandy Point—those were the life-saving stations, at the two lighthouses. They were the centers of all the activity."

I nodded, though he was beginning to lose me.

"So," Caleb went on, "there would be two ways for a person to come at the material. The website, which a fellow up in Boston is putting together, will be very straightforward, with all the documents listed and catalogued, easily downloaded. But here in the building, we'd also have a narrative version, for someone who wanted to leaf through books and get a sense of how the events transpired in real time."

"That makes sense," I said. "Who actually comes in here?"

"People here for the weekend, or on vacation. They wander in, especially on rainy days. They're not writers or academics, they're just curious. Most have never heard of the *Larchmont*."

"So this way," I said, "they'd be able to sit down and read the documents like a book, or flip through."

"Precisely. We want the materials to be user-friendly, for the average person who just drops by. We get a lot of retirees coming through. It's the nature of the island, really: you don't visit Block Island if you want your vacation to be a thrill a minute. People who come here tend to appreciate the past and be interested in it."

"Sounds good," I said. "I've brought some supplies, but I didn't want to order any materials until I knew exactly what we'd need. I'll go online and have some samples sent. We can see what looks and feels right with the documents. You get FedEx here, right?"

Caleb laughed and nodded. "It only *feels* like the nineteenth century."

The stories I read would stay with me for days.

At eleven o'clock at night in February 1907, as a fierce winter storm was whipping up the waters between Block Island and Watch Hill, Rhode Island, a schooner named the *Harry Knowlton*, packed with coal it was transporting from South Amboy, New Jersey, to Boston, rammed its bow deep into the side of a steamship called the *Larchmont*. Up to two hundred people were aboard the ferry. Nineteen survived. All of the children on the ship were lost.

A massive steamer with three passenger decks, the *Larchmont* had left Providence that evening on an overnight journey to New York City. A bitter wind was blowing in from the northwest as the vessel made her way through Narragansett Bay, but the ferry didn't encounter the full force of the icy gale until it rounded Point Judith and headed directly into Long Island Sound.

The boat's captain, who had spent the evening in the pilothouse and had just steered the vessel safely into open seas, was in his quarters, getting ready for bed. Startled to hear several sharp blasts of the steamer's warning whistle, he raced back to the pilothouse. The three-masted schooner had been spotted. It was headed directly toward the *Larchmont*.

The captain and his quartermaster blew the whistle again, and when the schooner failed to turn or slow down, they both grabbed the wheel and frantically tried to alter the *Larchmont*'s course, hoping to avert a catastrophe. Seemingly propelled by the storm's powerful winds, the schooner rammed into the side of the steamer.

The impact of the collision drove the sailboat's bow nearly halfway through the *Larchmont*. For a few minutes, the schooner plugged the hole it had opened in the ship's side. But soon, roiling seas separated the two vessels, and water rushed into the steamer.

The flooding could not be contained in the area of the ship that had been damaged. Frigid water poured over the cargo and into the hold, and when it reached the boiler that powered the vessel, great clouds of steam exploded into the air, blocking many passageways and staircases. The steam stranded the captain in the pilothouse and disabled the ship's communication equipment. The captain now had no way to communicate with the crew, to direct the response to the crisis.

The steam also killed scores of passengers on the port side of the boat. Up to a third of the people aboard that night may never have been aware of the accident, so quickly were they burned to death in their beds.

Other passengers, thrown from their bunks by the force of the impact, rushed to the decks in panic, not taking the time to bundle themselves in warm clothing. At first, terror kept them from even feeling the cold. But within moments, standing on deck in the sleet, wind, and ice, they began to freeze. And they couldn't return to their rooms, which had by then been flooded. With nearly a hundred people on deck and scores of men, women, and children trapped, dead, or dying below in their sleeping quarters, the *Larchmont* began to sink. All of this happened in about ten minutes.

Officers ordered the lowering of the lifeboats, while crew members attempted, for the most part successfully, to control the chaos and panic on deck. But already, the ears, noses, and fingers of passengers and crew members alike were turning blue with frostbite. By the time the lifeboats were in the water, just minutes later, cold had so affected the victims that they were not able to walk—they could barely stumble to the bobbing vessels. Wails of agony rose up from the boats into the frigid night air.

Conditions deteriorated further in the lifeboats, which had oars, and the rafts, which did not and had to be towed. Stormy waves sent sprays of foam and mist over the passengers, most wearing only their nightclothes, encasing the victims in layers of ice. The lights of Fishers Island, roughly five miles away, were visible on the horizon, so every vessel headed that way. But the lifeboats were weighted down by too many passengers, and by the additional burden of towing the rafts. Cold sapped the strength of the men at the oars, who were coated in layers of ice. The rafts soon broke away from the lifeboats towing them. They slowly drifted away, carrying their doomed passengers with them.

One victim, driven insane by the agony he endured in one of the lifeboats, committed suicide by cutting his own throat. Other passengers in his lifeboat, too dazed or weak to interfere, looked on vacantly as though the act made perfect sense. Several of the dead were later found with their hands frozen to their ears.

The first lifeboat reached Block Island at daybreak. The feet of the survivors were so badly frozen that the victims had to be carried to the lifesaving station. News of the catastrophe quickly spread from house to house across the island, and islanders flocked to the waterfront to try to help. Fishermen went out in their boats, and islanders waded into the icy surf to drag the lifeboats and victims to shore. Later in the day, it was bodies that drifted, one by one, to the shore, carried by tides that later turned and swept countless other victims out to sea.

Seventeen survivors were taken into the cottages and houses closest to where the boats had landed. Many of the victims seemed not even to realize that they had reached land, nor to care. Forty-five frozen bodies were recovered from the ocean and laid out in rows at the lifesaving stations at Sandy Point and New Shoreham. In the following days, two more survivors and ten more victims were brought to shore.

A week later, with her flag at half-mast, a sister ship of the *Larchmont*, the *Kentucky*, arrived at Block Island to transport eighteen of the nineteen survivors and forty-nine bodies back to Providence. One survivor refused to set foot on another ship. Over the following days and weeks, twenty-two more bodies were given up by the sea.

Chapter Five

Henry was painting a car when I arrived at the school. Not a picture of a car, an actual automobile.

It had been donated, I later learned, by a summer resident who hadn't used it in thirty years and had recently sold his vacation cottage, necessitating the cleaning out of the barn on his property. An old Dodge Dart that didn't strike me as anything Danny Zuko and his gang of slick hot-rodders would have gone anywhere near, it was nonetheless parked on drop cloths on the stage of the school theater. How they got it in there I wasn't quite sure; there must have been loading doors in the back. Henry and a dozen other kids of various ages, wearing extra-large T-shirts to cover their clothes, were painting the beige body a brilliant crimson, attempting to avoid what looked like a flame pattern marked off near the wheels in masking tape.

Henry caught sight of me smiling and waving but redoubled his concentration on the painting. I was clearly meant to understand that he was awfully busy with important work and couldn't drop his paintbrush this very second just because I happened to have arrived. Thinking of the note on which we had parted that morning, I sighed with relief and sank down into one of the seats. I was more than overdue for a stretch like this, given how many times he's had to wait for me to finish something to do with paper and glue.

The stage was abuzz. Another painting crew was working on a sign that read "Burger Palace." A third set of kids was assembling an enormous sculpture at the back of the space. They seemed to be attaching balls of Styrofoam to a fixed dome about four feet wide, using spokes of various lengths. The overall effect was vaguely atomic, though I couldn't imagine what the piece was going to be used for.

There was only one ghost in the audience, which was odd. This probably had to do with the newness of the building, because theaters—especially the ornate old movie palaces and opera houses—are usually filled with ghosts. These are often the spirits of people for whom real life was a dim, pale shadow of what transpired onstage, actors and actresses whose most precious living moments occurred behind the footlights. Sometimes, they can't bring themselves to bid good-bye to their stages and dressing rooms, where they were nightly transformed into Medea or King Lear, and where the evenings culminated in roses and applause.

Out in the foyer and drifting through the aisles, I often see the ghosts of ushers. Elderly and alone in the city, many had lived in boardinghouses and taken their meals in communal dining rooms with other men going through life alone or working to earn money for their families, who were living elsewhere. Stage managers, ballet masters, musicians—the walls of old theaters enclose the ghosts of them all.

The ghost at the back of this theater, though, had to be attached to one of the children. She must have been a grandmother or a great-aunt, for she didn't emanate disturbance or despair. Her long gray hair, pinned into a coil at the nape of her neck, and the worn wool cardigan held in place on her shoulders by a sweater chain gave her the appearance of a strict and spinsterish schoolmarm. But she smiled warmly and calmly, her attention engaged by the activity up front.

I loved seeing the kids all caught up in their tasks. Walking back to the Grand View a half hour later, I got the lowdown from Henry and began to understand how the week had been organized to accommodate kids of all ages.

Henry had opted to be a member of the "car crew." This meant he spent half his day working on the transformation of the donated automobile into a *Grease*-worthy hot rod. First they were painting it red—two coats, he explained authoritatively. On Wednesday, when the second coat was dry, they would work on the flame pattern, and on Thursday they would attach the decorative details that were being built in the woodshop: hubcaps with spokes and an oversized hood ornament shaped like wings in flight. These would be spray-painted silver.

The second big chunk of his day was devoted to learning a dance number, a preview of which I was treated to on the sidewalk. *Oh dear*, I thought. I had witnessed Henry's attempt to master some steps the previous month, for a Saint Patrick's Day assembly at St. Enda's, and I wasn't optimistic about his future on the dance floor. Though his moves had been breathtakingly enthusiastic, they bore little relationship to the music, a fatal combination for anyone being danced with. Whoever was choreographing Henry's dance was going to have their work cut out for them.

That left two recesses and lunch, all of which had apparently gone fine.

"What did you have for lunch?" I asked.

"Hamburgers."

"Hamburgers!" Even at Henry's school, a throwback to the kind I went to, parents pushing for local and organic sourcing of school lunches had made the weekly hamburger obsolete. While I knew this was all to the good, I thought back fondly on my own favorite grade school lunch: a bit of tuna swimming, unaccompanied by so much as a morsel of celery or onion, in a sea of mayonnaise and served in a white hot dog bun. For crunch, we packed potato chips in with the tuna.

"And Jell-O," he added.

"Did you meet any nice kids?"

He shrugged.

"Do you have a partner for this dance?"

"Ellen."

I held my tongue. Too many questions all at once usually caused him to shut down.

"Hmmm," I said as he took aim at a stone on the sidewalk and sent it into the dune grass with a resounding kick. We walked for a bit in silence.

"She cut her hair," he finally announced. "That's why it's kinda crooked."

"I see."

"Her mom was mad."

"I'll bet."

"Would you be mad if I did that?"

"I don't know. I wouldn't like you pointing the scissors at your eyes, but hey, it's your hair."

"So would you or wouldn't you?" He kicked another stone.

"It's a little different with boys, honey."

"How come?"

"Well, because boys usually wear their hair shorter, so if it looks sort of goofy, it doesn't take long to grow out."

"Ellen had pigtails," Henry said, shooting me a sly glance.

"Ooh," I said, suppressing an urge to laugh.

"Yup," he said. "And now she doesn't."

He looked over at me, and I couldn't help but smile.

"Oops," I said.

He let out a tickled whoop.

Mark, Lauren's husband, had taken to Henry as soon as he met him the previous evening. I'd figured this had to do with impending fatherhood, but it still had been sweet to see the way Mark had drawn Henry out with questions about the ferry and his life back in Cambridge.

We had no sooner reached the Grand View than Mark appeared on the front steps and announced that he was heading out in his truck. A buddy of his had caught a haul of striped bass off Ballard's Beach and had offered us some for supper. "Would Henry like to come along for the ride?"

"Okay by me," I said. Though I had only met Mark two days ago, I hadn't a reservation in the world about sending Henry off with him. Mark was warm, funny, and, though I tried hard not to notice, cute. He had sandy brown hair as straight as hay and favored carpenter's pants, plaid flannel shirts, and work boots.

"Just be back in time for supper," I added.

"We're *getting* the supper, Ma," Henry said.

"Oh, right," I responded, leading him on. "Duh!"

Henry grinned. "Duh!"

It was that beautiful time near dusk, when the sinking sun

throws horizontal beams onto the tops of trees and houses and everything seems bathed in a coral tint. They walked to Mark's green pickup, parked in the driveway, and Mark helped Henry buckle himself in. Henry waved as Mark backed the truck out of the driveway, and they disappeared down Water Street.

I was glad for a bit of time to myself. I thought about sitting on the porch for a while, savoring the loveliness of the light, but the winds were chilly, and I had spent the entire day reading about people freezing to death. I wanted a hot bath.

Unfortunately, I never got one.

As I climbed the stairs and headed down the hallway, I heard odd creaking sounds coming from the back bedroom. My first thoughts were of Lauren—was she in there? If so, was she all right? I tiptoed down the hall and listened. The creaking was regular and rhythmic in nature.

My next thoughts were of the ghosts described in *Inn of Phantoms:* the one that looked like Abraham Lincoln and the one with her hands pressed to her ears. If they were here now, maybe I could move them along before the ghost detectives arrived with their quasi-bogus ghost sensors. Before I could stop myself in the interests of the hot bath I so longed for, I had grasped the glass doorknob and eased open the door.

The ghost, who bore no resemblance whatsoever to Abraham Lincoln, was sitting in a bentwood rocker by the window. I should have played dumb at that point and pretended not to see him, as I pretended not to see every other ghost I didn't feel like getting involved with, but politeness kicked in. I slipped quietly into the room and closed the door behind me.

The phantom paused in his rocking and stood up. He was less than six feet tall, probably five ten or eleven, and he wore a sack coat over a matching vest and a dotted necktie with a starched, formal collar. Everything seemed too big on him, as though even before he'd been taken in death, he had shrunken away from the robust outlines of the man who'd been measured for the suit.

"Who are you?" I whispered.

He registered a look of surprise and appeared to struggle for words. Ghosts are so used to coexisting with humans who can neither see nor hear them that they're often shocked into silence when I speak to them directly.

"Why are you here?" I asked.

"You are able to see me?" he whispered. "Hear my words?"

I nodded. I detected a slight accent.

"But how?"

"Search me." I shrugged and smiled. "My name is Anza. Anza O'Malley."

"But I have never met anyone who—"

"I know. There aren't too many of us around. Are you a family member?"

"I am," he answered quietly.

"What's your name?"

"Baden. Baden Riegler."

"So you're Mark's—"

"Alby was my brother. This was his home." Baden's accent transformed the sentence into: "Dis vas iss home."

"Mark's great-grandfather."

"Yes."

I had to think a minute. I wasn't quick at sorting out family trees, once it got to branches of in-laws and cousins first removed, but this genealogical line was direct enough. Baden had been Mark's great-great-uncle.

"It's a beautiful place," I said.

"It was after the style of our family's summer home on Lake Attersee, in the Salzkammergut, Austrian Alps. My grandfather built that home. Perhaps you have seen paintings by Klimt."

"Gustav Klimt?"

"He spent his summers there. Made many paintings. And Mahler, Gustav Mahler, the famous Austrian composer. It was a wonderful retreat for the artists in summer. This paper—"

Baden gestured toward the luscious evergreen print of the wallpaper, which looked like some kind of historical pattern, expensively reproduced. "Like Alpine spruce, just as in the Alps. Here, I feel almost at home."

I would have been happy to sit right down in the club chair by the window and have a long conversation about the Alps in summertime and the music of Mahler, not that I know very much about Romantic music. But I didn't want Lauren to walk in on us. I'd have to tell her soon about my paranormal abilities, but I didn't want to do it with the ghost of Baden in the room.

"What are you doing here?" I whispered. "What happened to you? I'm here for the week, but we can't talk too long, not right now."

He paid no attention to my caution about time. It had been a long time since he'd talked to anyone who could hear him, and he seemed anxious to get his story out.

"It was a difficult time for the bank, for all banks. There were many, many pressures from the war between Russia and Japan, from the earthquake in San Francisco, the railroad expansion, the fall crops coming in so late. We were a small private bank, very exposed, and so Alby and I, we thought that perhaps I should go to Providence and talk to Mr. Webster,

Theodore Webster. He was the president of the Mutual Building and Loan, and a good man, an honest man. We had met him in New York and we thought that, possibly, we might bring our banks together."

I nodded. "When was this?" I asked.

"End of January, 1907."

It was as though a breeze all the way from the Austrian Alps had blown right into the room.

"How long did you stay?" I asked the ghost.

"I stayed for a week. I was a guest of Mr. and Mrs. Aldrich. Mr. Aldrich's brother was a member of the Union Club, my club in New York."

"Were you on the *Larchmont*?"

Baden looked puzzled.

"Did you board a boat to go back to New York? A steamer? At night?"

"Yes, yes. The weather was very poor. I nearly asked the driver to turn around and take me back to the Aldrich home. But I had been their guest for a week. I didn't want to put them to any more trouble."

"Then that's what probably happened. You died on the *Larchmont* and somehow ended up here."

"I don't know," he said sadly. "I only know that I have been here for a very long time."

"Why didn't you cross over? What kept you from going into the light?"

The ghost shook his head, as though the truth was too private to impart. He sank back down into the chair, and I held my tongue, trying to allow him some time to absorb what I had just said.

A doorway of light had certainly opened for Baden at the

moment of his death, as it does for every person who dies. If you have ever spoken to someone who has nearly died in an accident or during surgery, or read any accounts of that experience, you'll usually hear mention of a tunnel, which leads to a doorway of bright, white light.

Many people experience extraordinary bliss when their spirits leave their bodies at the time of death. They surrender easily and joyfully to the powerful force drawing them toward the light beyond the doorway. With every fiber of their beings, they resist being pulled back to life through medical heroics or a turn of the wheel of fate. Explaining later, they often utter the words, "I didn't want to come back."

This light burns brightly for two or three days, during which time a spirit who is lingering on earth can remain among the people they love, visit the places they long to revisit, and even attend their own funeral, which every ghost I have ever encountered has done. Shortly thereafter, though, the brilliant white light begins to fade, and then it goes out completely. If the earthbound spirit has not yet passed through the doorway to whatever is on the other side—and I have no idea what that is, none at all—he or she is trapped in a no-man's-land between this life and whatever comes next.

If there is a next. I, personally, believe that there is. Maybe not the heaven of my First Communion catechism, but something sublime and mysterious. I've never forgotten an essay I read long ago, in which a scientist, a biologist whose name I cannot recall, talked about the curious fact that his faith wouldn't go away, even though he had devoted his entire life to science. What it came down to for him—and I found myself agreeing with him—was the fact that he couldn't quite believe that a pool of primordial muck could eventually evolve to the point at which it had the ability to compose the Mozart Requiem. Not without a little extra help.

I suddenly felt a sneeze coming on and wondered, irrationally, if sympathy for the victims of the disaster at sea was causing me to develop a cold. *That's completely ridiculous*, I thought as I closed my eyes and sneezed once, twice, three times.

When I opened them, the ghost was gone.

Chapter Six

LAUREN BAKED THE bass with a topping of bread crumbs, spring onions, and chives, and she served the flavorful fillets on a pile of creamy mashed potatoes. I immediately resolved to make potatoes more often, for the first bite took me right back to the suppers of my childhood: the torn vinyl seats of our kitchen chairs, scratchy against the backs of my thighs when I wore shorts; the basket-weave pattern of the enamel tabletop that chilled my forearms in winter and summer. I tend to cook pasta as our starch, because it was Nona who taught me my way around a kitchen. Dad's repertoire isn't extensive, but he sure knows how to make mashed potatoes. When Joe and Jay and I were small, he often served them with thick chunks of kielbasa, coiled inside out from having burst in the boiling.

Henry had surprised me by nearly finishing the food on his plate. He would never have eaten this much fish at home, but I'd witnessed the satisfaction with which he carried the dressed fillets in from the back barn, where he and Mark had done the skinning and gutting, and presented them to Lauren in the kitchen. I noticed that he looked a little pale, but it was good for him to be reminded that fish didn't come from the counter at the Fishmonger. To be squeamish about consuming their haul, after all of his and Mark's work, might have elicited a little good-natured teasing, so for tonight at least, Henry managed to be a guy who ate fish. Enthusiastically.

Now he was a guy who was lying on his stomach on the floor in front of a crackling woodstove, feeding tidbits of bass to one of the most corpulent cats I had ever seen, a languid orange tabby named Frances. Frances was eighteen and not above entertaining herself by taking a gratuitous swipe at your ankle as you walked by—assuming that this didn't require her to move her unwieldy body.

She spent most of her time on a pillow near the woodstove. All that was missing was a crown. But like any good queen, Frances was gracious to subjects who bowed and scraped and offered her the fruits of their labors. As Henry was presently playing that role, Frances was at her imperial best.

And then she appeared, the little ghost girl. She sat down cross-legged on the floor beside Henry, and I noticed Frances pull her plump self to attention. Many animals are aware of ghosts, and Frances appeared to be among them. She began to sweep her tail back and forth across the floor, and for a moment, I feared she might be gearing up to release her anxiety by taking a swipe at my son's cheek.

"Don't get your face too close," I warned him.

But Frances wasn't interested in Henry. She had even lost interest in the fish, which, given the looks of her, had to have been a first. She arose, daintily for her size. She fluffed up her fur and hackles and padded cautiously over to where the ghost girl was sitting, grinning gaily. The cat pulled her ears back and produced the most alarming sound, like that of a partially blocked faucet being turned on at full force.

Henry sat back on his heels and glanced at me, eyes wide, gleefully anticipating drama.

"Frances!" said Lauren. "What's gotten into you?"

Mark stood up and began to clear the plates.

Frances hissed again, lifted her paw, and swiped right through the little ghost girl, which sent both kids into a cascade of giggling. The girl made a face and swiped back. Frances emitted a guttural growl that sounded like something right out of *Night of the Living Dead.* Forget ghosts. You want scary sounds? Just make a large feline murderously angry.

I felt sorry for the poor cat, but it was nice to see the little ghost girl smiling and laughing and behaving like a normal child. I just hoped that Henry wouldn't start talking to her. The ghost lunged toward Frances, and the cat pulled away, then shocked us all by attempting to rise up onto her hind paws, growling and hissing and scratching the air.

"What the heck?" asked Mark, glancing over from the sink. "All right, that's enough." Mark swooped down, caught the stunned Frances over his forearm, opened the back door, and tossed the baffled feline out onto the porch. "You," he said, "are sleeping in the barn."

"She's getting a little dotty," he explained, sitting back down.

"She's psychotic, is what she is. I think she needs some—" Lauren broke off, glancing at Henry. "Kitty medicine."

"No," said Henry, "she just—"

"How about the Stooges?" I said quickly, cutting him off. Henry popped his mouth open in an expression of exaggerated surprise, because he's not allowed to watch TV during the school week.

"It's vacation," I said.

"Yay!" said Henry, hopping to his feet.

The little ghost floated up to his side.

"Tea? Decaf?" Lauren asked.

"Whatever you're having."

Henry and the girl followed me into the den, where I fired up the DVD player and read the back of the case. Good! There were three episodes left: *Cuckoo Cavaliers*, *Squareheads of the Round Table*, and *Disorder in the Court*. At twenty-five minutes each, they'd take us right up to bath time. Henry clambered onto the couch, belatedly removing his shoes. The little ghost sat down at the other end, more interested in Henry than in the television. He ignored her, but that was normal. In a contest between the Three Stooges and a girl about his age, the girl didn't have a prayer.

It would remain to be seen whether she was still there when I came back; she might drift away out of boredom, as Silas, Henry's other "imaginary playmate," had often done. In the meantime, I could explain away any laughter or chattering coming from the room as evidence of Henry's getting overinvolved with the on-screen hijinks.

"Don't go anywhere without telling me," I warned him.

"Okay," he said.

"I'll be right in the kitchen."

"I *know*," he responded, flashing me a look that meant, *And now would you please leave?*

Back in the kitchen, the talk was still of Frances. I had assumed that she was Lauren's cat, and her story the classic tale of a doted-upon feline being supplanted by her owner's boyfriend and eventual husband. But Frances belonged to Mark, or more accurately, to the house. She had wandered into the kitchen almost two decades ago, a stray kitten, and proceeded to make the place her home. She had earned the family's affection by being a first-rate mouser, and had been sheltered and fed during the colder months by neighbors who stored their snow removal equipment in the Rieglers' back barn. Every spring, though, when Mark's family returned to the island, Frances took up residence again in the kitchen.

"Does she still catch mice?" I asked.

Mark grinned. "Look at her! What do *you* think?"

"Oh, she'll give it a go," Lauren said, "once in a while, just for old times' sake. But she's just too slow. Poor thing."

Mark shot his wife a look I couldn't interpret.

"This is *not* about Frances," she said cryptically. "I'm just *nervous.*"

"Lauren believes all the old wives' tales," Mark explained.

"They wouldn't have lasted for all these centuries if there wasn't some truth to them!"

"Oh, come on," Mark said. "Cats climbing into cradles and sucking the breath out of babies?"

"Maybe they suffocate them! Who knows?"

"She'd have to get into the crib first, and that ain't happenin'," Mark teased. "I'll tell you what. I'll build a little crib top—a crib canopy! And we'll rig the whole thing up with bells!"

"What if she gets through the bars of the crib?" Lauren insisted.

"Fat chance," said Mark.

Lauren, who had been experimenting with dessert recipes, offered me a choice: lemon pudding cake, a brownie with or without ice cream, or what she called a "pot de crème."

"Or all three!" she said. "I need feedback, I really do. I'm trying to figure out what to put on the menu."

I love brownies—I suppose everyone does—but you can

get a good brownie any time. I chose the pot de crème, having absolutely no idea what it was, only to be delighted when Lauren produced an antique English teacup in its saucer. It looked like something from which Miss Marple might have taken her afternoon cuppa. In the teacup had been baked an individual serving of a fragrant vanilla custard.

"Oh my gosh!" I said after the first bite. "This is wonderful!"

"Thanks," Lauren said. "In season, we'll have berries on top. But we're trying to stay seasonal. And local. I mean, pretty local, given that we live in New England. On an island."

"All the more reason," said Mark. "It's here and along the shorelines that you can really see the damage."

I was so intoxicated by my custard that I must have shot Mark a dumb glance. *Berries? Damage?*

"From erosion," he clarified. "Parts of Nantucket are losing fifty feet a year. Beaches, houses, just—gone. Some of it's natural, but not this rate of loss. The land's just washing away."

"Because the polar ice cap's melting," I guessed, hoping to redeem myself in Mark's eyes. I wasn't a complete moron when it came to global warming. I was familiar with the concept of carbon footprints and with the true costs of flying raspberries halfway around the planet.

"That and the nature of the storms we're getting now, which is also a result of the warming," Mark went on.

I'd always assumed that the storms we were getting now were no different from the storms we had always gotten. But I grew up in Ohio and have only lived around Boston for a few years. I have no real feel for what's "normal" in New England.

"What kind of storms *are* we getting?" I asked.

"Not as many hurricanes and nor'easters, but lots more

storms that are moderately severe. Add to that the way our beaches are shaped—they're long and broad and kind of flat—and well, let's just say it's not a good combination. If erosion keeps happening at the rate it's happening now, Nantucket will be under water in a few hundred years."

"You're kidding!" I said. "The whole island?"

"Yup. They've already lost twenty-five buildings. Expect to lose fifty or sixty more in the next ten years."

"That's terrible," I said.

"And we're not immune here. They already moved the Southeast Lighthouse once, back in 1993. The edge of the cliff was wearing away, so they had to pull the whole building back a few hundred feet. Took them ten years to raise two million dollars to finance it, but if they hadn't done it, the lighthouse would have fallen right into the ocean. The Bluffs are still taking a beating."

Lauren wore a patient, indulgent expression.

"This is Mark's passion," she explained, "in case you haven't figured it out."

I smiled. "You're preaching to the choir. I even recycle those little wire twisties from the bread bags."

Mark was apparently relieved to discover that I was a kindred spirit, environmentally. "Our entire renovation was green," he said, "though it did end up costing us more than we'd hoped."

"Don't things always go over budget?"

"Yeah, sure, and we'll save money in the long run."

"We hope!" Lauren added. "Half the island turned up at the open house. The real old-timers were the ones who stayed the longest, believe it or not. They couldn't get enough of the new technologies, inspecting the solar panels, checking out all the energy-efficient materials. I was really surprised."

"It makes sense, though," Mark said. "They're invested in the island, and not just here on the weekends or for a week in the summer. They've seen the changes happening over their lifetimes."

"To be fair, though," Lauren said, "everybody cares about the island. There are just different ideas about what we should do, and people worry about the impact on tourism of some of the proposed changes."

"What changes?" I asked.

Lauren shot Mark a look. "There's an initiative to build an offshore wind farm. Mark's the head of the committee. The debate's been pretty spirited."

"Spirited?" Mark said.

"Lively?" Lauren asked.

"How about *ugly*?"

"*Energetic,*" she declared.

"Vicious," he said.

———

"What's your name?" I asked the little ghost. I am able to hear what ghosts are thinking, but they don't usually think about their own names. The little ghost might have been used to young children being aware of her, but she seemed shocked that I could see her. Henry answered my question before she could recover her composure and speak.

"Vivi."

She had followed us up the stairs and into our room. It was nearly nine o'clock, time for Henry to go to bed, but Vivi showed no sign of being aware that she was expected to leave. I had no one but myself to blame for this, of course, given that I had let her curl up in my lap the previous night.

"Is that a nickname?" I asked her.

She stared at me and said nothing. I tried again.

"What's your real name?"

After a pause, she floated over to Henry and whispered in his ear.

"Viveka," said Henry.

"And what's your last name?"

She whispered again, and Henry said, "Riegler."

"Viveka Riegler," I said. "That's a pretty name."

She stuck out her tongue.

"Why are you sticking your tongue out at me?"

She stuck it out again.

"Okay, Vivi," I said, sighing. "I think we've all had a very long day. I know Henry's tired."

"No, I'm not," said Henry.

"Well, I am, and we all have to get up very early tomorrow. So Vivi, honey, maybe it's time for you to go back to—"

I broke off. To where? The hallway? The attic? Her cubby under the stairs? The truth was, I had no idea where this kid went when she wasn't with us.

Vivi glared at me, her skinny little arms crossed angrily.

"Can she sleep over?" Henry asked. "Could you ask her mom?"

Could I ask her mom? Okay, so this meant that Henry believed Vivi *had* a mom, either here on the premises or, possibly, reachable by phone. That indicated that Vivi seemed like a normal kid to him, a kid whose mother, like any other parent, would or would not grant permission for a last-minute sleepover. So far, this hadn't given me any new information.

"You know," I said, "I'm not sure tonight's the best night."

Vivi stamped her little foot and scowled at me defiantly.

"Why not?" Henry whined petulantly. "You *said* . . ."

"I said what?"

"You *said* it was vacation."

I sighed. "We still have to get up early, honey. You've got that car to paint."

"Greased Lightnin'," he said edgily. "We'll go to sleep right away, I promise."

I knew how the night would go. Just as it usually went when Delia and Nell, Henry's half sisters, ages four and three, spent the night: there would be laughing and whispering followed by tickling and kicking followed by fighting and crying.

Now I was the one feeling irrational. There was no reason to feel anxious about this little sprite, but I just didn't like the schizophrenic vibe she was sending off: curling up in my lap one minute and acting devilish and fresh the next.

Like most children her age, I reminded myself.

I understood. I did. She was desperate and lonely, and she had finally found a playmate her age, a playmate who could actually see her and talk to her. Not to mention a mother-type person who had let her curl up in her lap.

And now the person who had been nice to her last night was turning on her. I was saying no. No to the playmate, no to the sleepover, and no to the shelter and solace she had found in my arms. I was turning her out into the darkness.

"Vivi," I said quietly. "Henry's going to hop in the tub, and maybe you and I can have a little talk."

"I don't like you," she answered, in a squeaky little voice. "You're mean."

"Henry, honey, go in and run a bath. Go on."

"I don't want to," he groused.

"Now!" I snapped, a little more fiercely than I meant to. I

startled him. He got right up and went into the bathroom, and I heard the water begin to flow. I also heard him lock the door.

"Unlock that door," I called.

I heard him obey. I also heard him give the door a little kick, but I decided to let that go.

I wasn't aware until the moment I opened my mouth that I had changed my mind: I wanted her gone, *now!* I wanted this much more than I wanted to find out about Henry's paranormal abilities.

"Vivi," I said. "I know you must be really lonesome for your mommy and daddy. I can help you cross over and see them again. Right now. Would you like to do that? We can do it right this minute."

"No," she said, pouting.

"No?"

"I want to play with—him. I want to stay here."

"Well, you can't, honey. Your mommy and daddy really miss you, and they've been waiting a long, long time to see you. I want you to look over at that door."

Vivi refused to turn her head, but I went ahead anyway, confident that she would be mesmerized by the sight of the glowing doorway and would, upon seeing it, instantly change her mind and hurry toward the light.

I closed my eyes and imagined the light burning warmly and brightly inside me. I pulled the glow upward and outward and opened my eyes, and now the blinding beams of light from the other side were filling the room, and the door to the other side was right there, superimposed on the doorway to the hall. It was less than five feet away from us, just waiting for Vivi to walk through it.

THE ICE CRADLE 63

"Look, honey," I said. "Everyone you love is right through that door. Look! Look at the light! Go ahead! Maybe you'll see your mommy. Or your daddy."

She wanted to look, I could tell, but she refused to turn her head. I could see how hard she was working to control her own curiosity and longing. But she didn't like me. She had liked me last night, but now she didn't, and she wasn't going to give me the satisfaction of doing anything I asked her to do. Even at the cost of her own happiness.

"Sweetie," I said. "I'm sorry if I hurt your feelings. I really and truly am. I want you to be happy. I don't want you to be lonesome anymore."

"Liar!" she said. "You want me to go away."

I sighed. It was true. If I could have picked her up bodily, carried her over to the door of white light, and tossed her through it, I would have. But you can't pick up a ghost.

"How about we just look?" I suggested. "You don't have to go through if you don't want to, but we could just walk over to that door and have a little peek. See who we see." I winked, hoping my enthusiasm would be infectious.

It wasn't.

Fairly quivering with the effort required to resist my pleas, she shook her head angrily and disappeared. I had no choice but to close the shining door.

———

I don't know what woke me up.

I had been having a crazy dream about popping popcorn in my old dorm room. I had poured in too many kernels, and I was watching with horror as the volume of popped corn grew and grew, lifting the lid right off my old Revere Ware pan. And then there was all this noise in the hall; people were shouting, and people outside in the courtyard were yelling, and it was all because I'd been popping the corn on an illegal hot plate. I knew I was going to get busted.

There was the sound of shattering glass, and I opened my eyes.

The room was dark, but I could still hear the popping and crackling. I threw off the covers and stumbled over to the other bed, where Henry was sprawled out, sound asleep. I pulled back the heavy damask drapes and peered out in horror.

The crackling was real. The shouting was real. The sky was an eerie melon color, and I didn't know whether to stay or flee.

The barn behind the inn was on fire.

Chapter Seven

I DRESSED AS QUICKLY as I could. I was torn about whether to wake Henry, who hadn't been roused by the sounds and light in back of the house. I wanted to help Lauren and Mark if I could, and that would be hard with a five-year-old in the mix. On the other hand, I didn't want Henry to be terrified if he woke up alone in the room and opened the curtains to discover the barn in flames. Factoring in how soundly he usually sleeps, I decided to take my chances. I slipped into my jeans and boots and pulled a sweater over my head, then closed the drapes tightly and tiptoed into the hall. There, I broke into a run.

Vivi. It was all I could think. Furious at being banished from our room, I theorized, she had found a way to focus her anger on the decrepit old wiring in the barn, sending enough energy frizzing through a frayed antique tangle to cause sparking. That's all it would have taken, really. I'd seen the barn's interior a few hours earlier, when Henry and Mark had been scaling the fish, and it abounded with the usual clutter found in most people's basements and garages: firewood, half-empty cans of paint, doors removed from their original locations, furniture awaiting refinishing or repair.

Plans for restoring the hundred-year-old barn had fallen by the wayside as the costs of renovating the inn had skyrocketed, Lauren and Mark had told me over dinner. They'd had to settle, temporarily, for installing a new set of doors and freshening the clapboards with a new coat of paint.

Now, the stained oak doors stood open on their hinges. Mark and a couple of men who had arrived on the scene were using garden hoses and buckets of water to try to keep the flames from spreading. It didn't take a trained observer to perceive that the blaze was getting away from them.

"Where's the fire department?" I asked Lauren, who was pacing in her bathrobe on the grass behind the house. For an instant, I wondered if there *was* a fire department.

"On their way," she said, just as I heard the first sirens in the distance. "It's all volunteers. They have to get to the station from their homes."

I put my arm around her. She was shivering. I know that pregnancy doesn't make a woman frail or ill, but I still didn't feel that Lauren should be out here in her bare feet, breathing in all the smoke.

"You should go inside," I said.

"No."

"Really. Think of the baby. There's nothing you can do out here."

She shook her head firmly.

I broke away and moved toward the barn, and as I reached its doors, I could see flames beginning to lick up three of the four interior walls. The men seemed to have tapped all the water sources, so I ducked inside the barn, hoping I could save some objects by pulling them out onto the grass.

"No!" Mark shouted, seeing me. "Get out!"

"I'm fine." I grabbed a chair by its arms and hurried it out to the side lawn. Over the next few minutes, I was able to pull or push out five more chairs, a snowblower, a lawn mower, three tables—one of which weighed a ton—two bicycles, and half a dozen huge, expensive-looking ceramic pots. These I had to roll.

When the firefighters arrived in two trucks, tapped a hydrant, and brought in the heavy hoses, we were all ordered to get back. Mark crossed the grass, stood behind Lauren, and wrapped his arms around her shoulders. The other men drifted into the clusters of horrified neighbors who had gathered at the edges of the property.

I retreated to the back steps but had to move a short time later, when the firefighters decided to hose down the stairs and the exterior of the inn. This seemed overly cautious to me. I highly doubted that a stray spark, having jumped a distance of some three hundred feet, would have been hot enough to set the inn on fire, but what did I know? I scooted out of the way and joined an older couple lingering on the far lawn by a hedge of hydrangea bushes.

"Terrible," I said.

"Awful," said the woman, who was wearing a pink flowered nightgown under her trench coat. "I heard a whole string of explosions. Woke me right up. Course I don't sleep much. Bing bing bing bing! That's what it sounded like."

"Spray cans," mumbled the man.

"What?" the woman asked. She nodded at me and said, "I'm Mina Hansen. We live over there." Mina pointed to a shingled cottage tucked back behind the barn. Unlike the back steps, the cottage appeared to be well within reach of a stray spark, and I wondered why the firefighters weren't turning their hoses in that direction.

"Aerosol cans going off," said the man.

"I'm Anza O'Malley," I offered. "I'm a guest here."

"You think that's what exploded?" Mina asked. For my benefit she added, "This is my husband, Frank."

"I know damn well it is," said Frank.

"Frank was a volunteer firefighter for thirty-one years," explained Mina.

"Thirty-two," he corrected.

"He just retired last year."

"And I'll tell you something else," Frank went on. "There's something fishy about this fire."

Yeah, no kidding, I thought. "You think it could have been—electrical? The wiring out there must be pretty old."

"Electrical fires don't usually start by themselves," Frank explained.

It might have had a little help, I thought.

"Not in the middle of the night, anyway," he continued. "Not when everything's turned off. Now, if you left your clothes dryer running, say you turned it on before you went to bed, and you had a big backup of lint in there . . ."

"I'm good about lint," I answered reflexively and immediately wondered why in the world I had said it. And just as quickly I realized that Frank reminded me a lot of my dad, who'd always been a bear about dryer lint.

"You've got to clean the screen off *every* time," Frank said, before a crash and some shouts drew our attention back to the barn. Something had happened inside. Something had fallen or broken. Nevertheless, the men and two women handling the hoses seemed to be getting the fire under control.

"You smell anything?" asked Frank.

Mina shook her head. I mostly smelled smoke, but I took another deep breath.

"Gasoline?" I asked.

Frank nodded and set off along the line of bushes. He motioned for us to follow and we did, moving deeper into the lot until Frank paused under one of the pear trees. From our new position, we had a clear view into the barn.

"See how orange those flames are?" he asked. "See that black, black smoke?"

He was right. The flames were the color of tangerines, not the washed-out yellow of fireplace blazes. And the smoke was pluming up and out in big black clouds.

"What would cause that?" I asked.

"Accelerants," he replied. "No question."

"You think the fire was set?" Mina whispered.

"Not a doubt in my mind," said Frank.

▬▬▬

It was nearly three in the morning. Henry was still asleep, and since the trucks and the neighbors had all departed, and the lapping of the waves was the only sound in the air, it seemed likely that he would slumber on until daybreak.

I had finally gotten Lauren to come inside, and now she sat wrapped in an afghan at the kitchen table, nursing a mug of chamomile tea. Mark had cracked open a beer, not undeserved under the circumstances, I thought, but after taking one sip, he left it sitting untouched on the table. One of Mark's closest

friends, the fisherman who'd caught the bass we'd had for dinner, had arrived in his pickup just as the hoses were being
drained and the bystanders were dispersing. The wife of one
of the volunteer firefighters had alerted him to the alarm, knowing that he was close to Lauren and Mark. Alberto Azevedo,
who went by Bert, had now joined us in the kitchen for the
gloomy postmortem.

Bert asked for tea rather than beer, which surprised me,
given that he was all decked out in bulky sweaters and heavy-
weight canvas. He definitely struck me as a beer guy. With his
curly black hair and sunburned good looks, he could have
walked right out of one of those offensive high-fashion spreads
in which a supermodel is posed in a far-flung location among
exotic "natives" in their actual clothes, or lack of them.

How do they get away with those ads? I wondered as I plopped a
peppermint tea bag into a stoneware mug and poured in boiling
water. What were we supposed to make of a woman dressed, or
semi-undressed, for the red carpet, mugging for the camera before a council of Zulu warriors or from the deck of a wind-
tossed fishing boat?

"Thanks," said Bert.

I nodded and sat back down. Why in the world was I
thinking of Bert on the deck of a wind-tossed fishing boat
with a woman in a state of elegant undress? This was in such
poor taste. Lauren and Mark's barn had practically burned
down.

"At least no one was hurt," said Mark.

"That's all that really matters," said Lauren.

It was one of those bland, soothing things that people always say, and it was true, of course. But it wasn't completely
true. Other things did matter. They mattered a lot. Like how

much the repairs would cost and how much damage the old structure had sustained. Precious objects were now soaked and sooty, and no one had a clue as to where Frances had gone. They hadn't found the remains of the portly old feline, thank goodness, but who knew what daylight would reveal?

Then there was that little matter of arson. For nauseatingly selfish reasons, I sort of hoped that Frank was right. It was awful to contemplate the possibility that my own self-centeredness had prompted Vivi to act out in childish fury and ignite the blaze. I wondered if anyone had mentioned to Mark the possibility that the fire had been set.

"I've never seen flames that color," I said, hoping this comment might lead to the subject. "And all that black smoke."

"That's my fault," said Mark. "I had a couple of cans of gas out there, for the lawn mower and the snowblower. It's the first thing I thought of when I saw the flames, how stupid I'd been to leave gasoline lying around."

"Heck," said Bert. "Everybody does it. Or worse."

Mark shook his head. "I didn't dare go near them. I was afraid they'd blow up in my face."

"Good thinking," said Bert.

Lauren gave an exaggerated shiver, obviously imagining what might have been.

"What happened to them?" I asked.

"They both exploded. Didn't you smell the gas?"

"I did," said Bert.

"Me, too," said Lauren.

"There must have been some leakage from those old metal cans," Mark went on, "because that whole area back there lit right up before the cans exploded. It was just after the trucks got here."

"So those bright orange flames came from *your* cans of gas?" I asked.

Mark nodded.

I let out a deflated sigh.

"Well, the good news," said Bert, "is that everything can be fixed. Lou Markham and I went around and checked the foundation, and it held up pretty well, all things considered. I don't know about the stuff you had stored in there . . ."

"A lot of it was junk," said Lauren. "Well, not *junk,* but things we don't have room for in here, stuff we just collected over the years. Some of it was nice, definitely, but the reason it was out there was because we didn't know what to do with it."

"So the inn's completely furnished?" I asked.

"Oh, yeah," said Mark. "I was actually thinking we might have a barn sale this summer and get rid of a lot of that stuff."

"Oh you were, were you?" Lauren said.

"You're the one who hates clutter," Mark said. "Fussy little B and Bs with doilies on all the tables."

"Mama?" I heard.

It was Henry. He was standing in the doorway in his footed pajamas. His hair was sticking up in tufts, and he looked like he was about to cry.

"I woke up," he said.

"Oh, honey, come here. I'm sorry. Were you scared?"

He blinked rapidly in the bright light of the kitchen and looked around in bafflement. I put out my arms, and he padded over to where I was sitting, then crawled into my lap. He didn't want to admit that he had been unnerved to wake up and find me gone from the room, so he buried his head in my shoulder. I took a deep breath and suddenly felt exhausted.

I stood up. He was heavy. I wouldn't be able to carry him this way for much longer.

"I guess I'll head up," I said. "I hope you two can get some sleep."

Lauren and Mark nodded. "Thanks for all your help," Mark said.

"No problem."

Bert stood up. "You need a hand?" he asked.

"I'm okay," I said. "But thanks."

Bert reached over and laid a hand on Henry's back. "Sleep tight, sailor," he said.

At the sound of his voice, Henry looked up.

"See you in the morning," I said to Lauren and Mark.

"See you—sometime—maybe," I said to Bert.

"Good night," he answered.

"Where *were* you?" Henry demanded.

"Right there in the kitchen, honey. I was just talking to Lauren and Mark."

"And Bert," Henry added.

I laid him down on his bed, disentangled the covers, and tucked him in. I hoped he would close his eyes and drift right off, but I knew this was unlikely.

"I didn't know where you went," Henry said.

"You were sound asleep. I didn't think you'd wake up."

"You left me all by myself!" he whined.

"I was only downstairs. I just had to go down for a minute."

"How come?"

"I had to help Lauren with something."

This seemed to satisfy him momentarily. I thought I might be home free.

"Lauren has a fat tummy," Henry said.

"That's because she's going to have a baby pretty soon."

"*I know,*" he said.

"You do? How'd you know that?"

"Mark told me."

"When was this?"

"On the boat."

"The boat?" I asked. "What boat?"

"Bert's boat."

"You went out on Bert's boat?" My mind raced back to the afternoon. How long had they been gone?

"No," said Henry. "We just—walked over the gangplank and—"

Henry paused. The pauses between his sentences were getting longer and longer.

"The gangplank," I said quietly.

"Uh-huh," he finally said.

I waited a long time for him to go on. He was out.

Chapter Eight

Now I was the one who couldn't sleep. There's nothing more depressing than knowing that in three or four hours, you're going to have to be up again and functioning for a whole day and evening before you get another chance to lay down your head. But I couldn't stop replaying the night's events: waking from my popcorn dream to the crackling noises outside, to the chilling air and the sting of smoke in my eyes, the shocking explosions from inside the barn, and my grateful relief upon hearing the sirens drawing nearer and nearer on the boulevard.

I am not normally troubled by insomnia, but like most people, I have an uneasy night every now and then. It usually has to do with managing to forget somehow that drinking caffeinated tea or coffee after four in the afternoon always keeps me up. So I've read with interest those articles that list what doesn't help when you are wide awake in the middle of the night: continuing to toss and turn and hope for the best, glancing at the clock every two seconds and worrying about how you're ever going to get through the next day. The experts advise getting up, changing rooms, reading for a while. Since I didn't want to risk waking Henry again by turning on the light, I decided I'd slip downstairs and sit on the front porch for a bit. I hoped that the sound of the ocean might calm my restlessness.

I also thought there was a chance that Vivi might be ghosting around somewhere. Admittedly, we hadn't parted on the warmest of terms, but if she was desperate and reckless enough to wreak this kind of damage, who knew what else she was capable of doing? I had to find that devilish little minx and have a chat with her.

It wasn't Vivi I encountered on the porch, though; it was Baden Riegler. He appeared on the front steps just moments after I sat down in one of the rockers.

"Hello," he said. "It is very late."

"I can't sleep," I replied.

"I am not surprised. Come. Let us walk."

I'd been about to suggest something similar, in case I wasn't the only one still awake. That's all I needed right now: to have to explain to Lauren or Mark why I was carrying on a conversation out here in the middle of the night with—no one. They'd had enough drama for one night.

"I can't go far," I whispered. "My little boy's asleep upstairs."

"Shall we walk by the water?" Baden asked.

"It's too cold," I said. "Let's go over there."

Baden nodded and followed me to the side yard, where two Adirondack chairs had been placed under one of the apple trees. We sat down.

"Were you here for the fire?" I asked.

Baden nodded gravely.

"Do you know how it started?"

"Yes," he said politely. "But I'm still very surprised—"

"That I can see you and talk to you?"

"It is strange, no? Most extraordinary."

"I'm used to it. I've always been able to see and talk to spirits. But to tell you the truth, you seem a little different from most."

"In what way, may I ask?"

"You're very calm."

"Oh, no. No, I assure you."

"Well, you seem it. Most spirits are more demanding. There's something they want very much and it's all they can think about."

Baden smiled. "It is the way I was raised, perhaps; not to show everything I am feeling. To keep private what is personal."

I nodded. "It's refreshing. Though I suppose that means it would be impolite of me to ask you a personal question."

"Not at all. Though I may choose not to answer."

I smiled and nodded. "Of course. It's just that, if I knew more, I might be able to help you."

"Help me to do what?"

"To cross over."

"To cross over to what?"

"Well, I don't know, to tell you the truth. I see a white light, but I can't see into it, and I have no idea what is or isn't on the other side of it. I probably won't know until it's my own time to go, but a lot of people think it's God. On the other side."

"I'm afraid I don't believe in God," Baden said.

"Fair enough," I responded. "Then let me put it this way. Most spirits I've met really want to enter the light. You've seen it, I assume."

"Yes, I did. Long ago."

"And you—didn't want to enter it?"

"No."

I didn't entirely believe him. The light was a powerful and compelling force for every single spirit I had ever encountered, whether they thought of "God" as Jesus on the cross or the old man in the white beard or four-armed Lakshmi or, more simply, the concepts of love or oneness with the universe. As far as I could tell, their personal preconceptions about God's existence didn't seem to matter. As soon as I was able to help them solve the problems that had stranded them in time and space, ghosts could hardly wait to go through that shining white door.

Baden took a deep breath. "I had my own reasons, which I prefer to keep private, for not wanting to, as you say, 'cross over' when I could. But there's something else that concerns me now. Something very troubling, and that I *will* share with you. But first, may I ask *you* a question?"

"Sure."

"Do you see *all* spirits?"

"Well, I wouldn't know, now, would I? I see the spirits I see, but there very well could be spirits that I'm not able to see. But if I'm not able to see them, how would I *know* I'm not seeing them?"

A twinkle appeared in Baden's eyes. It seemed I had pegged him correctly as the sort of person who liked to play linguistic games and to parse the meanings of the most casual comments, things people said primarily to be polite or amiable.

"Be that as it may," he went on, "you *are* aware that there are dozens and dozens of beings like me all over this island and near the spot where we found ourselves. That night."

"Where the ship went down, you mean?"

He nodded tentatively. In one other way, Baden was unlike

many of the other ghosts I've known, nearly all of whom were acutely aware of the circumstances under which they had died. I suspected that Baden's uncertainty had to do with the *Larchmont*'s having sunk in the middle of the night, when he and most of the people on board were asleep. They'd awakened into their ghostly incarnations, not sure what had actually happened to them. It probably felt as though they were trapped in a dream, a dream from which they could never awaken.

"I've seen them," I said. "They're everywhere." When Henry and I had walked to the lighthouse and the Mohegan Bluffs, I had seen dozens of disoriented and despairing souls wandering uncomprehendingly through their eternal night.

"They are very unhappy," Baden said.

I nodded.

"And not for the reason you think," he went on.

"Oh?"

Baden nodded and let out a long sigh. He seemed to be choosing his words carefully.

"There is a movement on the island," he finally said, "to install what people are calling a wind farm." Baden gestured out to sea. "Out there in the banks."

"I heard that, yes. I think it's a great idea."

"It may or may not be. That's of no concern to me."

I felt myself getting a little irritated. "Then what is?" I asked. I didn't mean to sound snappy, but I must have, because Baden appeared startled.

"My family. My family is all that matters to me. I have watched my brother's great-grandson and his wife work night and day to repair this precious building, into which my brother poured his soul. But many of the spirits are furious with the boy."

"The boy? You mean Mark?"

Baden nodded. "They are conspiring to drive them both off the island. Mark and his wife."

I was suddenly wide awake. It was as though someone had doused me with a bucket of freezing water. *"What?"* I said. "But why?"

"He is determined to see the wind farm built. But the engineers have chosen the very area where the boat went down. If those windmills are erected, they will drill deep into the ocean floor. They will destroy the final resting places of everyone who went down with the ship."

It took me a moment to absorb what Baden had said, and when I did, I practically shuddered.

This was bad. This was very bad.

I remembered reading about the construction of the Quabbin Reservoir, a man-made lake that holds Boston's water supply. Dams had been built and four towns evacuated and razed in the 1930s to create the basin for the water, billions of gallons of it, but before they let in one drop, the engineers moved the cemeteries. Thirty-four of them. Six thousand graves. I've never forgotten those numbers.

Burial grounds are sacred. Granted, the undersea wreckage of the *Larchmont* wasn't your average cemetery, but it was the only cemetery those poor souls had, and it deserved as much protection as that afforded Native American burial grounds, churchyards filled with unnamed slaves, and the mass graves of anonymous victims of genocide and famine.

"You said they're conspiring," I went on tentatively.

"Yes. Certain *parties* are aware that there is a television person coming to the inn."

"By *parties*, you mean ghosts, spirits."

"Yes."

"And you're talking about the TV crew, the guys from Australia. The 'ghost detectives.'"

"I am."

I was beginning to catch on. Because Mark was publicly leading the wind farm initiative, the ghosts had identified him as the person on the island to target, the man responsible for the impending destruction of their communal graveyard. They hoped to defeat the wind farm proposal, and they planned to do that by driving away the man they perceived to be leading the effort.

"Let me guess," I said. "They know the ghost detectives are coming and they're going to put on a real show. Haunt the daylights out of the inn."

"You're very astute," said Baden.

"So the Grand View will come off on national television as not just haunted, but . . ."

Baden was nodding.

My mind raced ahead to envision all the things a few dozen angry, disruptive spirits could do to set off electromagnetic field meters and infrared thermometers and all the recording gizmos and wireless doodads that these Australian opportunists employed on camera. Heck, these guys found ghosts where there weren't any! I could only imagine the red lights that would blink and the sensors that would shriek if there actually *were* a few dozen spirits in the house.

And I had been worried about Vivi's being on the premises! Suddenly, Vivi seemed like a relatively small problem to have.

Then again, maybe not.

"Wow," I said, shaking my head.

"Indeed," answered the ghost.

I couldn't decide whether it was worth going to bed. It was nearly five o'clock now, and a thin, pale line of pink had just appeared on the horizon. The firmament above me was still slate blue, and in it, a couple of stars were shining so brightly that I thought they had to be planets. But closer to the line separating sea from sky, I began to make out tufts of violet clouds and the barest streaks of lemony light.

I hadn't seen a sunrise in years. The clouds, lit from underneath, from back behind the curve of the earth, were like lavender cotton candy, torn into clumps and shreds and tinged with outlines of pink. The sky behind them was streaked with shades of melon and peach, and slashes of bisque and pale turquoise portended the sky of day. The ocean, reflecting the light from above, was eerily calm and more salmon than blue. The outlines of several fishing boats were silhouetted blackly against the glowing sky.

I took a deep breath. The air, while cool and damp, carried the slightest note of hyacinth. Soon, at least back in Cambridge, it would be heavy with the fragrances of lilacs and lilies of the valley and apple blossoms, all of them, this morning, still enclosed in tight green fists of buds.

I had to remember to pay attention. So longingly awaited through the hard, flinty chill of January and the blizzards of February, through the slush and mud of March and the drizzling weeks of April, the blossoms and their hypnotizing scents came and went in a matter of days. You could easily miss them altogether, these quiet, precious rewards for having endured the winter.

As the light grew and gathered around me, I vowed to take Henry to the hilly woods around Fresh Pond, carpeted by millions of lilies of the valley, or maybe to the Arnold Arboretum for the blooming of the lilacs. There was an awful lot of beauty to be seen in the world, if you only remembered to look.

Chapter Nine

I NEVER DID GO back to bed. By five thirty, when the tantalizing scent of fresh coffee first drifted out of the kitchen, I had decided that I'd probably feel worse after an hour or two of sleep. This is a trap, as anyone who has ever pulled an all-nighter knows. You get a burst of energy first thing in the morning, then walk around wired for five or six hours, marveling at how perfectly fine you feel. Until, suddenly, you don't. I wasn't looking forward to that moment, having only a few days to get my arms around a fairly ambitious amount of work, but I'd figure it out.

In the end, I didn't have to figure out anything. At about eight thirty, just as I was leaving to walk Henry to the school, Caleb Wilder pedaled up on an old three-speed bike. A dozen friends and neighbors had already assembled to offer their support to Lauren and Mark. The women, two of whom carried boxes marked "Christy's Bakery," were now chatting and drinking coffee with Lauren in the kitchen, and the men were back in the barn with Mark, checking out the damage the fire had done.

"I just heard!" said Caleb. "Everyone okay?"

I nodded. Henry and I had just come back from inspecting the barn, or as little of it as the fire officials would let us see. Frances hadn't turned up, which I was insisting was a very good thing.

"You must be Henry. I'm Caleb."

"Hi," said Henry.

"Caleb has two girls at the school. Kara and . . ." I blanked on the second name.

"Louisa," Caleb said.

"I know Louisa," Henry offered. "She's painting the sign."

"What sign?" I asked.

He gave me an incredulous look. *"Burger Palace."*

"That's right, she is," said Caleb. "Speaking of which, you two had better get a move on. And Anza, if you need to take some time today, feel free. You were probably up half the night."

"Thanks," I said. "It was pretty crazy around here."

"Yeah, no problem. As long as we get everything organized and under way in the next few days, you can finish the work at home."

"Really?"

"Absolutely."

"Well, I'll probably fade sometime this afternoon, but I'm wide awake right now. Might as well make the most of it."

"I'll be in at about eleven." Caleb said. "You've got your key?"

"I do," I replied.

My task today was organizational. There were thousands of pieces of paper to examine: newspaper clippings, official and personal correspondence, reports of all the inquiries into the collision of the *Larchmont* and the *Harry Knowlton,* telegrams, lists of pieces of cargo that had washed up during the subsequent weeks, and intimate, handwritten accounts of the islanders' experiences with the dead and the injured.

There were also dozens of snapshots, and these were plaintive and haunting. According to Caleb, the pictures had been taken in the days following the disaster by a young woman named Honor Morton, an amateur photographer who had lived on the island. She had been a sickly child, asthmatic and often bedridden. When she was eleven or twelve and recovering from a bout with influenza, she had been given a Brownie box camera. These sold for about a dollar at the turn of the century, and delivered the means of photography, for the first time since the process was invented, into the hands of ordinary people.

Judging from her vision, the eighteen-year-old Honor had been anything but ordinary. Her evocative images offered a twist on the old Sufi adage "Blame the archer, not the arrow": her eye was unerring and her composition flawless, even though her "arrow" was little more than a cardboard box equipped with a lens. For me, these curled and cracked snapshots of the stunned and hollow-eyed survivors and the islanders who nursed them were the real treasures of the collection.

I heard a knock at the door and looked up. A robust, ruddy-cheeked man in a dark olive barn coat and crisp khakis was standing on the porch. The door was unlocked, so he hadn't needed to knock.

"I didn't mean to startle you," he said, opening the door and stepping inside.

"We're not actually open." I felt a little uncomfortable employing the first person plural. I wasn't really in charge here. I was also a little spooked by a strange guy's coming in while I was all by myself in the building, but I tried not to let that show. What was he going to do? Pull a knife and demand some newspaper clippings?

"I'm Porter Rawlings," he announced.

"Anza O'Malley," I replied. "I'm working on a project with the director."

"Caleb? Just the man I was looking for."

"He'll be here in about an hour."

Rawlings nodded but showed no sign of leaving. He looked me over, up and down, and I fleetingly regretted my rumpled appearance. Just as quickly, I reminded myself that first, I had been up all night trying to help put out a fire, and second, bookbinders wore old clothes to work, because new ones were immediately ruined by glues and dyes.

Rawlings glanced around the room, nodding. In Cambridge, I would have been on high alert by now, but I struggled not to overreact; this was small-town America, where people were friendly and not always in a rush.

"What's all that?" Rawlings inquired, indicating the clippings and photos.

"Oh, historical papers. Some old pictures." I tried to sound perky and unruffled, but I hoped my tone made it clear that I wasn't exactly inviting him to sit down and paw through the piles.

Rawlings nodded. "Tell Caleb I came by. My wife and I are having a little party tomorrow night—cocktails, hors d'oeuvres, nothing fancy. I just wanted to invite him and Sally."

"I'll tell him," I said.

He looked me straight in the eyes, disconcertingly, and

seemed to be about to say something, but apparently he thought better of it. He gave me a brisk nod and departed.

———

"Senator Rawlings?" Caleb said.

A senator? I thought. "He's having a party tomorrow night. He stopped by to invite you. And Sally."

"My wife," Caleb explained.

"I figured."

"So what is he, a state legislator?" I asked hopefully.

"He's the senior senator from Rhode Island, and head of the Senate Appropriations Committee. He and his wife have a summer house out on Harbor Point."

This explained a lot, particularly the way the man had felt entitled to walk right in, behaving as though the mere mention of his name would tell me everything I needed to know about him.

"Did he stay long?" Caleb asked.

"No."

"Did you discuss any of your ideas with him?"

The question struck me as strange: why would I? "He was only here for a few minutes."

"Sure, yeah, of course," Caleb said. "It's just that he's always been interested in what we're doing here, in the history of the island. But you'd have had no way of knowing that."

"No," I said. I sensed that there was something Caleb wasn't telling me, a detail missing from the overall picture, but I wasn't at my sharpest this morning. My head felt as though it was wrapped in heavy cotton batting.

"What's he doing here now, on the island?" I asked. "How come he isn't in Washington?"

"I'm a little surprised that they're down here this early. It might have to do with the Environmental Impact Review."

I was now officially lost.

"The Wind Farm Initiative," Caleb explained. "They've just done a huge study on the impact the windmills might have on birds, fish, noise levels, navigation."

And ghosts? I thought.

"The results were due at the beginning of the month."

"Has the senator been involved in the debate?"

"Oh yeah," Caleb said.

"For or against?" I asked.

"Against. Vehemently. He's a staunch environmentalist, and he's worried about migratory birds and fish habitats and all that."

"Oil spills aren't so great for them, either." I smiled, hoping to soften the edge of my comment.

"Oh, I'm all for putting them up, myself, but it's a real touchy subject. The island's split right down the middle."

"Really?" I knew that Mark had encountered resistance to his efforts; he and Lauren had used words like *ugly* and *vicious* to describe the tenor of the wind farm debate. I was also well aware of the fact that the ghosts were on the rampage. But hearing that half the island opposed the installation of windmills really surprised me.

Caleb nodded. "It's made for some pretty strange bedfellows, I have to say."

"How so?"

"Oh, folks who have literally nothing else in common. Windsurfing yuppies and lifelong year-rounders, fishermen and stockbrokers; it's crazy. Half the time they don't even agree on *why* it should or shouldn't happen—they've got completely different reasons—they just agree on the fact that it should or shouldn't be built.

"Take the environmentalists. You'd think they'd all be for it. I mean, climate change isn't just a theory anymore; everybody believes it's real and serious and happening much faster than anyone thought it was. But you've got people like Rawlings trying to protect the natural landscape and the ocean floor and the birds and the fish, and they're arguing with other environmentalists, folks who are more concerned about our carbon footprints and our dependence on fossil fuels. Not only is neither group wrong, they're both right. Then there's the impact on tourism and property values."

"How big are they?" I asked.

"The windmills themselves? Over four hundred feet. You'd definitely be able to see them from the island, but some people actually find them beautiful. I don't mind the look of them at all, but plenty of folks feel they'll ruin the view and take the tourism industry down with it."

"How many windmills are they talking about?" I asked.

"Forty."

"Wow. Yeah, you're going to see forty of them."

"My guess is that this little gathering tomorrow night has something to do with that report. I mean, Rawlings is a perfectly nice fellow, very down-to-earth, but he and his wife usually keep pretty much to themselves when they're here. They don't throw a lot of cocktail parties; or if they do, Sally and I aren't on the guest lists."

"It might be fun. Who knows?"

"I wouldn't go that far," said Caleb.

We turned our attention to the documents on the table. I

was starting to feel the effects of my sleepless night and hoped it wouldn't show.

"I do like the idea of working chronologically," I began. "I like that a lot. But we have an awful lot of material, and at some point, that concept is going to break down. People are going to want to follow the drama of the whole situation and may start to feel impatient or lose interest if the telling of the story, for lack of a better term, is being delayed by too much information. I don't know if this is making any sense to you."

From the expression on Caleb's face, I suspected that so far, my concept was as clear as mud.

"Go on," said Caleb.

"For example, at the beginning of the story, our story, meaning the book we create that *tells the story* of those hours, we might have, oh, profiles of some of the passengers and their reasons for boarding the boat. This would serve to draw in the reader and add a feeling of anxiety and tension, because we know what's about to happen to them. It's poignant, in a way, to think of them getting on that boat and having absolutely no idea that they'll never reach New York. That can really hook the reader emotionally. But later, we might be less interested in every last passenger and much more interested in how the news reached the island, who heard it and what they did first, how they felt."

"Okay," said Caleb.

"So I thought that the main book, the one people would look at if they were only going to examine one, might be a very creative if somewhat loose chronology using the most dramatic pieces we have, whatever we decide they are. Some passenger profiles, say, followed by a weather report, followed by that first-person narrative you have about the captain's retiring for the night, those quotes about hearing the ship's warning siren, maybe that lace handkerchief that washed up, anything that would make the story of that night come alive. I'm not saying that these would be the actual pieces, but the idea is that we'd find documents and maybe some objects that generate emotion of one sort or another and then we'd string them together like pearls on silk. All in the service of telling a dramatic story."

"That's great," Caleb whispered.

"Really?" I thought I'd sounded dense, slow, and inarticulate.

"I like it," he said. "And of course, there would have to be other books, given that we have so many other documents."

"Acid-free boxes might work for some of them. I don't see everything in a book. Also, I wouldn't rule out using some of the documents as the basis for exhibition pieces."

"Like what?" Caleb asked.

"You might record people reading the first-person accounts. Maybe the descendants of the islanders who actually wrote them. There could be an audio component to the exhibit. It wouldn't be very expensive."

"Maybe actors and actresses!" Caleb said. "We've had some fairly high-profile vacationers."

"Maybe," I said.

"This is great," said Caleb. "I like these ideas a lot."

"There's one more thing," I added. "Those snapshots, the ones by Honor Morton. We really should do something with them."

"They're amazing, aren't they?"

"You couldn't frame them all—it would be too expensive—but maybe you could have them put between mats."

"We could have an exhibition! Celebrate the opening of the—*Larchmont* Archive!"

"She deserves it," I said. "She had an amazing eye. Whatever became of her?"

"It was strange," Caleb replied. "It seems she left the island when she was twenty years old and never came back. There were rumors that she—" He broke off.

"Died?"

"Took her life," he said sadly.

Chapter Ten

I MET LAUREN IN the upstairs hall. It was about one thirty, and I had walked back to the inn from the Historical Society, planning to get a few hours' sleep before I had to pick up Henry. With Caleb's permission, I'd filled a sturdy plastic file box with most of the documents I hoped to include in our principal volume. My plan was to go to bed for the rest of the afternoon, pick up Henry and spend the evening with him, and then, once he fell asleep, settle down to a few hours' work before turning in myself.

Though Caleb had liked my idea for the main book's structure, I wanted to lay out all the pieces in the order in which I was thinking of using them, just to make sure that this concept really worked. I also planned to e-mail my favorite suppliers of leather and paper and ask them to FedEx us samples. We wanted to have a look that unified all the materials pertaining to the *Larchmont* disaster, so Caleb and I had decisions to make on everything from the shade of the papers and the texture of the leathers to the matting material we'd be using on the snapshots and the color and shape of the acid-free boxes.

"I was just bringing you this," Lauren said, handing me a copy of the book we had discussed over tea on Sunday, Antony Wicklow's *Inn of Phantoms.*

"Oh, thanks, great! I'll take a look at it."

"I didn't know you were around."

"I just got back."

"You must be ready to drop," she said. "I'm so sorry."

"It's not *your* fault. Did you get any sleep?" I'd found her in the kitchen when I'd come in for coffee at about a quarter of six this morning. She, too, had been tossing and turning for hours.

Lauren nodded. "I just woke up a little while ago."

"Good. Any sign of Frances?"

"No. I'm not surprised, though. There have been so many cars and trucks in and out of here that she's probably spooked. If she . . . I mean . . ."

"At least she wasn't in the barn," I noted quickly.

"No, no, they looked everywhere. No sign of her in there."

Lauren suddenly teared up.

"I'm sure she's *fine,*" I said. "She's probably just hiding somewhere until things quiet down."

Lauren sniffed and shook her head, obviously trying to get her emotions under control, but the tears spilled over.

"It's not that," she whispered.

"You poor thing. Come here." I took her arm and steered her over to an upholstered chair by the hall window. I pulled out its matching hassock and we both sat down.

"I'm fine," she said. "Really, I am. I don't know what's the matter with me."

"You don't? I could offer some possibilities."

"They think the fire was set," she announced abruptly.

"You're kidding. You know, I didn't want to mention anything last night, but Frank—your neighbor Frank?"

"Frank Hansen?"

"He said the same thing. He claimed he could tell by the color of the smoke. But then when Mark was talking about the cans of gasoline . . ."

"They found signs of accelerant all along the exterior foundation. The gasoline caused those black plumes inside, but somebody poured something on the outside and lit it."

"That's terrible! Who in the world would do that?"

"We don't know. We have no idea. It's such an awful feeling, to be asked if you have any enemies!" Lauren began to cry again. "*Enemies*? We thought everyone—liked us."

"Everyone *does* like you! You should have heard the way Caleb talked about the two of you—how much admiration everybody has for you both."

"Not everybody, obviously."

"So they have no clue as to who might have done it?"

Lauren sniffed and shook her head. "There's one weird thing, but it'll probably turn out to be nothing."

"You never know. What is it?"

"You remember Bert?"

Did I remember Bert? "Uh, yeah," I said.

"Bert has a sister, Aitana. She has her own catering company; she does a lot of the weddings and parties on the island. She had a last-minute request from the Rawlingses."

"Senator Rawlings? For the cocktail party?"

"How'd you know?"

"He came looking for Caleb this morning. He wanted to invite him."

"The senator?"

"Yeah, but I had no idea who he was."

Lauren laughed. "Did he give you the once-over?"

"He did."

"He's famous for it. Anyway, Aitana wasn't actually up and running yet; it's too early in the season. So she really had to scramble. She took the ferry over to the mainland yesterday and did all the shopping and came back last night. She has a commercial kitchen over on the other side of the island, and she was there until the middle of the night, trying to get a lot of the preliminary cooking done. On her way home, this couple in a station wagon practically ran her off the road."

"When was this?"

"About three this morning. She was driving back to her house."

"Were they drunk?"

"She didn't think so. But they were driving really fast. They forced her over onto the shoulder, passed her, and sped off."

"Did she get a license plate number?"

"She tried, but it was too dark. She thinks it began with *L* or *E,* but that was all she could see."

"How far from here did this happen?"

"Just down past the National, three, four blocks."

"How'd you hear about it?"

"Bert came by a little while ago. Aitana's over at the police station in New Shoreham now."

"Did she see what kind of a car it was?"

"It looked like an old Legacy, light green or maybe gray."

"The island's not that big," I said. "They ought to be able to find it."

"Yeah, but even if they do, it could have nothing to do with the fire." Lauren paused and then said, "You should really get some sleep. Want me or Mark to pick up Henry?"

"No, I'll be fine. I'll set the alarm on my cell phone."

"You sure? It's really no problem."

I shook my head. "Thanks, though."

"Thank *you*. I still can't believe you managed to get all that stuff out of the barn."

"Just in time to sell it!" I joked.

"In his dreams," said Lauren.

My cell phone rang at about four thirty. I was sleeping so heavily I felt practically drugged, but I hauled myself up to a sitting position and peered at the caller ID. It wasn't my alarm. It was my brother. I struggled to catch the call before it went to voice mail.

"Jay!" I said. "How *are* you? *Where* are you?"

"I'm at work." My brother likes to refer to himself, only slightly tongue in cheek, as a "civil servant." He works for the city of Chicago in a program called Green Alleys, the purpose of which I don't fully understand; it has something to do with making sidewalk and road construction more environmentally friendly. I tease him by calling it "Green Acres" and "Guys with Trucks" and regularly give him grief about finding a profession that pays him to muck around with steam shovels and excavators, his childhood obsessions.

"Where are *you*?" he asked.

"We're on Block Island."

"*That* must be nice." As payback, he always ribs me about my not having a normal nine-to-five job.

"I'm working," I said.

"No!"

"Yes."

"Hold on, I feel faint. And speaking of feeling faint, are you sitting down?"

I would have handed my brother lots of ammunition if I told him I was actually in bed, so I just said, "Yeeesssss."

"We're having a baby!" he announced. "In fact, we're having two!"

"Oh my God! Jay! *Tell* me!"

Jay laughed. "I just told you!"

"You're having twins?"

"Well, *I'm* not. Louise is."

Louise and Jay have been married for almost four years, but since I'd already moved east by the time they met, I don't really know her that well. We only see each other once or twice a year, on holidays. She's a corporate litigator on the partner track at her law firm, and I've always suspected that she thinks I'm kind of a slacker, if not a bona fide black sheep. She, on the other hand, works such long hours that I was surprised she even agreed to get a dog, which they did last year.

"This is wonderful!" I said as tears began to prickle the backs of my eyes. "I'm so happy for you!"

"Thanks. We're—well, we're a little shocked, to tell you the truth. And it wasn't even IVF! It was just—"

"Luck," I said.

"I hope so," Jay answered.

"How far along is she?"

"Fourteen weeks. We didn't want to tell anybody until, well, you know."

"How's she feeling?"

"Like crap."

"Well, that's a good sign. Or so they say."

"No, it is, it is. It's all going great. It's two little boys." Jay's voice caught on the final words, and I had a surprising reminder of the softheartedness that lies beneath his all-guy demeanor. Jay's so much like my dad: all bluff and bluster but soft as a July peach.

I thought about my mother, and how unfair it was that she had to miss this, too. I didn't go through life longing for her at every turn, or if I did, I wasn't very aware of it. I hadn't really known her, so her absence at all the milestones of childhood and adolescence was felt more keenly by others than by me.

All that changed when Henry was born. In fact, it changed the minute I knew I was pregnant. I missed everything about her and everything I imagined about her. I envisioned her listening to my troubles through all those long months and finding me clothes that were comfortable and pretty, helping me get a nice nursery together and coming to stay when Henry arrived. I never contemplated the possibility that had she lived to see that day, she might have been disappointed in me, or angry, or distant and distracted. I just didn't want to go there, so I didn't, claiming instead the sad privilege of children who lose a parent early. I was free to imagine her any way I wanted, so the mother I created was perfect.

"I wish Mom were here," I said.

"Me, too," Jay whispered. He was five when she died.

"What did Daddy say?"

"I haven't told him yet."

"You haven't? What about Joe?"

"Him, either."

Now my own tears spilled over. "You told *me* first? Jay!"

"I'm kind of surprised myself," he said.

On my way out the door to pick up Henry, I offered to make a stop at a pizza place I'd noticed between the inn and the school, unpromisingly named Vito's Sub and Slice. You can't judge a pizza joint by its name, though. My all-time favorite had been called, simply, Joe's.

Lauren looked askance at the pizza idea.

"I could get a couple of extra-larges and a salad or two. Couldn't you use a break?"

"That place is a dive!"

"Is there another one that's better?"

"Not at this time of year," she insisted. "Anyway, the meat's already marinating."

I'd had no choice but to relent, and now, sitting at the kitchen table a couple of hours later, I was glad I had. Mark was grilling London broil over wood charcoal, and Lauren had just removed from the oven a pan of tiny red potatoes roasted with cracked pepper and fresh rosemary. A simple green salad with dried cranberries and toasted pine nuts sat in a wooden bowl in the center of the table, and I could only dream of the desserts lined up in the mahogany-paneled pantry.

Vivi made her appearance as soon as we sat down. I'd expected that she would turn up before long, but my heart sank at the sight of her slight frame materializing in the rocking chair by the woodstove, not five feet from where we were all sitting. I hoped she wasn't strong enough to get the rocker going, and I wondered what Henry would do. Would he start talking and playing with her right there in the kitchen, with all of us sitting around? Or would he be restrained by some vague awareness that he should wait until the two of them, or the three of us, were alone?

I didn't dare take a chance.

"You are *not* to talk to Vivi! Or mention her to anyone," I whispered sternly while Lauren and Mark were in the backyard, conferring about the doneness of the meat.

"Why not?" he responded.

"Just don't," I growled, and in case he was thinking of not taking me seriously, I added, "And I *mean* it! I'll explain later."

He gave me a hurt and bewildered look, and rightly so. He'd done absolutely nothing to elicit what probably felt like a reprimand, and I hated myself for acting like one of those adults who pushes a kid around just because they can.

"I'm sorry, sweetie. I'm not mad at you, but I—just need you to do this." Lauren was coming back into the kitchen as I leaned over to give him a conciliatory kiss. He pulled away. Things could then have gone either way. Henry can be fractious when he feels like it, which is often, but tonight, as Mark sliced the meat and Lauren tossed the salad, I watched him sink into a morose little funk. I felt terrible. I almost wished he would act up and defy me.

Over the course of the next twenty minutes, Vivi practically hung from the chandelier in her efforts to get Henry to talk to her. She made faces at him and danced around the table like a possessed little demon. She called him stupid and accused him of eating like a pig. She tried to squeeze in next to him on his chair and blew in his ear. Henry shot me look after desperate look, but there was nothing I could really do except try to get us out of there as quickly as possible and into the relative privacy of our room.

He beat me to the punch.

"Can I be excused?" Henry asked halfway through our main course. *"Please?"*

"Aren't you hungry?" I inquired, feeling phony and disloyal.

He shook his head but fixed me with a killer gaze.

"You're probably tired, " I said. "It's been a long day." This was another small betrayal. We both know that when he's overtired, he doesn't lose his appetite, he eats like a horse.

"He does look a little pale," Lauren noted.

"More steak for me," Mark teased, and a flicker of a grin passed quickly over Henry's features.

"Sure," I said. "I'll be up in a bit."

Henry got up and pushed in his chair.

"What do you say?" I prodded.

"Thank you for dinner."

"I'll send some cookies up with your mom," Lauren told him. "In case you get hungry later."

"Thanks," he said and skipped out of the room. The ghostly little wraith fled with him.

Chapter Eleven

❧

I DIDN'T INTEND TO leave Henry with Vivi for long, but I was eager to know if there had been any news about the blaze. According to Lauren, two investigators from the state fire marshall's office in North Kingston had arrived at about one thirty, while I was asleep upstairs. They'd spent most of the afternoon talking to Mark, taking photographs, and collecting wood and soil samples. Though they were reluctant to render an official verdict before the results of the lab tests came back, Mark had no doubt in his mind: it was arson.

They had showed him a suspicious burn pattern where the fieldstone foundation met the wood of the barn. They'd managed to determine that the fire had originated from several places at once, unlike in the usual scenario, they'd explained to him, when a single object or area catches fire and the flames spread outward and upward. They also discovered an empty five-gallon kerosene can in the marshy brush between the barn and the Hansens' house. They took this back to North Kingston, to test it for fingerprints and to see if they could determine where it had been purchased.

"Who would do this?" I asked. Privately, though, I felt

enormously relieved that the evidence was pointing to live human beings.

Mark shook his head and shrugged.

"This seems like such a peaceful place," I went on.

"They're not from the island," Lauren announced. "Whoever did this."

Mark smiled. "Lauren's got it all figured out. Women's intuition."

"No, I don't," she protested. "And don't start in with that. I'm not saying I know who did it, I'm just telling you that I seriously doubt it was anyone who lives here."

"Why do you say that?" I asked, though I had a feeling she could be right.

"Because around here, people come right out and tell you what they think, and that's that. Like when they were building the new school?" Lauren glanced at Mark. "Remember?"

Mark shook his head.

"The first design for the building was really out there," Lauren explained. "Personally, I thought it was kind of neat, but I agreed that it probably wasn't right for the island. It was a famous architect from Switzerland who designed it. I've forgotten his name now. God knows how he got the job."

"I know how he got it," Mark put in. "He was at RISD at the same time Rawlings was at Brown. They played softball together, and they've been friends ever since."

"Figures," said Lauren. "Anyway, nobody pulled any punches that night. Don't you remember that meeting?"

"What meeting?" Mark asked.

"In the school cafeteria! You remember!"

Mark shook his head. "I don't think I was there."

Lauren appeared to consider this for a moment. "You're

right, you weren't. I went with Aitana. Well, anyway, the architect's model for the school was sitting right there on the table, and the building was all these crazy, slanty angles. If you could have seen the looks on some of the old-timers' faces: Hiram Whitehall and Stu Cavanaugh, and that guy who sells eggs out in front of his house."

"Makem," Mark said. "Gibby Makem."

"Right. But my point is, there was a respectful debate. It was lively, sure, and there was plenty of smoke and steam about preserving the character of the island, but the issue was resolved in a civilized way, in public. Nobody was sneaking around."

Sneaking around? I wasn't sure where this was going, and I didn't know if I should ask. My mind raced ahead to the question of whether a phalanx of earthbound spirits, fiercely opposed to the planting of windmills in their deep sea graveyard, could possibly have (a) purchased a five-gallon tank of kerosene, (b) transported it to Lauren and Mark's backyard, (c) doused the barn's foundation, and (d) lit it.

Fortunately, the answer to all these questions was simple. No.

"I know you think I'm crazy," Lauren said to her husband.

"I don't think you're crazy, honey. I think you're— pregnant!" A wide grin broke out on Mark's face.

"I hate it when you say things like that!" Lauren sprang to her feet and began clearing our dishes. "This has nothing at all to do with whether I'm—"

"I'm sorry."

"No, you're not!" Lauren insisted.

Mark stood up and grabbed the plates from her hands. Lauren sat back down. "You could very well be right," he conceded.

"I know I'm operating on a sleep deficit here," I put in, "but I'm not following."

"Lauren thinks that someone was trying to intimidate us, get us to back off," Mark explained.

"Yeah, somebody too cowardly and immature to walk up the front steps, knock on our door, sit down with us, and discuss the matter like a civilized human being. They can't have a problem with the inn, whoever they are, or if they do, I can't for the life of me imagine what it would be. This place was an eyesore. It was bringing down everyone else's property values. All *we* did was pour close to a million dollars, which we don't really have, into bringing the old wreck back to life.

"Mark gets along with everybody," she continued, "and so do I. Heck, the islanders who are most opposed to the wind farm were all here today, trying to help out. Bud Brady, Andy Miller . . ."

"She's right," said Mark.

"I know I'm right," said Lauren.

I was about to attempt some kind of lame, reassuring response when our conversation was interrupted by an impatient howl.

Lauren wheeled around and flew to her feet.

"Frances!"

Sure enough, there she was, round and regal.

"Oh, my baby," Lauren said. "Are you okay?" She hurried over to the door, opened it gingerly, and scooped Frances up. "Where have you been? We've been so worried!"

Frances didn't appear to be any the worse for wear. There were so many questions I wanted to ask my hosts, but my thoughts had turned to the scene upstairs, and I suddenly felt a wave of anxiety. Frances's homecoming offered me a timely opportunity to slip away.

"I'm going to check on Henry," I said. Lauren nodded distractedly, and Mark hardly seemed to hear me.

"You must be starving!" he cooed. "Poor old thing!"

"Reow!" mewed Frances.

———

I love to eavesdrop. I know it's sneaky, but that just makes it more fun.

I tiptoed down the upstairs hall and paused outside our door, which Henry had neglected to close. I'd heard some reassuring hoots on my way up the stairs, so I gathered that once Henry had been released from my glowering interdictions, he and Vivi had settled back into their curious little relationship, in which they alternately ignored and bickered with each other, and occasionally rode a wave of escalating hysterics that culminated in breathlessness.

"And then he lit it!" I heard Vivi shriek.

I caught my breath and tried to remain motionless.

I hadn't told Henry about the fire. As we'd made our way home from the school, he'd been animated and chatty, full of stories about the progress on Greased Lightnin', the items he'd eaten for snacks and lunch, and a boy named Brian. As any parent knows, when your child is in a talkative mood, it's wise to keep your mouth closed; you never know when they'll be forthcoming again.

"He did not," Henry said.

"He did, too!" Vivi shot back.

There was now a long period of silence. From the squeaking of bedsprings, I deduced that Henry was bouncing, from a sitting position, on the bed. If he progressed to outright jumping, I would have to step out of hiding.

"Did you see *The Lion King*?" Henry finally asked.

"What?"

"*The Lion King*! The movie!"

"No," Vivi answered.

"*Never?*" Henry sounded incredulous.

If Vivi responded, I didn't hear her.

"But did you ever hear the songs?" he pressed.

"I don't know," Vivi said quietly.

"Like, 'Hakuna Matata'!" Henry said.

I almost laughed out loud.

"What?" I heard her say.

"Hakuna Matata," he continued, "is a wonderful day! Hakuna Matata——" And here he broke off.

"Ha-do-do duh-doo-do!" Vivi mimicked.

Henry upped her one. "Ha-poo-poo puh-poo-poo!"

Next came uproarious giggles and the groan and screech of seriously aggrieved bedsprings.

"Hey, hey, hey!" I said, stepping out from behind the door and into the room. Henry immediately plopped onto his bottom on the bed. Vivi kept jumping, but being as insubstantial as a breeze, she posed no threat to the furniture, the windows, or herself.

"No fair!" Henry complained.

"No fair what?"

"No fair sneaking up on us!"

I hadn't been fair in imposing a gag order at the table, either, but this seemed to have slipped his mind. I would probably hear about it later, or be treated to some kind of misbehavior that revealed that he was still really, really miffed at me about *something*, he just couldn't remember what.

I decided to dive straight in.

"I heard you talking about the fire," I said. "Pretty scary, huh?"

"No," said Vivi. She wasn't going to give me the satisfaction of agreeing with anything I said.

"How come you didn't wake me up?" Henry asked accusingly.

"I did," I lied. "Don't you remember?"

"No," he said petulantly.

I shrugged.

"Was someone *smoking*?" Henry asked.

I had to hand it to the antismoking folks: they sure had managed to drive home the message that smoking was *bad*. I was used to hearing the dripping scorn in my son's tone of voice when we passed a hapless tobacco addict on the street, but this was impressive: he automatically assumed that any fire had to have been caused by a carelessly tossed butt.

"I don't know," I said. "What do you think?" I glanced at Vivi.

She appeared to be torn about whether to talk to me. She was obviously still wary after the events of last night, but I was confusing her now by being nice.

"I bet someone fell asleep while they were *smoking*," Henry pronounced, predictably.

I plopped down on the other bed and divested myself of my bulky sweater.

"I dreamed I was making popcorn. But when I woke up, I realized that the sounds were really happening, and they were coming from the fire."

Henry dropped his jaw. This gesture was new to the repertoire and was usually accompanied by rapid blinking.

"Didn't that ever happen to you?"

Henry shook his head. "Sometimes I think I'm walking down stairs but they disappear."

"Stairs? And you step off into the air?"

"Yeah," Henry said.

"And you kind of jump?"

He nodded.

"That's happened to me, too," I said casually, stealing a look at Vivi. I had to remember that she was only a child, and that she had been alone for more than a hundred years. I didn't rush in to fill the silence. After a moment, she surprised me by speaking up.

"One time when I was sleeping," she volunteered, "I heard a really big boom. And then I dreamed I was swimming underwater." There was no longer any trace of a smirk on her face. She looked tiny and cheerless.

"Then what happened?" I asked gently.

"I woke up," she finally whispered.

"Woke up—like you are now?"

She didn't answer. She didn't have to. It was clear to me that Vivi was not recalling the familiar human transition from sleep to wakefulness, but her own baffling passage from life to death. Though she had never actually told me about being on the doomed steamship, I felt all but certain that she had met her death there. She had probably been asleep and had been awakened by the *boom* of the *Harry Knowlton* hitting the *Larchmont*. No doubt she actually remembered being under water, before "waking up" into her present incarnation.

"Were you afraid?" I asked gently.

She nodded.

"Were you alone?"

She frowned and bit her lip, but before she could say any more, Henry burst in.

"Can she sleep over *tonight*?" he wheedled. *"Please?"*

"Okay, but you have to let her have your bed."

"How come?" he demanded.

"Because that's the polite thing to do. When somebody sleeps over and there aren't enough beds, you let the guest have your bed."

"Can we make me a bed on the floor? With pillows?"

"Sure."

"You call her mom," Henry instructed me.

Vivi looked over to gauge my reaction, but as I caught her eye, I just shrugged. She shrugged back.

I was rewarded for my patience after Henry fell asleep. Vivi was lying on top of his bed, barely visible in the moonlight streaming through the window. It had taken all my strength to remain awake, but the moment arrived when I was sure that Henry had finally drifted off.

"Vivi?" I whispered.

She looked over.

"You were talking about the fire."

She watched me and said nothing.

"Did somebody set it?"

"Yes," she said quietly.

"Who?"

"I don't know."

"Kids or grown-ups?"

"Grown-ups," she responded.

"Do you know how old?" I realized immediately that this was a stupid question. Children can't tell how old adults are; anyone old enough to babysit would probably be classified as a grown-up.

"Just guess," I said. "Did they seem older than me or younger?"

"The same," she said.

"So, about my age?"

She nodded.

"And were they men?" I asked.

"A man and a lady."

"Thank you for telling me. This will be really helpful." How, I wasn't sure. I couldn't exactly head over to the police station in New Shoreham and pass on the information without having to reveal how I'd learned it.

We were quiet for a few moments. I struggled to keep my eyes open.

"Is there anything you want to talk to me about?" I finally asked, with my very last ounce of waking energy.

"No," she said.

"You remember that I can help you cross over, right? Whenever you're ready. Any time at all, you just tell me."

"I don't *want* to," she said vehemently.

"Why not?"

"Because of my brother. I can't leave until I get him."

I sat up. "What?"

"He let go of my hand. When we were swimming."

I felt a chill run through me. "When you were under water?"

She nodded.

"How old was he—*is* he?"

"Three," Vivi answered.

I took a deep breath. "Well, honey, he's probably already crossed over. I'm sure he's with your mom and dad."

"No, he *didn't*."

"How do you know?"

"He's here. Down by the lighthouse. He's—like me."

"A spirit? A ghost?"

Vivi nodded. "A lady has him. She was on the boat. He *wants* *me* but I can't get him. She lets me play with him, outside, but when I try to get him back, she picks him up and takes him away, and she doesn't let me come."

"What's his name?" I asked.

"Jamey," she whispered.

Chapter Twelve

CALEB WAS ALREADY in the office when I arrived at nine. I had little to show for the previous days' efforts, but he seemed unperturbed by my lack of visible progress and excited about the leather and paper samples that would be arriving, I hoped, tomorrow.

"You know, I really liked that idea," he said.

"Which idea?"

"The audio component. Having the letters and diary entries read by the descendants of the people who actually wrote them. Or by actors."

"I can't take credit for that," I said. "I've been to a couple of museums where they've done that. It's spooky: you're looking at all these sepia-toned pictures and hearing those people's words. It's almost like listening to voices from beyond the grave."

"It would be great if we had a special room we could dedicate to it. I'm going to have to think about that."

"Do you have the space here?" I asked.

Caleb shook his head. "Well, not downstairs. There are rooms up on the second floor, but they need a lot of work."

"Maybe in the future," I suggested.

"Maybe."

I spent the morning doing what I had planned to do the previous evening: laying out all the documents and sorting papers and mementos into pertinent piles. Two hours of thinking and rearranging convinced me that the concept of relying on a dramatic story line really would work, and I set my mind to putting together a rough assembly of the most poignant and heart-stopping individual documents I could find.

I had dozens to choose from. The Joy Line Company, in gratitude for the efforts of the islanders to aid the stricken survivors, had turned over to the Historical Society all its correspondence with the *Larchmont*'s passengers before the evening of the fateful voyage.

There was a handwritten note from a Mr. Redmond Mullins of Providence, requesting the private use of the small library on the steamer's second level between the hours of nine and nine thirty: he intended to propose marriage to a Miss Evelyn Brosman.

There was the carbon copy of a letter from the *Larchmont*'s head chef, Coleman Birmingham, to a Mrs. Dedrick Hoskins of New York, who had booked passage back from Providence for five in her family. Mr. Birmingham had received the request for a birthday cake and asked that Mrs. Hoskins telephone him with further directions. Would little Miss Hoskins like decorative rosettes or candied violets? Lemon or rose-water icing?

There were full-length statements taken from the few survivors. I intended to break these up into short paragraphs and drop the fragments into the story line, in effect juxtaposing a human voice with hard copies of the wireless dispatches, weather reports, and after-the-fact newspaper fragments detailing the

events of that evening as they unfolded. My only problem
was, I had nearly five hundred documents I really wanted to
use.

I popped into the adjoining room, where Caleb was working at his desk. "We might need to do two volumes," I announced.

He looked up. "Is that a problem?" he asked.

"Not for me."

He smiled. "Go for it."

"Great," I said.

"Oh, and gosh! I completely forgot I was supposed to ask
you..."

"Ask me what?"

"To the party. At the Rawlingses'. Tomorrow night."

"What? *No!*"

Caleb nodded. "He called the house last night. He made a
special point of it, mentioned several times that he *really* wanted
me to invite you."

"He's just being polite," I said.

"Polite? Rawlings? I doubt it."

"I can't."

Caleb gave me a skeptical look. I was sure he was thinking
that my social calendar couldn't be *that* overcrowded, given
that I'd been on the island all of three days and knew hardly
anyone.

"How often do you get invited to a senator's house?" he
nudged. "Besides, you really should see it." His tone was suggesting *something*, but I wasn't sure what.

"The house?"

"Let's just say it's one of a kind." He leaned back in his
chair and put his feet up on the desk. I noticed that he was not

wearing socks with his Top-Siders, a habit I had often observed among guys who seemed to get their clothes at J. Crew or Brooks Brothers.

I sighed. I *was* curious, no question. It would be so much fun to call Dad and my brothers and let drop the little tidbit that I had been invited over for cocktails by the head of the Senate Appropriations Committee. It would really surprise Louise. Then again, I couldn't call Dad just yet. Jay might not have reached him with the news about the babies, and I didn't trust myself not to spring the surprise.

And what about Lauren and Mark? Had they been invited? After how welcoming they'd been to me, I couldn't imagine announcing that I had scored what had to be, on the island, a fairly coveted invitation and bouncing out their front door, leaving them behind. Besides, I had nothing to wear. And I had Henry.

"We've got a sitter coming," Caleb said, after I elected to rely on the latter excuse. "Bring him over. We'll be home by eight or eight thirty."

"I'll think about it," I replied.

―――

At one thirty, I decided to take a break and get out for a breath of fresh air and some lunch. Caleb had left at about twelve o'clock. Running the Historical Society, as it turned out, was not his full-time job; he was "of counsel" to a law firm in Providence, specializing in wills and trusts. This meant that he made his own schedule, working from a home office, advising mostly people of a certain age on matters of estate planning. A few times a month, he took the ferry over to the mainland to file documents, show up at probate court, treat clients to lunch or drinks, and generally maintain the steady flow of work that enabled him to telecommute year-round from Block Island.

I locked the door behind me and took a deep breath. The wind was brisk, and the cool temperature—somewhere in the fifties, I guessed—suppressed the aromas of spring. I didn't want to go back to the Grand View. Lauren would insist on making me a nice lunch, and I wasn't up for either the socializing or the volume of food. A quick slice of pizza would do.

I headed up toward the school, half hoping that the kids would be out at a recess, affording me the opportunity to spy on Henry and assess for myself whether he was having fun and making friends. The schoolyard was deserted, though, and that made sense. They'd probably had outdoor playtime right after lunch and were now back to the serious business of car painting and dance rehearsing.

A pickup truck pulled up behind me just as I was opening the door to Vito's Sub and Slice.

"Wait!" I heard someone say.

I turned around. It was Bert.

"You really don't want to do that," he whispered.

"I don't?"

He shook his head.

I peeked into the shop. No one seemed to be around, so I wouldn't be hurting any feelings by retracing my steps. I closed the door quietly.

"But I'm starving," I said.

"We can fix that," Bert replied.

"Who's we?"

"My sister." He grinned. "I'm bringing her some flounder."

"Oh, and I'm sure she'd appreciate a surprise guest for lunch."

Bert laughed. "You don't know Aitana. I'll have you back in an hour. I promise."

I was still hesitating, and I didn't know why. Well, actually, I did. I had developed an immediate and alarmingly intense crush, and I didn't entirely trust myself not to reveal this somehow. Also, I didn't want to ruin the pleasure of a perfectly harmless and enjoyable escape by finding out that in fact, Bert was a dope.

Then again, that might a very good idea. He lived here. I lived in Cambridge. He probably had a girlfriend, and if someone as cute and nice as he was *didn't*, there had to be a good reason why. I'd do well to nip this thing in the bud.

I walked around to the passenger side and got in. I could just tell that I hadn't pulled off a fetching and mysterious Juliette Binoche–type half smile; I had produced a goofy and unattractive squint.

"Buckle up," Bert said.

The interior of the truck was pretty tidy, unlike those of most trucks I've been in. Of course, I'm in no position to point a finger in the vehicle cleanliness department. Once every few months, I fill a shopping bag with empty coffee cups and candy wrappers and sheets of paper covered with directions I no longer need, but the inside of my car hasn't seen a vacuum cleaner or a bottle of Windex in a long time.

"So, what are you doing here, again?" Bert asked by way of a conversation starter.

"Just grabbing a quick lunch."

"No, I mean on the island!" Bert pulled out onto Ocean Avenue and headed in the direction of the Mohegan Bluffs.

"I'm a bookbinder. Freelance. I'm working on a project for the Historical Society."

"Oh, right, yeah. What is it? Or can't you say?"

"There's nothing secret about it. They had boxes and boxes of stuff related to a disaster at sea back at the turn of the century. The twentieth century, I mean. A steamship was hit by another boat and it sank."

"The *Larchwood*," Bert said.

"*Larchmont*, but yeah, that's the one. I'm pulling all the materials together. They got a grant of some kind."

"From whom?"

I paused. A sexy guy who used *whom* correctly? This could be dangerous.

"I don't know," I replied. "It was anonymous."

"Hmmm," Bert said, eyebrows knit thoughtfully. "So that's probably a person, right? It's usually people who want to stay anonymous."

"Now that you mention it, yeah, probably."

"You think it was someone from the island?" he asked.

"I don't know. It could be anybody, really. I thought maybe it was from a descendant of one of the passengers who died. Anyway, I'm binding some of the materials and getting some others ready to be displayed. The Society is hoping to have some kind of event this summer."

"What kind of event?"

"Maybe a lecture or two. An exhibit, probably with a reception."

"I've never set foot in there, to tell you the truth."

"I'm the same way at home. The only time I go to a museum or a monument is when I've got company from out of town."

"Where do you live?" he asked.

"Outside of Boston. Cambridge."

"I used to live in East Cambridge!"

"You're kidding! When?"

"When I was in high school. My uncle owns a fish market by the courthouse. I used to work the counter during the summers."

"And where'd you live the rest of the time? Here?"

"New Bedford. Aitana, my sister, she married a guy from the island," he went on. "We really got to like it over here. My— wife and I."

I felt my stomach drop. His *wife*?

Bert glanced over. "She passed away three years ago."

"Oh my God! I'm so sorry. She was—young."

"Twenty-eight. She had a heart rhythm disorder. Genetic. She was on medication, but . . ." He trailed off.

"Gosh, I don't know what to say."

"There's nothing *to* say. It happens." Then, as though to re-direct the conversation as quickly as possible, he added, "You've got a nice kid."

"Thanks," I said.

"What does your husband do?"

"I'm not married."

Bert seemed to mull this over for a minute. "Divorced?"

"Nope." I was torn about what and how much to reveal. I tend to view my situation as one variation of normal, but people don't always agree. Then again, Bert had just revealed some fairly personal information to me.

"Henry's dad is a police officer in Boston," I began. "We got together when he was separated from his wife. They were thinking about getting a divorce, but then, fortunately, they were able to work everything out."

"Fortunately?" Bert asked.

"For them."

Bert burst out laughing, and surprisingly, so did I.

"Though I did get Henry out of the deal, so I'm not complaining."

"Not much, anyway," Bert quipped.

"Not out loud," I added with a grin.

———

Aitana's kitchen was located on Lakeside Drive, on the other side of the island. As we pulled into the driveway, I turned to Bert in disbelief.

"This is it?"

He nodded, got out, and walked around to the back of the truck to retrieve the flounder.

The one-room building looked nothing like a commercial kitchen; it seemed hardly bigger than the maple sugar shacks you see tucked just inside the edges of the Vermont woods. Though tiny, it had all the charm of an antique one-room farmhouse. It was framed with substantial beams and clad in what looked like reclaimed barnboard, and white sheers breezed lazily out of open windows on both sides of the oversized front door.

"You like?" Bert asked as I closed my door.

"It's adorable!"

"We built it, Peter and I."

"You *built* it?"

He nodded. "My brother-in-law's a plumber. It was a crime what Aitana was paying to lease a cooking space, and her in-laws had the land, so we went for it. Come on in."

Bert led me around the side of the building and up the wide back steps to a deck that ran the length of the structure. Sliding glass doors opened into the kitchen and afforded the chef a soothing view of the woods out behind. A woman about my age and height, whom I took to be Bert's sister, was standing at a stainless steel-table rolling out a sheet of piecrust or puff pastry.

Bert slid the door open. "Hi," he said, motioning for me to step inside. "We came for lunch."

Aitana looked up. It was eerie how much she resembled her brother—same dark chocolate eyes, same black hair, nearly identical wry grin.

"It wasn't my idea," I added quickly. "I'm Anza O'Malley. Nice to meet you. Sorry to drop in so—"

Aitana attempted to wipe her floury hands on her white apron. They were covered with sticky dough, though, so she just said, "Sorry! Nice to meet you, too."

"You're on your own," she announced to Bert. "And make some for me, too. All I've had today is coffee."

"What have you got?" Bert asked, scanning the contents of one of the two refrigerators that spanned the entire side wall.

"You've got eyes in your head, don't you?" she shot back.

"Mmmm! Quiche!"

"No! Do *not* touch those!"

"What about the—what is that, onion pizza?"

She paused in her rolling and gave him a long look. "Pissaladière," she corrected. "And that's off-limits, too. It's for tomorrow night."

"What's the flounder for?" I asked.

Bert snapped his fingers and said, "Lunch." He must have seen me look at my watch because he added, "Don't worry. You'll be back by two thirty."

Twenty minutes later, we were seated on tall stools at the far end of the steel table, tucking into poached flounder with butter sauce, roasted green beans and parsnips left over from a thank-you luncheon Aitana had catered for the library volunteers, and French bread plucked from the freezer and tossed into a hot oven. I'd been dismayed to witness Bert's ease at the stove and the comfortable teasing he gave and took. A secret infatuation was one thing, but here we were with his sister, laughing like old friends over an impromptu lunch. I needed to find something not to like about him, and quick.

"You can have some cookies," Aitana announced grandly, sliding off her stool as Bert scooped up our plates and placed them in the sink.

"Gee, thanks," he shot back. "Coffee?" he asked me.

I nodded. Aitana retrieved two huge plastic Tupperware boxes from a high shelf and pried off their lids. They were filled with dozens and dozens of tiny cookies, all laid out on sheets of parchment paper: shortbread drops with chocolate chips, crumbly squares with layers of jam, rounds of pastry topped with pecans, shards of chocolate-topped toffee, and thumbprint cookies emblazoned with glazed apricots.

"We can't eat *these!*" I said.

"Why not?" Aitana replied.

"They're too beautiful!"

"Trust me," Bert teased, "they look better than they taste."

"Very funny," Aitana shot back.

I helped myself to two. Aitana put a couple more on my plate.

As we waited for the coffee to brew, I fought an urge to ask Aitana about the events of Tuesday night. I must have withdrawn and gone quiet all of a sudden, preoccupied with thoughts of Vivi and the fire and the pain I'd heard in Lauren's voice as she tried to puzzle out who might hate them and why.

"What's up?" I heard Bert say.

"What? Oh, sorry! I was just—thinking about the other night."

"The fire?" Aitana asked.

I nodded, and before I could stop myself, I said, "I heard you—might have seen someone . . . !"

"I've been looking high and low for that car!" Aitana said. "I went out on my bike first thing this morning, before it was even really light out. I took all the back roads and peeked in people's garages."

"Aitana!" Bert said.

"I don't care!" she replied.

"Well I do!" said Bert.

"That son of a b—pardon my French—practically ran me over!"

"You leave that to the police," Bert said sternly. "They've got all these guys in from North Kingston, and they don't need you poking around."

"So you didn't really see them?" I asked.

"It was a man and a woman, I know that."

"I heard that, too," I admitted, then immediately wanted to strangle myself for opening my big mouth before thinking it through.

"From whom?" Bert asked quickly, eyes wide.

"Lauren," I blurted out, covering my tracks. If there was one thing that could stop a budding romance dead in its tracks, it was a badly botched version of my ghost disclosure. I'd learned that the hard way.

Aha! I thought. Wouldn't Dr. Freud have something to say about this! I had thoughtlessly blurted out a detail I might have to explain, if I were being truthful, as something a ghost had told me, just moments after realizing that I was falling for Bert and had better find something to dislike about him. Soon.

Or—maybe something he might dislike about *me*.

He lived here. I lived in Cambridge. And guys who seemed to be too good to be true usually were.

"Okay," I said. "You're both probably going to think I'm totally bonkers, but—well, here it is: I have the ability to see ghosts. And talk to them. I always could, ever since I was little."

Bert's smile faded a little.

"And?" Aitana prompted.

"And . . . there's a ghost at the Grand View. A little girl. She saw the people who set the fire, and she said it was a man and a woman."

"I knew it!" Aitana shouted.

She knew it? No stunned silence? No exchange of awkward looks?

Bert had turned his back to us and was pouring the coffee, so I couldn't gauge his reaction to all this.

"So you believe in ghosts?" I asked her.

"I sure do," she replied. "In fact, I've seen ghosts. Twice."

"You have?" My heart was thumping.

Bert turned and handed me my coffee.

"I don't," he said. "Sorry."

"But you believe *I* saw them, don't you?" Aitana pressed.

"No, as a matter of fact." He got a container of cream out of the refrigerator. "I think you had one too many margaritas."

"I did not!"

"I could probably convince you," I said to Bert.

"Oh, yeah? Well, I'm not very suggestible. People have tried to hypnotize me before and it didn't work."

"This is a little different." I took a sip of my coffee.

"How so?"

"Well, sometimes I'll see a ghost in the vicinity of a person, hanging around them. If I speak to the spirit, I can usually learn some things about the person that I would have no way of knowing, because the ghost is usually someone the person was close to in life, a relative or close friend."

I saw Bert look away quickly, and I was suddenly really sorry I had started down this avenue. He'd just told me that he lost his wife not too long ago.

"I see," he said, sipping his coffee. "Any ghosts hanging around me?"

"Nope," I was happy to reply.

Chapter Thirteen

"Can we drive by the lighthouse?" I asked Bert as he pulled the truck out of the driveway. "If you have time, I mean."

"I've got all the time in the world. Until I get serious about catching some fish, anyway."

I had time, too, now that I really thought about it. It was obvious that I wasn't going to be able to finish the binding and mounting while I was on the island. Caleb and I hadn't been able to select our final materials; the samples that would allow us to choose them hadn't even arrived. Feeling sure that Lauren or Mark would almost always be around, I had arranged for the FedEx packages to be delivered to the Grand View rather than the Historical Society. I was hoping they would arrive today, but until they did, and until Caleb and I could sit down together and decide which leathers and stocks of paper would be best, there wasn't a whole lot more I could do. Besides, Caleb had hired me to complete the project by sometime this summer, not to work nine to five in an office. I might play a little loose with my schedule while I was here, but the project would be done on time.

"Oh, darn, hold on a sec," Bert said suddenly, pulling over to the side of the road and shifting into park. "There's something I meant to pick up. I'll be right back."

"No problem. Take your time." I watched him cut across the grass toward Aitana's cabin. I rolled down my window and breathed in the scents of the sea and of pine.

So he didn't believe in ghosts. He would one day, if anything ever developed between us, and in the meantime, I would leave the subject of proof to him. If he wanted to put me to a test, I'd be more than happy to take it, but I wasn't about to force the issue. Bert came back into view, hurrying toward the truck with a brown cardboard box in hand.

"Sorry!" he said, placing the box in the space behind the seat. "She had a couple of old sconces she wanted me to rewire."

I smiled. He was a nice guy. I reached over and touched his hand.

"You think I'm weird?" I asked, feeling suddenly vulnerable.

"No! What do you mean?"

"Ghosts and spirits and everything?"

He shook his head. "Look, I thought I knew everything until a couple of years ago. Now I realize I don't know a damn thing."

I didn't know what to say. I knew he was probably talking about how his life had been turned upside down, but I didn't want to go there, and I didn't think he did, either.

So I did something that shocked me even more than I think it shocked him.

I leaned over and kissed him.

The kiss turned into two, then three, at which point Bert had the presence of mind to pull the truck down the road a little and into a sheltered turnaround in front of a split-level ranch.

"Don't worry," he said. "I know the owners. They're not coming down until June."

"Should we be doing this?" I asked, now that the train was on the express track to trouble.

"Probably not," he said.

"You're right. Sorry."

He leaned back against the headrest and took a deep breath. "No apologies necessary." He looked over. "You just beat me to it."

"I did?"

He nodded.

I leaned back myself and let out a relieved breath.

"So I guess my secret's out," he went on.

I hoped that I knew which secret he meant—the same secret I intended to keep from him—but I had to be sure. Believing that a spark usually goes both ways, and that you don't feel it unless the other person does, too, I leapt into the void.

"You mean our little—*frisson*?" I asked.

He gave me a puzzled frown.

"*Frisson*. It's French."

He shook his head and shrugged.

At last, I thought! *Something!* A gorgeous fisherman who used "whom" correctly, liked my son, got along famously with his sister, and knew how to cook, build cabins, wire sconces, *and* speak French would have been completely and utterly irresistible.

It sort of took the *frisson* out of *frisson* to have to define the word for him, but this was my fault for trotting it out in the first place.

"It's kind of like a—sizzle," I said.

"Ah." He smiled. He pointed to himself, then to me, then back to himself.

I nodded. He nodded.

Neither of us spoke for a few minutes. An enormous robin made a rough landing on the grass nearby and proceeded to peck around. Off in the distance, someone took a chain saw to a tree or a log, and the whirring sound reminded me that I had to make a dentist appointment when I got back; one of my back teeth had gotten sensitive to cold. The silence felt companionable for a couple of minutes, but pretty soon it started to feel awkward. Then really awkward. Since I was the one who had made this moment all but inevitable, I figured it was up to me to speak first.

"I didn't mean to . . ." I trailed off. I didn't mean to—what? Kiss him? Yes I had. I hadn't meant to make him uncomfortable, though.

Bert looked over.

"Sorry if I jumped the gun."

"You didn't."

"I mean, maybe you're not ready to . . ."

"Make out? Oh, I wouldn't say that."

"Get involved again," I clarified, though freewheeling tomfoolery was A-OK by me.

"Now *that*, I don't know," he finally said. "I guess we'll find out, won't we?"

My heart leapt at the prospect of having the chance to find out. I couldn't, however, let him glimpse my delight.

"I guess we will," I said dryly.

"Are you seeing anyone?" he asked.

I shook my head.

He gave me a skeptical look.

"I'm *not!*"

"Since when?"

"Since—forever! It's not that easy. I've got a kid." I waited for him to jump in, but when he didn't, I went on. "Well, I was seeing someone last fall. Briefly."

"Why briefly?"

I shrugged.

"He didn't like your having Henry?"

"No, it wasn't that. He had a daughter himself. But he had a problem with the ghost stuff."

"Really?"

"I think it freaked him out."

Bert nodded. I wondered if he'd take the opportunity to quiz me on the subject, but he just reached over and pushed a lock of hair out of my face.

"So," he said.

"So," I responded.

"We could go for it in the back of the truck," he suggested, deadpan.

I must have looked kind of shocked, though the idea had instant appeal, because he hastened to add, "I'm kidding."

"Damn," I said, but I couldn't keep a straight face.

He hooted at this remark, then leaned over and kissed me like he really meant business.

"Rain check?" I whispered.

"Rain check," he replied.

I've probably seen thousands of ghosts in my lifetime, but the scene by the Southeast Lighthouse unnerved even me. Granted, the sky had abruptly darkened with a low layer of portentous storm clouds, and fat, intermittent raindrops had begun to dot the dust on Bert's windshield. But even if the sky had been cloudless and the air clear and bright, I would have been struck by the eerie pathos of the dreadful scene.

It was hard to believe that the lighthouse had been moved to its present location, as Mark had told me it had. To begin with, it was constructed of brick and set on a monumental granite base, and its stolid octagonal form conveyed the distinct impression of permanence. It was attached to a structure twice as wide, a cheery brick edifice that resembled nothing so much as a taut and tidy gingerbread house. Its window frames were painted a brisk shade of azure, and a charming little porch with jigsaw trim was tucked into a sheltered alcove between the lighthouse and one of the walls of the residence.

Henry and I had rested on the porch steps when we walked over here on Saturday. He'd made several circuits of the lighthouse's granite base, leaning into the brick structure to offset the sloping angle of the base's topmost molding. I had only seen one ghost that day, on the upper of the two cast-iron balconies that encircled the beacon. I had pointedly ignored him, being preoccupied with thoughts of Henry and Vivi and worried about the presence of a lighthouse keeper, who might not appreciate strangers lounging on his or her steps. But we hadn't encountered anyone (live). No one seemed to be around.

Today, though, mesmerized by the sight of forty or fifty earthbound spirits, I barely heard Bert's voice when he asked, "You want to stop?"

The ethereal creatures were everywhere: pacing wretchedly

on the rocks between the grass and the sea, ambling slowly around the beacon's cast-iron balconies, lying motionless on the grass, oblivious to the clouds and the raindrops, staring up into the endless dome.

"Anza?"

"Sorry! What?"

"You want me to stop?"

I did and didn't. These had to be ghosts from the *Larchmont*. Their clothing gave them away, as did the fact that they were all clumped together in little groups, as though still living out the shared tragedy of the lifeboats and rafts.

Ghosts can see and speak with each other, but they almost never do. Just as we usually ignore the people we pass on the street every day and sit beside on buses and planes, ghosts live in their own little worlds, preoccupied with their own histories and memories. Just like us, they keep largely to themselves when encountering strangers in public, even if those strangers happen to share their existential predicament.

But these ghosts, I knew, had banded together. If Baden Riegler had his story straight, at least some of these phantoms were united in a furious plot to try to drive Mark and Lauren off the island. If I had been alone, I might well have approached one or two of the spirits on the fringes, if only to learn the identities of the group's ringleaders. But I wouldn't do it with Bert here.

"I should probably get back," I said. "It's beautiful, though."

Bert gave a little shiver. "It gives me the creeps. I don't know why."

I did, but I kept the presence of so many ghosts to myself. "Well, lighthouses exist because of danger and shipwrecks. If I were a fisherman, they might give me the creeps, too."

"Maybe. I suppose that's it."

"Do you ever go out at night?"

"Sure, yeah. I mean, I don't *go* out at night, but sometimes I *am* out at night. Tuna and swordfish are farther and farther out, these days. It's barely worthwhile unless I'm out there for a couple of days."

"Really? Wow!"

"Don't be too impressed."

"I am! Are you all by yourself?"

"All by myself?" He made a sad little face, teasing me for using such a childlike phrase. "Sometimes."

"Who steers? When you're sleeping? I know that's probably a stupid question." The sky was growing darker and darker, gearing up for a storm. I heard the rumble of thunder in the distance, and this struck me as odd. I think of thunderstorms as phenomena of July and August, when scorching days just seem to heat up and burst.

"It's not stupid," Bert said. "The boat's got a lot of navigation gear. It's not like in the old days."

The truck had rounded a bend, and my heartbeat was returning to normal. I was vaguely aware of the fleeting form of a ghost, beginning to run from a point to the right of us toward the road ahead. She seemed to be in her late twenties and she was barefoot and wearing a tattered nightdress. Her arms were outstretched and her expression was frozen in a mask of fear and horror. She was headed toward the corner our truck was about to turn.

My gaze flew to the road before us.

There, at a point we would reach in a matter of seconds, was a small child, a boy.

I gasped instinctively and grabbed Bert's arm.

His gaze flew to my face. "What?"

"Look out!" I screamed, realizing that it was already too late, we were too close, the child's mother would never have time to reach him before the truck hit him. I squeezed my eyes shut and turned away, my stomach muscles tight and braced for the sickening thud of an impact.

The truck swerved slightly to the right, but I heard nothing: no squealing of brakes, no outcry from Bert, no sound of hurling metal colliding with vulnerable human flesh.

I opened my eyes. It had all happened so fast that I'd been unable to make my usual distinctions. The figure had not been a child, but a ghost, and I believed I knew who he was.

Jamey.

"Oh my gosh! I'm so sorry," I said.

"Let me guess," Bert responded. "You saw a ghost."

I couldn't tell if he was teasing me or not. "We drove right through him."

Bert's eyebrows shot up. He gave a long, low whistle and appeared to be trying to take this in. "So you can't tell the difference between a ghost and a live person?" he finally asked.

"No, no, I can! Ghosts are transparent: you can see right through them. But it all happened too fast."

"*What* happened too fast?"

"The little boy ran into the road. I mean, the ghost. My mind couldn't make the adjustment quickly enough."

Bert cleared his throat and stared straight ahead. He was silent for several moments, concentrating on the road. He turned on the windshield wipers.

"The little boy," he finally stated flatly.

"Yeah. I know you don't believe in ghosts, but—well, there was just a little kid, a ghost boy, in the road."

"Okaaaay . . ."

He looked over at me. I smiled apologetically.

"But he's all right," I went on. "We didn't hurt him or anything. I mean, he's already dead. But we didn't make him—any *deader.*"

"Awful glad to hear it," he drawled.

Chapter Fourteen

❧

I WISHED I COULD have just sneaked out of the Grand View with Henry, dropped him off at Caleb's house, and gone to the senator's cocktail party without getting into it all with Lauren, but there was no way I could do that. This is one of the trade-offs of the intimate B and B experience, especially when your hosts are warm and welcoming: you don't feel right treating the place like a hotel and coming and going without offering explanations.

Besides, this was a very small island. Given Lauren's friendship with Aitana and Mark's with Bert, word was sure to get back to my hosts that I had been at the party. I didn't see any alternative to handling it directly.

Lauren was sitting on the front porch having a cup of tea when I climbed the steps. It was a little after three thirty and I had done everything I could possibly do at the Historical Society, at least until our samples arrived. I was hoping to squeeze in a quick nap before picking up Henry at five. I was still trying to recover from that night of no sleep.

"Cup of tea?" Lauren asked.

"No thanks." I sat down beside her. "Listen, I hope this isn't a problem, but I don't think we'll be having supper here tonight. You haven't already started anything, have you?"

"No, no, but..." She was probably wondering where we were going to eat.

"Henry's spending the evening with Caleb's girls, and, well, to tell you the truth, it feels a little like a command performance, but the senator asked Caleb to bring me."

"To the party?"

I nodded. "I can't get out of it. I tried."

"Why would you want to get out of it?" Lauren asked.

Because he didn't invite you guys, I thought. I would have loved to have said this aloud, but drawing attention to my hosts' exclusion was almost as insensitive as the omission itself.

"I'd kill to see the inside of that house," Lauren continued.

I was vaguely curious, I supposed, but Rawlings had struck me as arrogant and entitled, and I really hadn't liked the way he'd given me the once-over, as though I was a horse he was contemplating buying. To top it all off, I strongly disagreed with him about the windmills.

"I'm not a big cocktail party person," I said, though this wasn't entirely true.

"Oh, I love them!" Lauren responded. "Or at least the idea of them. Martinis and Manhattans and perfume and cigarette smoke—it's so romantic and glamorous. So . . . fifties!"

"I won't stay long," I said. "I'll have one drink to be polite and get out of there as fast as I can."

"You may not be able to," Lauren said. "You'll probably have to listen to a speech. I'll bet you anything that he wants something from you."

"What could he want from me?"

"It's just how he is." She sniffed. "He's not the type of guy who gives a party to be nice."

———

I'm partial to old houses. I love worn floors and antique wainscoting, and I'll happily tolerate the wind whistling through cracks and crevices and windows that rattle and stick. I admire modern residences, with their lines all elegant and sleek, but I can't really see myself living in one. If there were ever a house with the power to change my mind, though, it looked to be the house we were now approaching.

Caleb, Sally, and I had decided to walk the half mile or so to the Rawlingses' beachfront estate. Henry had immediately joined in a badminton game in the Wilders' side yard, a loose jumble of flailing arms and flying racquets that involved, counting Henry, six children and at least twice as many shuttlecocks. Players on one side of the net were volleying randomly with kids on the other, and a babysitter who appeared to be of college age had hot dogs and hamburgers sizzling on a gas grill off the back porch.

I had an immediate fantasy of moving here. Bert and I would get together, and Henry would suddenly have a childhood like mine—*better* than mine, in that it would include a mother. A few seconds later, I came to my senses. Bert and I hadn't even had a date yet. And how in the world would I earn a living here? Working in a restaurant or a hotel five or six months a year? Not likely. Besides, Declan wouldn't be keen on the idea. Not the me-and-Bert part—Dec was in no position to object to that—the part that involved living eighty miles and an expanse of the Atlantic Ocean away from his son. And what Dec didn't like, Henry didn't like.

Oh, well.

The driveway and walkways leading to the Rawlingses' house were lined with little gold bags stabilized with sand and enclosing flickering candles. We tried this back in Cambridge two years ago, when the pumpkins we had carved were stolen and smashed by local ne'er-do-wells the night before Halloween. We didn't have time to carve any more, so Ellie, the arts-and-craftsy septuagenarian from whom we rent our apartment, came roaring to the rescue with an issue of Martha Stewart *Living*, a stack of brown paper lunch bags, and a tray holding what appeared to be every votive and pillar candle in her cozily cluttered house.

We cut faces into the bags and made up for in volume what we lacked in pumpkins, and in the end, even tearful Henry had been dazzled by the flickering brown goblins that lined our sidewalk and porch. Then, alas, it started to pour.

There were no clouds in sight tonight, though, so the dozens and dozens of bright gold bags with little star cutouts appeared to be in no danger of being reduced to pulpy piles. Set back from a rocky bluff, against which the waves were crashing, sending up sprays of fine mist, the house simply glowed. I was surprised that the senator, reputed to be an ardent conservationist, didn't object to what seemed like every light inside and out radiating brightness and warmth at the environmental cost of zillions of megawatts, but this made the residence a sight to behold. That, I suppose, was the point.

Massive panel windows revealed that inside, dozens of guests were already happily chatting and drinking cocktails out of festive flutes and martini glasses. The deep, wide porch was dotted with revelers in twos and threes, seated in teak armchairs facing the ocean or leaning against the slim columns that supported the porch's graceful roof.

"I'm underdressed," whispered Sally.

"You look fine," Caleb responded unreassuringly.

Easy for you to say, I thought. Men are lucky to have a basic uniform. Add a tie or a jacket, change to nicer shoes, and they can go almost anywhere. As far as I could tell, Caleb had simply put on a fresh shirt, traded his Top-Siders for loafers, and slipped on a sports jacket. Sally, on the other hand, had clearly put time and effort into her choice of outfit, and I thought she looked really pretty in her flowered blouse, coral cashmere sweater, black linen slacks, and black satin ballet flats. But glancing around, I could see her point: we were in the land of heels and silk.

As for me, I had only brought one dress, and it was black and polyester, so even though I had gotten it at TJ Maxx for $19.99, it passed for dressy. My relative good luck ended at my hair, though. Not only had I forgotten conditioner, I'd neglected to pack the round hairbrush that was the one beauty tool I owned. Without aggressive subduing with this brush and a hair dryer, my bangs crimped up in a wavy little curtain. I tried to smooth them down, but they sprung resolutely back. Then I tried to think like a person who might style her hair that way on purpose—say, a performance artist who lived in Brooklyn and wore pigtails and Doc Martens and looked cute in bright lipstick. That didn't work, either. This left only the deflating consolation of the phrase Nona used to fling at me whenever I went on *ad nauseam* about my appearance: *Nobody's going to be looking at you.*

Sadly, this was probably true.

As we climbed the front steps and opened the door, I heard slow, sexy jazz that turned out to be live: a man in a tux was playing a concert grand piano on the far side of an expansive room that stretched out widely on each side of the front entrance. To our right was the living room, lined with built-in walnut bookshelves and decorated in shades of cream and rose, and to the left, the living room's mirror image: a dining room with a glossy walnut table that looked long enough to seat twenty. Huge black urns of pink peonies, purchased and transported to the island at a breathtaking sum, no doubt, since peonies wouldn't be blooming for months, adorned the table. *The decorator is really good,* I thought. Despite its ultramodern design, the house was warm and inviting, and the antiques scattered throughout the rooms looked as comfortable in the space as did the sleek modern chairs and minimalist silver fixtures.

A woman dressed in black stepped forward to take our coats, but Sally and I had only worn sweaters and we both decided to keep them on. Sally helped herself to a glass of wine delivered by a waiter with a tray and drifted into the living room, where she had spotted some friends. I gazed longingly at the martini glasses held by some of the guests, obviously filled with drinks that looked like Cosmopolitans or those trendy "-tinis" made with vodka or gin and fruit liqueur. I really wanted one of those. And I had to remember to eat. I always came home starving from parties like this; I'd get talking to somebody, have a drink or two, and completely forget to hit the hors d'oeuvre table.

I reached for a plate. There were scallops in broiled bacon, runny cheeses with seeded flatbreads that looked homemade, and bowls of macadamia nuts and Marcona almonds. There were bite-sized pieces of the onion tart we'd been warned not to touch yesterday, tiny quiches in puff pastry, and polished silver bowls filled with strawberries and grapes.

My plate was half covered and my mouth completely full when I heard a voice behind me.

"I'm glad you could make it."

I turned around. It was Senator Rawlings.

I nodded brightly, trying to gulp down the little quiche I had just popped into my mouth.

"Take your time," he said as I struggled to swallow, then to have a sip of wine, in case there was egg or crust in my teeth.

"Sorry," I said. "Thank you."

"For what?"

"For inviting me."

"My pleasure. I hear you're from Cambridge."

Where had he heard that? "I didn't grow up there, but I live there now."

"I did my undergraduate at Harvard."

"Really? I thought you went to Brown." *Oops!* I immediately realized that perhaps I shouldn't have said this.

"For my PhD," he explained. "But I'm curious—how'd you know that?" He attempted a disarming smile, but it was anything but disarming.

I couldn't think of a plausible bluff, so I had to go with the truth. "Someone was talking about the local school, and how it was designed by a friend of yours from Providence who's an architect."

"Yes. Adrian Gerstner. He did this house, too."

"It's gorgeous. Really beautiful."

"Thank you. But I can't take any credit. Adrian and Helen really did it together."

"Helen?"

"Mrs. Rawlings." He glanced around, apparently looking for his wife, but she wasn't in sight. "She's here somewhere."

"Caleb tells me you're pulling together the *Larchmont* papers. How long do you think it will take?"

"Yes, I am. The volumes themselves are pretty straightforward, but a lot will depend on some other decisions we have to make."

"What kind of decisions?" He took a sip of his drink, which was one of those appletinis, or whatever they were.

I didn't know whether I should tell him anything about my high-flying ideas. The conversations I'd had with Caleb were just that, conversations.

"There's a lot of material," I commented vaguely. "If the money were available, the Society could do some really great things."

"Like what?" he pressed.

I glanced around for Caleb, but I didn't see him nearby. Rawlings had fixed me with a disconcertingly direct stare, and I found myself bumbling ahead like a child being grilled by the principal. After all, he *was* the head of the Senate Appropriations Committee.

"There are some amazing photographs," I said. "If they were properly matted and framed, they'd make a terrific exhibit. And there are other ways to bring parts of the story to life: audio recordings, other types of installations. But that would require a dedicated space."

"And what would that cost?"

"I have no idea. There seems to be room in the building, but the space would have to be renovated."

"And how long would that take?"

"I really don't know. I could talk to Caleb."

"Great," said the senator, interrupting me. "Get back to me as soon as possible."

"All right," I said meekly, and then he was gone.

———

Lauren had been right about one thing: Rawlings had some kind of agenda, though I wasn't quite sure what it was. And now it appeared she was going to be right a second time: the senator was getting ready to make a speech. I was sipping my melon martini when a young guy who looked like he might be an aide-de-camp came into the dining room and attempted to usher everyone into the opposite space.

I had every intention of following him, but Aitana had just appeared at the door to the pantry and was waving me over with a frantic gesture.

"I'll be right there," I said to the aide.

"Everything's great!" I told Aitana.

"Thanks," she answered distractedly. "But listen! The woman in the car . . ."

"What car?"

"The one that almost hit me! I think she's here!"

"I thought you didn't see them."

"So did I! But I guess I saw more than I thought. I couldn't have described her face to the police, but I swear it's her."

I glanced across the foyer, where people were settling in, all facing the back of the house, where Rawlings was presumably standing. I heard him say something I couldn't make out, and the guests erupted in polite laughter.

"What should we do?" I asked.

"I'm stuck back here. But maybe you could talk to her—find out where she's staying, I don't know. If we could find the car, that would be a start."

I nodded. "What does she look like?"

"She's young. Early twenties. She's wearing a red jacket and a denim skirt. Blond hair."

"I'll see if I can find her," I said.

Aitana nodded and closed the door. I made my way across the foyer and into the living room, where I found a place at the very back of the crowd. I was actually able to sit on the windowsill, so deep were the walnut-framed enclosures into which the picture windows were set. I scanned the backs of the guests and found her almost immediately: the jacket wasn't just red, it was bright red, almost fluorescent, the only red jacket in the crowd. I would have to wait until the speech was over, though, before I could try to talk to her.

Caleb turned out to be right about the reason for the party. Rawlings warmed up his neighbors and guests with amiable chitchat featuring tales of local characters, apparently all present, before moving on to the substance of his presentation: the results of an environmental impact study on the effects of the proposed wind turbine installation. At this point the lights were dimmed, and slides began to flash across a screen set up to the senator's left.

For the next half hour, we heard ominous "proof" that construction of the windmills would be disastrous to just about everything that flew in the air, swam in the ocean, and nested in the dunes. I found this really annoying. You don't invite people to a party and then hold them hostage while you hammer home some point, forcing them to stand there and pretend to be interested when they really want to be eating hors d'oeuvres and listening to jazz. Then again, I hadn't been to any parties given by senators. Maybe that was *exactly* what they did.

At the point at which I tuned back in, Rawlings was intoning the first of a series of chilling predictions. The 440-foot windmills would kill, harm, and "harass" dolphins, seals, and whales. They'd slice six million migratory birds into shreds, especially during stretches of bad weather, when birds abandoned their customary "Atlantic flyways" and flew at lower altitudes. The building of the electrical service platform was going to destroy all kinds of habitats, and tens of thousands of gallons of transformer oil would always be in danger of spilling into the ocean just off the island's shores. At this point, a pathetic image of a tiny, oil-soaked duckling appeared on the screen.

And that was just the tip of the iceberg. Gray harbor seals would lose their "pupping sites." Terns, sea ducks, and piping plovers would be driven right out of their nesting grounds. Leatherback, green, and loggerhead turtles would be in the market for new digs. Boats and ferries, search-and-rescue efforts, and even airplanes would be "endangered" by the wind farm. *Airplanes?* I thought. Couldn't they just plan to fly around the 440-foot windmills? Last but not least, the wind turbines would have a deleterious and permanent effect on "beloved historic vistas."

Bingo, I thought. *Now we're getting somewhere.*

Because it hadn't escaped my notice that the Rawlings manse looked directly out onto the area of the sound where the *Larchmont* went down. Caleb had confirmed this earlier in the evening, pointing off into the distance when he and Sally and I rounded the edge of the point on which the senator had built his home. But if that was where the *Larchmont* had gone down, it was also the very spot where the windmills would go up. Forty of them, smack-dab in the center of the senator's "vista."

Now, it's not that I don't care about dolphins and whales. Of course I do—everyone does. The thought of harbor seals losing their "pupping sites" is heartbreaking. But so are the prospects of the oceans warming and whole species disappearing, not to mention endless cycles of wars fought over access to fossil fuels.

And I couldn't help wondering whether all these predictions were actually true, or completely true. Who had done this study? An impartial third party with rigorous scientific standards and no vested interest in the outcome? Or an allegedly progressive, "green" front of some kind, funded behind the scenes by people who claimed to be all about protecting birds and fish, but who were really looking out for their property values and ocean views.

I'd have loved to have asked right then and there, when the lights came back on, who had underwritten the study, but Rawlings's self-important aide-de-camp was holding a stack of brochures and starting to pass them out to the people who were leaving. These would certainly identify the organization behind the study, so I decided to keep my mouth shut, snag a brochure on my way out, and do a little snooping on the QT.

As the senator was surrounded by neighbors with questions, I stepped back into the hall. Sally came into view, and just behind her was the girl in red; and she really *was* just a girl—no more than nineteen or twenty. As she made her way through the room full of guests, I tried to come up with a conversation opener. I had to hurry, though, because she was walking right toward me.

"I love your jacket," I said.

She stopped short and looked at me. "Thanks."

"It's a great color," I added. And it was. Maybe not for a jacket, but then again, maybe she was a performance artist from Brooklyn.

"I got it in Boston." She smiled slightly. "At the Salvation Army."

"You're kidding!"

She shook her head. "The one on Berkeley Street."

"Near the Mass. Pike there?" I asked.

She nodded. "You know it?"

"I know where it is. I live in Cambridge. Anza O'Malley." I extended my hand and she shook it. Hers was cold and bony and I noticed deep, dark roots growing in beneath the blond curls that nestled inside her collar like baby birds.

"Elsa Corbett."

"Do you live near Boston?" I asked.

"Kind of," she answered evasively. I wondered whether she *kind of* lived there, or if where she lived was *kind of* near Boston. But she didn't seem inclined to get chatty. She looked past my shoulder, as though scanning the crowd for a face.

"Are you here on vacation?" I prodded.

She met my gaze again and took in a breath, as though she was about to say something, but then she didn't. She had apparently caught the eye of a guy across the room, whom I judged to be in his mid-thirties. He was wearing a retro golf jacket and a shirt that struck me as kind of dorky. But I think that dorky might be the new cool, now that I've gotten rid of all the clothes that might have qualified. Whatever fashion boat there is to miss, I somehow manage to miss it.

"I'm here for a couple of days," she answered, before

whispering a breathy "Excuse me" and slipping through the guests to join up with the guy in the golf jacket.

I couldn't let her get away. I hoped that they had walked to the party and not driven, because I was just going to have to follow them.

Chapter Fifteen

I ALSO HOPED THEY weren't going too far, because I didn't have a lot of time. I'd given Caleb and Sally the slip by ducking out through the Rawlingses' back door, but the fact remained that Henry was at their house, waiting to be picked up. I could plausibly claim that I'd thought they had left, that we'd somehow missed each other in the crush to claim coats and say our good-byes, but I had to get back to the Wilders' at about the same time they did. I didn't want to take advantage of their babysitting largesse or raise any eyebrows about my whereabouts.

The night was chilly, and a few stars were beginning to appear. A low, hazy web stretched like a membrane between sea and sky, and veins of cloud glowed faintly blue, like capillaries on the eyelids of a sleeping infant. It was lucky for me that most people had walked to the party, so the road was thronged with dozens of departing guests. In the fading light, the saucy red of Elsa's jacket waxed and waned in reflected radiance created by widely spaced streetlights.

Most of the walkers peeled off to the right, where the point jutted out from the mainland, but there were plenty of people who turned to the left, as Elsa and her boyfriend did. I assumed he was her boyfriend. They held hands as they walked, though there wasn't much chatting or laughing, especially for a boyfriend and girlfriend who had just been to a cocktail party. Their pace was purposeful and deliberate. I was relieved when they took a right turn onto an unpaved road marked Ballard's Way. From exploring the island on Saturday with Henry, I knew that this street was only a few houses long.

A low stand of pines lined the road on my right and ended at a small cottage that looked deserted. Its shutters had been bolted closed, and a dilapidated brown sedan was on blocks in the driveway. *Perfect,* I thought: I could cut through here without arousing suspicion. But I was just past the trees when I was stopped in my tracks by one of the largest, and most outraged, dogs I had ever seen.

I caught my breath, stopped short, and tried to remain completely motionless. I say *dog,* but the blood that ran through this collarless creature's veins could easily have been that of a wolf. He stood in my path about ten feet away, his eyes glittering, his head slung low between powerful shoulders, his gray lips pulled back in a ferocious snarl, the hackles on his back in full intimidation mode.

His low, throaty rumble was broken only when he stopped to draw a breath. I didn't dare look him in the eye, because I couldn't remember if that was what you were supposed to do or never supposed to do. Suddenly, his growling stopped. The dog looked up, and everything about his demeanor changed before my eyes: his shoulders relaxed and he began to make little submissive circles, glancing warily up to the left of me. Only when this had gone on for a while did I dare to glance around myself.

Just behind me stood Baden.

"Thank God!" I whispered.

Baden remained silent but began to advance on the animal. The dog paused briefly, but when Baden made a wild run at him, he turned tail and raced away.

My hands were trembling as I took the first deep breath I had taken in a while. I turned to Baden.

"Thank you," I said. "You might have saved my life."

"You might be right."

I don't know for sure if animals can actually *see* ghosts, but I absolutely know that they can sense them. They may feel a change of energy in the air, sense an unsettling aura of heat or cold, or even hear sounds that are out of the range of human hearing, like the sounds produced by dog whistles. I suppose it's like the changes you feel on a sultry summer afternoon, when you can smell approaching rain in the air.

"Were you following me?" I asked.

Baden gave me a dismissive look, then turned back to the path. I'd probably missed my chance to learn where Elsa and her friend were staying, and there was no way I was going to leave Baden's side, not with that creature on the loose. I'd telephone Aitana later tonight. Maybe we could come back in the morning.

Not one to let an awkward situation pass without trying to turn it to his advantage, Baden asked, "Why would I be following *you*?"

"It's a fairly unlikely place to run into someone."

"One could say the same to you."

Baden fell into step beside me as we walked back to the main road. Though I was dying to ask him what *his* reason had been, I remained quiet as an older couple approached us on the road, leisurely making their way home from the party. I didn't want to seem like a psychotic woman, talking animatedly to no one in particular on a dark and lonely street. I smiled and nodded when the man said, "Evening." Baden kept pace beside me.

"I'm here on account of *your* family," I whispered. "Lauren and Mark need my help. And they need yours." The time had come for Baden to declare himself. His own personal history and desires aside, he seemed to really care about Lauren and Mark. But he had to do more than care. He had to jump in and help.

Suddenly, his expression softened. He squared his shoulders and addressed me, for the first time, with feeling and concern in his voice. "For them," he said, "I will do anything."

"Really?" I couldn't quite believe it. Could it actually be this easy?

Baden nodded. "Tell me what you require of me. Tell me how I may help."

"I'm not really sure," I said. "I need your help even to figure that out."

"Then you have it," he said.

"Okay, then maybe we could begin by being honest with each other. I'll tell you why I was here if you tell me."

He gave a slight nod.

"Do you know who Aitana is?" I began. "Bert's sister? She runs a catering company."

"I do."

"Okay, well, the night of the fire, she was working really late getting the food ready for the party at Senator Rawlings's house. That's where I was tonight."

"Go on."

"And when she was driving back home from the place where she cooks, a car practically ran her off the road. It was right around the time that the fire broke out, so we think the two might be related. Tonight, at the party, Aitana saw someone who she believes was in the car. Aitana was stuck in the kitchen, so I followed the woman and her boyfriend here. They turned off onto Ballard's Way."

"You intended to confront her? That might have been dangerous. Like the dog." He smiled.

I could hardly believe it. Humor without bite? Maybe we were getting somewhere.

"The car was green or gray, a small wagon. I thought if I could find out where she was staying..."

"Perhaps you may locate the car. But you still may not know if the two are related."

"No. But if this woman and her boyfriend have the right kind of car, it might contain traces of accelerant."

"This is true," he said.

"She isn't from the island, as far as I know. She said she's only here for a few days. But I can't help wondering what she was doing at the party."

"Was she alone?"

I shook my head. "She was with a man. They weren't very dressed up and I didn't see them talking to anyone else—they didn't seem to *know* anyone else. So how did they get onto the senator's guest list?"

"There is no way to know. Perhaps the senator knows her family, or the young man's. Does the senator have children?"

"I don't know," I answered.

"What is his age?"

"Close to sixty, I'd say."

"They may be friends of his children," Baden suggested.

"I suppose."

"But you believe they are staying back there." Baden indicated the road back to our left, where I had seen Elsa and the man turn in.

I nodded. "Do you know who owns those houses?"

"I do not. My only knowledge is of the next street, where we met." He wore a nervous look, as though fearing he had opened the door to further questions.

He was right. I stopped and looked at him. I kept looking at him. I didn't intend to stop looking until he told me more about himself.

"You knew someone who lived on that street," I guessed.

He nodded.

I guessed again. "At the time your brother lived here."

He looked away and then let out the most surprising and pitiful moan. He covered his face with his hands and his shoulders began to shake.

Now *that* was a secret he'd been keeping for a very long time.

"A woman," I guessed.

He nodded almost imperceptibly.

"Who was—not your wife," I said quietly.

He took his hands away from his eyes, and what I saw was both grief and relief. Someone finally knew. The Catholic Church has gotten a lot of things wrong, grandly and tragically wrong, but it sure has an appreciation for the relief that follows confession.

It would have been cruel to press him for details. I knew enough, or at least I could imagine enough. He'd probably had an affair with a woman who lived here, and when the *Larchmont* went down, he found his spirit marooned on the very island where his lover still lived. Perhaps this was why he didn't cross over when he could, and for all I knew, Baden spent the rest of his lover's life watching her and loving her and being by her side. It might have been enough for him, even if she didn't know he was there.

Trapped in his own personal circle of Dante's hell, he may not have wanted to leave. But when she finally died, he had no *way* to leave. Or maybe he harbored just the tiniest fear that there *would* be an afterlife, and his furious wife would be waiting for him! They might both be there! *Then* what would he do?

I couldn't say any of this, of course. Nor did I have the heart to probe the matter any further. I would have taken his arm if I could have, but you can't take a ghost by the arm. Slowly and quietly, we walked toward the lights of the town.

Chapter Sixteen

Henry was wired. His evening had involved Coca-Cola, apparently unlimited access to M&Ms, and a trampoline—how had I managed to miss *that* in the backyard?—and within minutes of picking him up, I knew that it would be at least two hours before his buzz wore off. To complicate matters further, Vivi was waiting for us on the front steps of the Grand View. She flew excitedly toward us the minute we came into view.

"Where did you *go*?" she asked Henry accusingly.

"My friends'," he answered, a little smugly.

"Who?" she demanded.

"Kara and Louisa," he replied. "They're sisters."

The woebegone look that appeared on Vivi's face made me feel like giving my son a good clip. He was being mean on purpose, and enjoying it.

In moments like this, my father would fix us with a stony stare and intone, slowly, "I ought to give you a good..." Once in a while, he'd draw his hand back as though *this time*, he really *was* going to give somebody a good... But the threat was usually enough to stop misbehavior in its tracks.

On the rare occasion that it wasn't, Dad would add, "Go ahead. Keep it up." The unspoken end of this sentence was *and you're going to be really, really sorry*. Not even Jay, the boldest of the three of us, ever dared to cross this line.

"Yes, well, the playdate's over now," I said curtly. "And how are you today, Vivi?"

"*They* have a trampoline," Henry added.

I turned and gave him a flinty look. "Knock it off."

"What?" His expression said, *I'm not doing anything! What's your problem?*

"You know *what*," I answered.

He made a face. I decided to let it go. My mind was racing ahead to what the next two hours were going to be like. I had hoped to get him to bed as soon as possible so I could call Aitana with my news, but that wasn't going to happen, not with Henry this jazzed up. I had to wear him out a little. Abruptly, I made a decision.

"You guys want to take a midnight walk on the beach?" I asked. It wasn't anywhere near midnight, but I knew that the word would add excitement to the idea.

"Yeah!" Henry shouted.

"Yeah!" Vivi echoed.

"Okay," I said. "Can I trust you to wait right here on the steps while I run upstairs and change? I'll be back in *one minute*."

"Okay," Henry said.

"*Right* here? I mean it."

"*Yeessss*," he said. "But hurry up."

"I just want to get jackets."

"I'm not cold."

"Well you might be in a few minutes. And I want to put my jeans on."

"Would you *go*?" he said freshly. One more flip answer and I would have to crack down.

I dashed inside. Lauren was nowhere in sight, and as I passed the window in the upstairs hall, I caught a glimpse of her and Mark out back by the barn, illuminated by the glow of the back porch light. I closed the door of our room behind me, pulled off my boots, and peeled off my sweater and dress. I grabbed my jeans from the back of the chair, slid them on, stepped into my running shoes—Running! Ha!—and pulled a heavy turtleneck out of my suitcase. I could hear the kids on the front porch, whooping and shrieking about something, so I sat on the edge of the bed for a second, sifting through the binding materials that had arrived earlier.

The rich, heavy paper ranged in color and texture from the tone and feel of a supermarket bag to the creamy, polished vellum of formal stationery. I was eager to open the various packets and pore over the fliers for boxes and mats, and I suddenly regretted having offered to take the kids for a walk. The room was warm and the bed intoxicatingly inviting. I lay back against the pile of pillows and closed my eyes, dreading the prospect of going back outside. But it was too late now.

I know I didn't fall asleep. I couldn't have had my eyes closed for more than fifteen or twenty seconds.

But suddenly, I sat up. Something was wrong.

I couldn't hear the kids.

My heart thumping wildly, I raced down the hall and down the stairs. I purposely called up images of Vivi and Henry sitting right there on the steps, whispering confidentially, or waiting patiently in the Adirondack chairs in the side yard. But I already knew I wouldn't see them, and the minute I stepped outside onto the porch, my intuition was confirmed.

"Henry!" I shouted, trying not to panic. "Henry!"

He was nowhere to be seen, and neither was Vivi.

My first thought was that Mark or Lauren had come around the side of the house, and the kids had followed them out back. I sprinted across the front lawn, peering toward the barn. But in the shadow of the side trees, which all but blocked the pale light offered by the moon and the stars, I couldn't see anything or anybody.

I'd had moments like this before, of course. Every parent has. Your child is right there beside you, and then, in the blink of an eye, he's gone. Panic rises like a tsunami, and horrible images fly through your mind. He's in the back of a stranger's van, having been spirited away while you were chatting with another mother at the playground. He's lying somewhere, unconscious and bleeding profusely, perhaps in the street, as a car speeds away, or under the branch of a tree he was climbing. And then, after a hallucinatory moment or two, you find him: playing in the little clubhouse under the climbing structure, or absorbed in a drama involving stick swords, oblivious to the sound of your voice.

Tonight, though, I wasn't finding him. But as I ran toward the back of the house, I heard a far-off little shriek. I stopped in my tracks, breathing raggedly.

I heard it again. It was Henry. And it was coming from the direction of the beach.

I turned and raced toward the road, a winding boulevard that encircles the island and echoes the shape of the coastline. I couldn't see Henry, or Vivi, for that matter, but I could hear him now, and the sounds he was making were chilling.

I raced across the street and scrambled up onto the breakwater. There he was, down in the water, splashing through the shallow waves as fast as his legs would carry him. Vivi was right there with him, chasing him and swooping around, flying right at him in a way that caused him to dart and stumble in the water, covering his face with his hands.

"Henry!" I screamed. "Stop!"

"Mama!" he shrieked as Vivi let out a ferocious laugh, a sound that startled even me. It was shrill and sharp and otherworldly, like a ghostly hyena braying before its intended victim. Henry regained his footing and started to run. Vivi flew right behind him. She was chasing him in the direction of the rocks.

"No!" I screamed. "Stop! Vivi! Henry!"

I jumped down from the wall and tried to run in the sand. Henry was only a few hundred feet away from me, but he was nearing the black and no doubt slippery rocks, and I felt the way you feel in a dream, when the normal motions of walking or running just don't move you forward the way they do in life. I made a diagonal dash for the water's edge, seeking the compacted sand.

Henry had reached the rocks by now, and I saw him lean over and use a hand to steady his progress. He began to scale the middling rocks that led to the shiny boulders stretching out into the sea.

"Vivi!" I screamed. "Stop it! Right now!"

Henry turned at the sound of my voice, and the motion caused him to slip sideways and go thumping down onto one of the rocks. He let out a little cry as Vivi alighted on a nearby boulder. Perhaps shocked into stillness by the sudden awareness that the game had gotten out of control and her playmate—or prey—could really hurt himself, Vivi stood still and silent. But as though a switch had been thrown in a primitive neurological center governing self-preservation, Henry continued to scramble upward and toward the water. She might have stopped, but he was getting away. As far away as possible.

I knew he wouldn't listen, couldn't listen, even to me. So as I neared the rocks, I watched in terror as he scrambled farther and farther out over the crashing black sea. Twice, he slipped, landing, sliding on his bottom before scrambling once again to his feet and heading farther into the darkness. I could barely see him. There were stars in the sky, but clouds had covered the fingernail moon.

"Henry! Stop!" I said anyway. "Mama's here! It's all right."

He wheeled around.

"Get out of here!" I growled at Vivi. "Go! Now!"

I must have sounded a like a monster myself, because she disappeared immediately.

"She's gone," I screamed, reaching the rocks and scrambling toward my son, using my hands to steady my progress toward the flat and substantial boulders. "Honey! Stop! Do not move! Stay right there!"

And then I witnessed the second miracle of my life, the first being the birth of the creature who was scrambling into the darkness not fifteen feet from me.

He stopped. And he turned. And before he could be snatched away by the wind or the sea or the rocks and the slime, I had him in my arms.

"She was chasing me," he explained. He was sitting up in bed in his pajamas. I'd calmed him down with a long, hot bath, after which he climbed into my lap as I sat in the rocker by our window, trying to collect myself and figure out what to say. I'd wrapped him in a down comforter and rocked him slowly, and even when tiny beads of perspiration broke out on his forehead and upper lip, and he tossed off the comforter, he still seemed to cling to the comfort.

"I know," I said. "Do you have any idea why?"

He shook his head.

"None?" I asked.

"No."

"Well, I do. You hurt her feelings and she was mad at you."

"What did I do?"

"You rubbed it in that you were off having a fun playdate. That made her feel sad and lonesome. And maybe a little mad. Because I don't think she has a lot of friends."

"Yeah, because she's *mean*."

"No," I corrected, though at that moment, I would have loved to have wrung her scrawny little neck. "Because not very many people can see her."

"Why not?" he asked.

The moment had come. We had to have the conversation. I took a deep breath.

"Okay, sweetie," I began. "You know how—some people are really good at baseball and some people can play the piano?"

"Or drums," he offered.

"Yeah. Drums, or flute or . . ." I drew a blank: should I go with a sports metaphor? A music metaphor?

"Dancing," he continued.

"Sure, yeah, dancing! Well, that's called a talent."

"What is?"

"Being really good at something not everybody can do. It's almost like a—present just for you."

"From who?"

"From . . . God." I gulped.

"But you still have to practice," he offered sagely.

"Yeah."

Might as well aim for the bull's-eye.

"In our family, we have a very special talent. We can do something almost nobody in the world can do. We can . . ."

I panicked. How should I finish the sentence? *See ghosts? Talk to earthbound spirits? Help people who have died?* Henry looked so puzzled and trusting. I deeply disliked being in the middle of this conversation.

"We can talk to ghosts," I finally said, struggling to keep my voice cheerful and casual.

"Is Vivi a ghost?" he asked.

"She is. So was Silas."

He gave me a disbelieving look. "He was?"

"Yup," I said.

He took a moment to absorb this. I reminded myself not to overwhelm him with information, but just to answer his questions directly and honestly.

"I never see Silas anymore," he said.

"He went away," I explained.

"Where did he go?"

"He crossed over."

"To where?" Henry asked. "Heaven?"

Oh. So he had the general contour of an understanding. Someone lived, died, became a ghost, and went to heaven.

I paused. "As far as I know."

We sat in silence for several moments. "Is there anything you want to ask me?" I finally said.

"Can Daddy see ghosts?" Henry asked.

I shook my head.

"You *said* our family," he shot back.

"On my side," I explained.

"Then who?" he demanded. "Pop?"

"No. Just you, me, and Nona."

I could see he didn't like this, so I added quickly, "Pop has other talents. And so does Daddy."

"Like what?"

"Daddy? Well, what do *you* think?"

"He's a good driver. He's good at putting up the tent."

"And . . . ," I prodded.

"And he makes good cocoa. And . . . he's a good policeman."

"And what about Pop?"

Henry hesitated, and my heart sank a little. Henry seldom sees my father, and when he does, it's not for long.

"He tells funny jokes. He makes good pancakes."

"Chocolate chip," I said.

"Yeah, and he makes his letters nice. Nice and—square."

I smiled. My father has beautiful handwriting, and even nicer printing.

"So you see," I said, "everybody's good at different things. If Pop's talent was to talk to ghosts like you and me and Nona, you'd never get chocolate chip pancakes."

This seemed to settle everything.

"So now, let *me* ask *you* a question," I said.

Henry sat up straight. He was kind of getting into this.

"When you walk down the street," I said, "do you see lots of ghosts?"

He gave me a puzzled look. "What does a ghost look like?"

"Like a regular person, but like Silas and Vivi."

"You mean see-through?"

Yeah, I meant see-through. "That's right."

"Then . . . lots," he said.

I caught my breath.

"But you don't talk to them," I said.

"Only to the kids. Sometimes."

"That's good. That's a good idea. Plenty of time for that later."

"For what?" he asked.

"Talking to grown-up ghosts."

"Okay."

"And there's just one more thing," I said. "I know it might feel hard, but this has to be kind of a secret. At least for now. The fact that I see ghosts and you do and Nona does."

"How come?"

"Because lots of people are afraid of ghosts. It would make them really scared if they knew how many ghosts were around all the time. It might even make them afraid of *you*. Or *me!*"

"Whaaa?" he said, in a cartoon character voice.

"I know, crazy, right?" I didn't remind him that an hour earlier, a ghost had practically driven him into the ocean. "It's because of everything on TV and in the movies, all that stuff those movie people make up. You and I know the truth."

"And Nona."

"Right. And Nona."

I could see how tired he was getting, and now a fretful look came over his features.

"Daddy?" he whispered.

"What about Daddy?"

"It's a secret . . . ?"

I sighed, took him back into my arms, and shook my head.

"Nothing," I said, "is *ever* a secret from Daddy."

———

Vivi never came back that night. She probably didn't dare.

I waited for Henry to fall asleep and then searched through my bag for the cocktail napkin on which I had written Aitana's cell phone number. It was nearly ten thirty. Normally I wouldn't call someone this late, but people who cater parties and work in restaurants are up half the night. She was probably still at the senator's house.

The phone rang six, seven, eight times. I was mentally rehearsing the message I was about to leave when I heard her voice.

"Hello?"

"Aitana? It's me, Anza. Can you talk?"

"Oh, Anza! Sure! Hold on." I heard some clanging of pans and a door slamming shut. It was suddenly quiet at her end, and I suspected she had stepped outside. "Hi."

"Hi," I said. "How's it going?"

"We're just packing up. Did you have any luck?"

"I didn't find the house, but I think I found the street."

"You did?" She sounded excited. "Where?"

"Ballard's Way. About half a mile from the center of town."

"I know where it is. It's a little short street, right?"

"Yeah. I was right on their tail until this dog came out of nowhere."

"I'll ask Bert to take me," Aitana said.

"Maybe you should just call the police," I suggested warily.

"And say what?" she asked. "I told them I couldn't describe

the couple in the car, and now I'm claiming to recognize them? Oh, hold on a sec."

I heard a muffled conversation at her end. When she came back on, she said, "Sorry, we're just finishing up here. Thank you *so* much."

"No problem. Let me know what happens."

"We're seeing you tomorrow, aren't we?"

"We are?"

"Lauren asked us over for supper. I know she's planning to invite you."

"Great," I said, before hanging up.

Great, indeed.

———

I wanted to sleep, but I wanted to think.

So Henry had the gift, if you could call it that. Now that I really thought about it, there had been some clues.

A couple of times, I'd seen him do double takes when spirits were in his vicinity. Then, for a while, he had a recurring nightmare involving a "skeleton in a dress." This started shortly after we took a trip to Boston's North End, where a couple of centuries ago, the immigrant Irish found dirt-cheap housing. Famine victims had collapsed and died on the streets of that neighborhood. I'd seen several "skeletons in dresses" myself that day.

Henry and I just hadn't talked about it. I suppose he figured, as I had at his age, that everybody saw the shadowy people. I know he mentioned Silas to his preschool teacher, relating the story of how Silas had jumped off the back porch roof and landed on his head. She'd laughed with relief when I explained that Silas was Henry's imaginary playmate.

But why hadn't he spoken to spirits in public? Here, again, I could only guess. Tonight, he'd said he "sometimes" talked to the spirits of children, though I had to admit, I hadn't been aware of this. There was Silas, of course, and now Vivi, but like lots of kids, Henry sometimes talks out loud to *himself*. At least that's what I always assumed he was doing, alone in his room, playing with toys and action figures.

As for the ghosts of adults, I wasn't surprised that he avoided *them*. Most of the time, so do I. He's pretty shy around strangers. If he can avoid interacting with just about any adult, he will.

I wasn't looking forward to telling Dec. For all my blather about "gifts" and "talents," I actually felt guilty, as though I'd passed down a really quirky gene, of the type not everyone would be thrilled to have.

There are huge satisfactions that come with being able to do what I can do. It's gratifying to ease suffering that has been going on for hundreds, sometimes thousands, of years. I make a lot of unhappy ghosts really happy. But when you're a kid, you don't want to have a "gift" that sets you apart. You don't want to be one of a kind. You want to be just like everyone else.

Chapter Seventeen

THURSDAY

W ITH MEMORIES OF the trampoline still fresh in his
mind—and recollections of his terror on the rocks
apparently repressed—Henry fairly bounced out the door on
Thursday. He couldn't wait to get to the school, now that he
had a couple of friends among the strangers, and now that
Greased Lightin' was all decked out with dazzling hubcaps
and silvery flourishes.

As we walked to school, I was practically holding my
breath. The elephant had appeared in the room. Would I now
be deluged with questions about all things ghostly, or would
the subject just be dropped?

"How's the dance coming along?" I asked.

"Good!" he answered brightly.

"How's Ellen?"

"Good."

"How's the hair looking?"

"She got a haircut."

"You told me."

"No, another one. Her mom took her."

"To fix it?" I asked.

"Yeah."

Henry spied an enormous worm at the edge of the sidewalk, the kind so long and fat that it seemed to be two worms joined together by a wide rubber band. He sprinted over and knelt down.

"If you cut a worm in two," he announced, "both parts stay alive."

"What?" I'd heard this factoid when I was a kid, too, and though I doubted it was true, I wasn't actually 100 percent sure. After all, some species don't need a male and a female to reproduce. This could fall into that same category: facts of biology that seem ludicrous but are accurate.

"It's true," he said, picking up a flat stone.

"Don't!"

"It won't hurt him," Henry insisted.

I grabbed him by the arm and pulled him to his feet.

"Mama!" he protested.

"Worm blood stings," I lied. "It's worse than a bee sting. *Way* worse."

Henry dropped the stone.

It was a relief to arrive at work. Caleb had just brewed a fresh pot of coffee, and for the next two hours, we immersed ourselves in the world of luxurious binding and storage materials. By noon, we had selected our papers and leathers, the acid-free boxes we would use to store the documents we weren't binding into books, and matting materials for Honor Morton's photographs.

Most of the work I would have to do at home, but that was fine. It was already Thursday, so even if I called in my orders today and had all the materials overnighted to the island, they wouldn't arrive until sometime on Friday. If there were a problem with the shipping, I could miss the packages entirely. It made a lot more sense to have the boxes sent straight to Cambridge.

"I'm awfully sorry," Caleb said. "I really underestimated how long things would take."

"It's okay," I said.

"No, it isn't."

"Believe me, it happens all the time."

"That may be true, but we're going to have to revisit the issue of money."

"What do you mean?"

"It's a much bigger job than I thought. You've been here nearly a week, and look how much work you still have ahead of you."

"The fee we agreed on was perfectly fair. This is all part of the process; I knew that."

"Well, I didn't," he insisted.

I shrugged. I didn't want to turn my back on more money, if he was offering to pay me more than the fee we'd agreed on, which he seemed to be doing. But I'd had my share of distractions this week, too. I couldn't honestly say that I'd been overworked.

"Let's just table it for now," I suggested. "I'll keep track of how much time everything takes and we can talk about it again when the project is done."

"We certainly will," he said.

When I heard from Lauren that we were going to have dinner in the dining room, I made an immediate executive decision: Henry was not going to be part of the evening. We hadn't laid eyes on Vivi since I'd screamed at her on the rocks, and I had no idea whether she was gone for good or just off planning the details of her next ambush. But if Henry was eating with all of us, and Vivi felt inclined to visit, she'd end up in the dining room, too. I really didn't want that to happen.

I carried Henry's supper—a grilled cheese sandwich, a bowl of tomato soup, and a piece of apple pie—into the TV room on a tray and popped in the DVD of *The Parent Trap*.

"Do not *move* from this couch," I ordered sternly.

"What if I have to go the bathroom?" he asked.

"Do you?"

"No, but I might."

"Then go," I answered. "And come right back. I mean it. I don't have to remind you about what happened last night, do I?"

"No!" he said, a little freshly.

If he hadn't said it freshly, I would have let the subject drop. But because he did, I took the opportunity to rub it in a little. "I told you to wait on the steps and you didn't."

"I *know*," he said. "I'm *sorry*."

He didn't sound sorry, but everyone was sitting down to dinner. I had to pick my battles.

"Okay," I responded, and I left.

Aitana had news. I'd met her and her husband, Peter, on the porch when they first arrived, and she'd indicated that she had quite a story to tell, but that she wanted to wait until we were all sitting down together and she could do it justice. As we finished our soup, it seemed that the moment had arrived.

"You want to do the honors, or should I?" she asked Bert.

"Be my guest," he responded, winking at me.

"Then don't interrupt me," she said. "You always butt in when I'm halfway through and take over."

Bert turned his palms to the ceiling and gave a look that said, *Who, me?*

Then he glanced at me, taking measure of how I'd reacted to this little display. I hoped that I was coming across as cool and enigmatic.

"Don't give me that," Aitana said good-naturedly. "Okay, so we're up at the crack of dawn."

"What else is new?" Bert said dryly. "That's late for me."

"Just for the record," Peter explained, "I was not in favor of this little . . . expedition."

"Which was why we had to go before you woke up!" Aitana chirped, batting her eyelashes at Peter in a Betty Boop fashion.

Peter shook his head, but he was grinning, probably used to his wife's cheerily disregarding his opinions.

"So we drive over there," Aitana continued.

"Over where?" Mark asked.

"To where Anza followed them."

Lauren turned to me. "Followed whom?"

"You didn't tell them?" Aitana asked.

"I haven't seen them!" I explained. "Not to talk to, anyway."

"The couple in the car!"

"From the other night?" Mark asked.

"Yes!"

Lauren shook her head, looking baffled. "But I thought you didn't see them."

"So did I," Aitana responded. "But then, at the party, I was refilling a platter of cheeses, and I saw this woman across the table, and I knew it was her! I just knew!"

"That she was the woman in the car?" Mark asked.

"Yeah. And she gave me kind of a funny look, like maybe she recognized me, too. But I couldn't leave, so Anza followed her."

"Them," I corrected. "She was with a guy. They turned off onto Ballard's Way."

"Where's that?" Mark asked. "I forget."

"Dan Koslowski's street," Bert replied.

"Right, right," murmured Mark.

"But then this dog came after me," I said.

"Mavis Crocker's, I'll bet," Bert put in.

"Whoa!" Mark hooted. "I wouldn't want to meet *that* mutt in a dark alley. Mavis used to keep him tied up, but lately I've seen him roaming around out on the street."

"He definitely wasn't tied up," I said.

"So *anyway*," Aitana said, anxious to get the story back on track, "Bert and I went over there this morning, before it was light out. Dan's away, and he and Bert are buddies, so we parked in Dan's driveway."

"What about the dog?" Lauren squealed.

"I brought a harpoon," Bert said evenly, and my heart did a little swoop. A *harpoon*? How cool was that? Of course it wouldn't have been cool if he had actually had to use it, either for the dog or for the owner who loved him, but owning one and bringing it was pretty cool. Then again, if Dec is any indication, I obviously have a soft spot for guys who are comfortable with weapons.

"But we never saw him," Aitana said. "He must have been inside with Mavis."

I couldn't wait any longer: I had to pop the million-dollar question. "Did you find the car?"

Aitana's eyes were sparkling.

"Yes! And that's not all!" she said excitedly. "We grabbed their trash bags!"

"You *grabbed* their *trash* bags?" Lauren echoed, a look of distaste on her face. "Whose trash bags? Where are we talking about?"

"The old Lawlor place," Peter replied.

"Doug Lawlor's?" Mark asked. "But he's not down yet, is he? He never opens it up until June."

"Well someone's there," Bert said. "The green Subaru was parked behind the garage. And you wouldn't believe what we found in the trash."

"What?" I asked.

"Empty kerosene bottles. Lamp oil."

"But everybody uses lamp oil," Mark protested. "We've got hurricane lamps ourselves."

"Yeah, but sixteen bottles?" Aitana said. "All empty?"

"Seventeen," Peter corrected, sounding a little excited in spite of himself.

"Hmmm. Yeah, that does sound a little fishy," Lauren said. "So what did you do?"

"Drove straight to New Shoreham and dropped the bags off with Chief McGill. He put Denny Lombard on the ten o'clock ferry with all the empty containers. They'll see if the residue matches the samples the fire marshall took, and if it does, they'll bring the two of them in."

"Can't they bring them in *now*?" I asked. "What if they leave the island?"

"Oh, they won't," Bert replied. "The cops are keeping an eye on the ferries. McGill could go over there and talk to them, based on the car alone, but he said it would be easier to hold them for questioning if there's a materials match."

"When will they know?" I asked.

"This afternoon, they hope," Aitana replied. "Tomorrow morning at the latest."

"But I'm afraid they'll get away!" I protested.

"They really can't," said Peter. "They definitely can't sneak the car off the island, and there aren't that many people going back and forth at this time of year. It's mostly islanders. Aitana gave McGill a good description of the girl. He's going to call Doug Lawlor and find out who's staying in the house."

"So, what do you all think of Rawlings?" I asked. We were working our way through generous helpings of coconut-crusted chicken, lentil salad, and roasted beets.

Bert turned the question back on me.

"What do *you* think of him? You're the one who got invited to his party!"

"I'm sorry! I feel terrible!"

"What was the house like?" Lauren asked.

"Gorgeous," I admitted.

"He's got two of everything in the kitchen," Aitana added. "Two Vikings, two Sub-Zeroes, two dishwashers."

"They probably do a lot of entertaining," Lauren said. She turned to Aitana. "Didn't they have a big thing there last September? Some kind of 'retreat'?"

"In October, over Columbus Day weekend. Sixteen people. Except for the Annapurna wedding, it was my biggest job all fall."

"Who were they?" I asked.

"I don't know."

"Politicians?" Mark inquired.

"I don't think so," she said. "The wives drove me crazy."

"How so?" asked Lauren.

"Oh, no butter, no white flour, no this, no that! This one's on South Beach and that one wants a nutritional breakdown for every morsel of food she's putting in her mouth. You'd think I was running a spa."

"What about Mrs. Rawlings?" I asked. "Did she help?"

"She was in and out. Mostly out. She didn't seem to know any of the women."

"So it wasn't a social thing," I suggested.

"No, it was like—meetings during the day and then a dinner. One night they went out for a sunset sail, another night there was a jazz band and dancing."

"You think they were lobbyists?" I asked.

"I really don't know," Aitana replied. "The check said, 'The Lenox Consortium.' No address."

The Lenox Consortium? I had just read that name somewhere—today. Where?

"You never answered the question," Bert said to me. "What's *your* take on Rawlings?"

"Honestly?" I asked.

People nodded and murmured assent.

"I—I—don't know," I replied, backing off a momentary impulse to answer the question directly. It wasn't a secret that everyone at the table supported the construction of the wind farm, so I wasn't in any danger of offending my dinner companions, but I didn't like gossiping about people I barely knew, *with* people I barely knew. The truth was, Rawlings kind of gave me the creeps. He was smooth and polished, but my conversation with him at the party hadn't changed the impression I'd formed at the Historical Society: that the man had an agenda, that he thought I could be useful to him, and that if I turned out not to be, I had better get out of his way.

I decided to deflect the question. "The presentation was really something. And I guess that was the point of the party, to publicize the results of the study."

"Which were . . . ?" Mark prompted.

"The end of life on earth as we know it, the minute those windmills go in."

Then it hit me! The name!

"Excuse me a minute," I said. "I'll be right back." I got up and headed toward the stairs.

"Everything okay?" Lauren called, apparently startled by my abrupt exit.

"Just checking on Henry," I responded. And I did. I looked in. He was sitting right on the couch where I'd left him, and Vivi was nowhere in sight.

I raced up the stairs and down the hall. I opened the door to our room, located my purse on the floor near the bathroom, and rummaged through it until I found a copy of the report the senator's aide had handed out. I turned the brochure over and scanned the back page. The top of my scalp began to prickle.

I hurried back downstairs, report in hand, and threw it on the table.

"What?" Mark said. "What *is* this?"

"The summary of the findings," I said. "Look on the back, on the bottom. Look who paid for the study."

"The Lenox Consortium," Mark read.

Lauren grabbed the paper out of his hand.

"Who do you think they are?" I asked.

"I'll find out, believe you me." Mark was leaving on the morning ferry for his trip to Boston. He was working on an article for the *Wall Street Journal*, something to do with stimulus funds and the national infrastructure. He would stay in Boston Friday night, meet the Australian ghost detectives in Providence on Saturday morning, and accompany them back to the island on the midday boat.

"How can you find out?" I asked.

"I have my ways," he replied.

Chapter Eighteen

HENRY FELL ASLEEP during *The Parent Trap*, and for once, I was able to get him upstairs and into bed without his waking up.

I had hoped that the evening would end with Bert and me having a little time alone, but that didn't happen. And it was probably just as well. I had some issues to resolve, and plans to make, and I wasn't even sure where to start.

First, there was the matter of the ghost detectives. They might exaggerate their findings and work digital magic aimed at thrilling their audiences, but sensors like the ones they carried *did* actually register temperature variations and changes in energy fields. If, on Saturday night, the Grand View were filled with angry spirits, the gear would definitely vibrate, blink, and squeal. This wouldn't be the end of the inn—the publicity might well fill every bedroom—but Lauren and Mark didn't just want to fill the rooms, they wanted to fill them with a certain class of vacationer. The kind that read *Town & Country Travel*.

I could rely on Baden to make himself scarce while the TV guys were here, but I definitely couldn't count on Vivi. She was probably furious, or scared, and either way, I could imagine her acting out defiantly, purposely doing the opposite of anything I asked her to do. I had to make a deal with her, but the only thing she seemed to care about was Jamey.

I lay in the low light, listening to the sound of the waves from across Water Street. As I reached for *Inn of Phantoms*, longing for a break from my troubled introspection, I heard footsteps in the hall. Someone had paused outside my door, and I heard a quiet, tentative knock. I sat up, then got up and padded across the room in my stocking feet.

"Hello?" I whispered through the door.

"Hi," came the quiet reply.

I felt a little burst of happiness—not fireworks, exactly, but at least the lighting of a sparkler. I opened the door.

It was Bert.

"You weren't asleep, were you?"

I shook my head, thinking, *And even if I were, I'd be thrilled to be woken up by you.*

"What are you doing?" he whispered.

"Nothing."

"Henry asleep?"

I nodded.

"Kind of clips your wings, huh?"

That was an understatement. "Depends on what you had in mind."

He did a Groucho Marx imitation, making his eyebrows flutter up and down.

"Right," I said.

"Only kidding," he insisted. With one hand, he held up a

squat and unfamiliar bottle, and with the other, two brandy snifters. "Sit on the porch?"

"It's freezing!"

"We could build a fire."

"And wake everybody up?"

"I was thinking, on the beach."

I looked back at Henry and sighed. I'd been freewheeling it ever since I'd gotten here, leaving him on his own, entrusting him to other people, talking myself into believing that he really didn't need me as much as he obviously still did. I didn't want him waking up and finding me gone, again, down on the porch or on the beach. It didn't make any difference that I wouldn't be far away; he would still be upset to discover that I had left him all alone at night, when he had fallen asleep trusting that I would be here.

"I can't," I said.

"Okay." Bert nodded toward the little sitting area at the end of the hall, and I pulled the door almost closed behind me. Fortunately, I was still dressed, and I hadn't washed off the makeup I'd applied earlier, so I allowed myself to imagine that I resembled a sultry French starlet, the kind with long, mussy hair who lights cigarette after cigarette and drinks coffee from a cup that was somebody's grandmother's and who always seems to be just out of bed, or just about to fall in.

Nah. I probably looked like—me.

Two upholstered chairs formed an inviting reading alcove at the end of the hall, and Bert chose the one that looked less comfortable. He held up the bottle and I nodded.

"What is it?" I asked.

"Rémy Grand Cru. My weakness." He poured about an inch into the bottom of a snifter and handed it to me. Then, with a surprising lack of self-consciousness, I mentally prepared to do what Earl, a pompous ass I once dated in college, had taught me to do with a snifter of brandy. Though I'd had several opportunities in the past ten years, I hadn't actually gone through the steps of the ritual.

I waited for Bert to pour his own glass and we clinked.

"*Sláinte,*" I said, the Irish toast to good health.

"*Saúde,*" he replied, which probably meant about the same thing.

I wrapped my hand around the bowl of the snifter. This, I had been informed, allowed the cognac to be heated slightly from the radiant warmth of the palm. I held the glass up to the light, admiring the clarity of the amber fluid, and I sloshed it around gently, watching for what Earl had called "legs"— little rivulets that testified to the precious liquid's age. I waved the glass under my nose and inhaled, then had a sip.

This was where my cognac knowledge ended abruptly. It just tasted hot and strong and burny. But I could tell that Bert was impressed by my performance, and this made me want to confess to him immediately that it had all been for show, a hollow and affected act picked up from a hollow and affected blowhard, and that I knew absolutely nothing about Rémy Grand Cru or any other cognac. I didn't even like it!

But I didn't get to say any of this, because I took another fraudulent sip, a much bigger one this time, and this one met an obstacle in my tense and overexcited throat and ended up going down the wrong way. What ensued was a coughing fit so severe that I was surprised, later, when I examined my appearance in the bathroom mirror, that I hadn't managed to pop a couple of blood vessels in my eyes.

It served me right.

Bert hopped up, trying to help, but there was nothing he could really do. I wasn't choking, so he couldn't perform the Heimlich maneuver (though I was sure he would have known how, being the kind of guy who was comfortable with a harpoon). But my windpipe wasn't obstructed. Even the water he hurried away to get me didn't help, because it went down the right way, which was to say, down my throat.

We just had to wait it out. It took almost five minutes before I returned to normal, the only upside of the whole, embarrassing episode being that my coughing extravaganza hadn't woken up Henry.

"Well," Bert said, when I finally took a deep breath and wiped away the tears I had been unable to check.

I smiled weakly.

"Bet you're glad I came by."

I *was* glad! I just couldn't talk yet. But I started to laugh. It was ridiculously funny, when you came right down to it, how one minute we were living out a romantic French movie, and the next, we were washed up on the shores of a cheesy cable melodrama. It must have been nerves, because once I got started, I couldn't stop laughing, and soon Bert was laughing with me, and before I knew it, we were back in Paris and my hair was all mussy and we had to keep stopping to listen, to make sure that in all our laughing and moving furniture and getting down to some serious hanky-panky, we hadn't awakened Henry.

Chapter Nineteen

FRIDAY

HENRY WAS POURING way too much syrup onto his French toast, but I was far too blissful to interfere. I dawdled over my coffee and toast, reliving every delicious detail of the minutes between eleven or so last night and 12:07 this morning. Had Bert and I really been together for only an hour?

"Mama?" Henry looked up.

I hit the Pause button on the delectable little film that had been playing in my mind.

"What?"

"Can we call Daddy?"

"Right now?"

Henry nodded. He looked a little glum.

"How come you want to talk to Daddy?"

"Because I *do*."

I glanced at my watch. I knew Declan's schedule, and I knew that if we caught him on his cell phone right now, he wouldn't be able to talk. It would be frustrating for both of them.

"Well the thing is, sweetie," I launched in, "Daddy's on the day shift today, so he's probably still at roll call. He wouldn't be able to pick up right now."

"Why not?"

"Because he can't be talking on the phone while his boss is talking."

"Why not?"

I sighed and had a sip of my coffee. "What does Miss O. do when you guys interrupt her?"

"She gets mad."

I smiled and nodded. "That's what happens at roll call, too."

Henry took a minute to chew and to absorb this. Then he put down his fork. "Daddy's coming to my play, though, right?"

Oh. I sighed. There was no way to soften the blow, so I didn't try.

"No, honey. He isn't."

A look of surprise appeared on his face, and it wasn't hard to understand why. Declan came to everything: every T-ball practice, teacher conference, end-of-something picnic. It had never occurred to me that Declan would come to see Henry in *Grease*, but it had probably not occurred to Henry that he wouldn't.

Or maybe it had.

"It's a pretty long trip," I reminded him.

"Yeah, on the boat."

I nodded. "I brought my camera. I'll take a ton of pictures."

"Okay," he said sadly.

"And we'll call Daddy tonight. I promise."

"Yeah, we don't want him to get in trouble."

I gave him a puzzled look.

"For talking out," he explained.

———

I dropped Henry off at a quarter of nine, walked to the Historical Society, and sat for a moment in the cool sea air, waiting for Caleb to arrive. My time here today was going to be brief. Caleb was bringing packing materials and we were going to spend the morning preparing all the documents and photographs so that I could transport them safely back to Cambridge, where all the work would be done.

Over the next few weeks, I would chip away at all the binding and matting. I would come back to the island sometime this summer, whenever the *Larchmont* Collection was ready to be unveiled. Maybe I could unveil to Bert a whole new me then, too; somebody a little better dressed, with a much better haircut, and—at least temporarily—without a five-year-old in tow.

As I sat on the porch steps, I took up the thoughts I had abandoned last night. As I lay in bed trying to fall sleep, after Bert left around midnight, I still had no idea what to do about the ghost detectives and the ghosts who planned to wow them. Or about the volatile Vivi, or the understandable desire of the lighthouse spirits if not to be actually commemorated, then at least to be protected from an undignified disinterment.

As for Baden, who knew what he wanted or what would make him happy? I could only offer him what I offer every other earthbound spirit I try to help: a sincere effort to resolve the problem that's keeping him or her connected to earthly life, and one more chance to walk through that bright, shining doorway.

But now, thanks to the miraculous three-pound organ that had worked the night shift while I slept, I had some answers. Well, maybe not answers, but at least ideas.

The first involved the ghost detectives. They were after ghosts, right? Well, I'd give them ghosts! Just not at the Grand View! If I could somehow redirect the attention of the TV guys with persuasive stories of the haunted lighthouse, then maybe I could get them to do their segment on that, rather than on the Grand View. For that to work, though, I'd need the cooperation of the ghosts at the lighthouse. I didn't know if my next idea would appeal to them, enough to get them on my side and off Mark's case, but it was worth a try.

I doubted they really *wanted* to derail the wind farm. *They* didn't care about politics or piping plovers or property values or historic vistas. Their problem was with the proposed location. But the *reason* the location was so important to them was because it was all they had to commemorate their lives.

What if I offered them something else? After all, I was the person putting together the *Larchmont* Collection. What if I found a way to commemorate each and every person who went down with the ship? Hadn't the tens of thousands of names chiseled into the Vietnam Veterans Memorial done much the same thing? Maybe we could get a grant for some kind of wall, with every single name engraved in granite, or build a meditation garden or plant a grove of trees or construct a walk that ended at a beautiful private place, where the families of the victims could pause and linger. Something like this might not satisfy each and every disgruntled spirit, because spirits are just like the people they were, and you can't please everybody. But maybe, just maybe, I'd be able to take the focus off Mark and Lauren and the Grand View. And that's what I had to do.

Timing would be everything. Before the midday boat arrived tomorrow, I had to visit the lighthouse. I had to locate Vivi and find a way to keep her far away from the Grand View, and that would probably involve the ghost of Jamey and the desperate earthbound spirit who'd taken him. I definitely had to enlist Baden's help because there was no way I could take on the dozens and dozens of spirits I'd seen hanging around the lighthouse. He would have to agree to be my go-between, and I hoped I could get him to do it, because I couldn't imagine any other way of pulling this off.

And there was Henry. And Bert. It wasn't as though I had nothing to do but solve everybody else's problems.

I felt tired and overwhelmed just thinking about what I was going to try to do in the next two days, much of it in secret, but I didn't have time to be tired. I didn't have a minute to lose.

***

I found Baden in the room with the evergreen wallpaper, sitting by the window in the bentwood rocker. Caleb had driven me back to the inn with all the boxes we had packed, and together, he and I had lugged them up to my room. Mark had left for Boston on the early ferry, and Lauren was down at the kitchen table paying bills, so as soon as I bid good-bye to Caleb, I went looking for Baden and Vivi. It was Baden I came upon first.

"Hello," he said politely.

"Hi." I closed the door securely behind me. "How are you?" I asked, not anxious to get to the reason for my visit.

"Very well, thank you. And you?"

"Fine. Looks like we're going to get some rain."

"It does, yes." There was an awkward pause. Baden ended it by indicating the only other chair in the room. "Sit, please."

"I don't mean to disturb you."

"Not at all."

I sat down in the chair. "I need to talk to you about something, but to tell you the truth, I don't know where to start."

"The beginning?" he suggested.

"Well, I suppose that would be—your brother's building this house."

Baden stopped rocking and appeared to give me his full attention.

"And his great-grandson's deciding to restore it," I continued. I thought I saw a flash of relief cross his features. I suppose he'd been worried that I was going to grill him about his love affair.

"Please, continue," he said.

"Mark and Lauren need our help."

"What can *I* do?"

"It's kind of complicated," I said.

"Most things are."

I smiled and sighed. "So, the ghost detectives are arriving tomorrow."

"Yes."

"Are the ghosts still coming?"

He nodded dejectedly. "I've attempted to dissuade them. I've been unsuccessful."

"Well, that's what I want to talk to you about. What if I were to commit to building them *another* memorial. Something real and permanent, like a wall with all their names, or a garden."

"And move their bones?"

"Do you think the bones are that important? The bones themselves?"

"We have no way of knowing what is important to another human being."

"Yes, we do. We just have to ask."

"You're intending to do that?" Baden said. "Ask dozens of

ghosts if a memorial on the island could take the place of . . . of what they have now?"

"Not me."

Baden frowned. He didn't understand.

"You?" I whispered.

"No."

"Please?" I begged.

"No. Three times I have tried. Three times I have failed. That's enough."

"But you had nothing to offer them before. Now you do!"

"What? A promise? From someone they do not know?"

"Yes," I replied. "Look, I'm not asking for myself. It's for *your* great-great-nephew and his wife! I thought you cared about them." My voice was rising.

"I do care. Very much."

"Well so do I, and I'm not even related to them!" I was trying not to get angry, but I could feel myself becoming tenser and more annoyed.

Suddenly, there was a knock at the door.

We both froze. I watched the doorknob turn slightly and then the door squeaked open. Outside in the hall stood Lauren.

―――

"Anza?"

"Hi!" I said, way too brightly. I glanced at Baden. He looked paralyzed.

"What are you doing?" she asked.

Oh, I thought, *just having a fight with myself in this empty room.*

I sighed. I had been hoping to manage all this without having to have the ghost talk with either Mark or Lauren, but now I had to rethink my strategy. Lauren had just heard me having what must have seemed to be a one-sided conversation.

"I'm talking to a ghost," I admitted.

She smiled, obviously not believing me.

"Really."

Her smile faded.

"Sit down," I suggested, motioning to the bed.

"It's nothing to be afraid of," I began, "but you do have a couple of ghosts in this house."

"We do?" The color seemed to drain from her cheeks. "How do you know?"

So I told her. Everything. I started with the four-year-old me, and Nona, and Vinny Sottosanto and his dog, Lola. I answered all the usual questions about what I can do and what I can't, what ghosts can do and what they can't, then I moved on to what I know and what I don't, and finished up by explaining the white light. All of this took close to an hour. When she seemed not to have any more questions, I asked, "Does this frighten you?"

"No, not really, not the way you explain it."

"Good. Because there's no reason to be afraid."

She nodded. "Who are they?"

"Who are who?"

"The ghosts we have in the house."

"One is a little girl. Her name is Viveka—Vivi for short."

"Oh my God! How old is she?"

"Six or so, I think."

"The poor little thing! What happened to her?"

"I think she went down on the *Larchmont*."

"That's so sad. But why is she here? I mean, if she was with her parents on the boat, why didn't she . . . what did you call it?"

"Cross over?"

"Cross over, yeah."

"I'm not sure," I lied, having decided that very minute not to go into the subject of Jamey, because that might bring us dangerously close to the topic of the ghosts at the lighthouse, which I was determined to avoid. Lauren had plenty to digest already. If I told her about the ghosts at the lighthouse, I'd probably put my foot in my mouth and somehow blurt out the fact that they were planning to descend on the inn en masse.

She sat back in her chair. "Wow," she said.

"Yeah, I know. It's pretty wild."

"So that's who you were talking to," she concluded.

When I didn't answer right away, she added, "The little girl."

"Actually, no," I admitted. "It was someone else."

The someone else was standing in the doorway and had been for much of my conversation with Lauren. I looked over at him, a question on my face. Slowly, he nodded.

"He's right here with us," I said.

"Who?" Now Lauren appeared distressed, so I took her hand.

"His name is Baden," I explained, and before I could say any more she sat up straight and swept her gaze all around, searching for the face she would never be able to see.

"*Uncle* Baden?" she cried. "He's *here*?"

"He is."

"Where?"

"In the doorway, right there."

I saw Baden stand up very straight and lift his chin. He smoothed one side of his hair down with one hand and then the other side with the other, and a vulnerable, hopeful look appeared on his face. I barely recognized the spirit that stood before us; his hardened, chilly reserve had all but vanished.

"Can he hear me?"

"He can," I said.

"Hello, Uncle Baden," Lauren whispered.

His voice caught when he replied, "Hello, my dear."

That was all it took. Baden was on board. Well, it took a *little* more than that, specifically about forty-five minutes in which I acted as a go-between while Baden and Lauren talked about the construction of the house and about Mark's father and a few other members of the Riegler clan, now deceased, people Lauren had known as frail and elderly and whom Baden remembered as children. The transformation in the ghost was remarkable. It was like watching a time-lapse film of the effects of water and sun on a plant long abandoned in a dry, dark room. In the end, Baden would have walked into a tornado for his great-great-niece.

Which, come to think of it, was pretty much what he was going to do.

"She's a lovely girl," he said after Lauren left. I had asked her not to tell anyone but Mark about my abilities, and she promised to keep it quiet.

"She is."

"When is the child to arrive?"

"End of June. It's a boy."

"They know this? It is impossible to be sure, no?"

"No. There are a couple of tests you can have nowadays. Not everyone wants to find out the baby's sex, but some people do."

"How strange," he said. "To know before the child is born." He was quiet for several moments. "It's best that I go alone," he finally said.

I could hardly believe my ears. Had he actually agreed to help me?

"Will they meet with you? Will they listen to you?"

"Colonel Hannah and Mr. Duffield will. Will I be able to persuade them to abandon their plans? That I do not know. You have no funds, correct?"

"No, but I'm sure I can—get some." I hoped.

"Where, may I ask? You forget: I was a banker. All my life, I worked with people who had plans to do things, to build things, to buy things, and for this, they needed capital."

I sighed. He was right. I didn't have a cent. And a lack of money to make good on my promise wasn't my only problem. "The little ghost, Vivi. Do you know her?"

"I do, yes. An irksome child. My nephew and his wife were indulgent parents."

"She's not irksome," I said. "She's just . . ."

"Bold, impolite, disobedient, insolent."

"True," I admitted, suppressing a grin. "I don't trust her. She could doom the Grand View when the ghost detectives are here, just for the fun of it."

"Decidedly," Baden said.

"I had a little run-in with her last night, and I haven't seen her since. I have no idea where she is."

"I know where she is."

"You *do*? Where?"

"In the barn, with the cat."

"Tormenting the poor animal, no doubt."

"No, no. They are inseparable."

"What? But the other night in the kitchen, Frances acted like she was completely spooked."

"They are rarely apart," Baden said. "The child occasionally turns on the cat the way she turns on everyone else, but Frances can take care of herself."

"That's for sure," I replied.

"So—what are you asking of me? Regarding the girl."

"I need to get her to cooperate. But I'm not one of her favorite people right now. I'm sure she's furious at me because I lost my temper with her."

"Yes, so?"

"Would you take her to the lighthouse with you? There's a baby there. His name is Jamey. He's Vivi's little brother, and he's been taken away from her by one of the women, one of the ghosts."

"She lost her own child," Baden explained. "The infant was drowned that night."

"Who did?"

"Emilia Davis. The woman who has young James."

"Oh, my God! So her own baby crossed over and Emilia was left behind?"

Baden nodded. "She was certain that he was among the spirits who remained on—this side."

I completed the story. "So she waited too long. By the time she realized he was gone, the white light had disappeared. And Jamey had lost his own mother."

"Precisely," Baden replied.

"But not his sister," I continued.

"It's no excuse for how the girl acts," Baden commented. "That child behaves disgracefully."

"She's a kid," I said, surprised at myself for defending a creature I would happily have throttled the previous evening. "She feels responsible for her baby brother. So why don't the other ghosts help her?"

"To do what?" Baden asked.

"To get her brother back."

"That won't be easy. Emilia believes that young James *is* her child."

"Is she mad?"

"Entirely. There are many at the lighthouse who are mad, especially the ones who met their ends in the lifeboats. Emilia may be—wholly insane, but she loves the little boy."

"But it isn't fair!" I protested.

"That child brought it upon herself. She's turned on even the people who tried to help her."

We sat for a moment in silence. In less than an hour, I would have to pick up Henry. I fought a growing dread that this whole house of cards was headed for collapse.

"Would you just take her with you tonight, when you go?"

"She'll not agree to accompany me, I'm sure. No one can make her do a thing."

"But I have to verify that I have the right little boy. And, to be honest, I need to be able to bribe her."

"To do what?"

"To stay out of the house while the ghost detectives are here. It won't do any good to lead them to the lighthouse if Vivi's having a grand old time setting all the gizmos off back here. And you know she will."

"She's fond of your son," Baden said.

"Yeah, well, that's another whole set of problems."

"I know who the child is," Baden said. "And I also know Emilia. I can take you to them whenever you like. But I will not take the girl with me tonight."

"Fair enough," I said. "Then good luck. And thank you again."

"Don't offer me thanks until I have accomplished something."

I shook my head. "Thank you for trying."

Chapter Twenty

THE THEATER WAS abuzz. I was early, so I took a few moments to check out what had happened onstage in the last couple of days. The set was impressive, and I didn't think I was biased, because the only piece Henry had had anything to do with was the car, and that was nowhere in sight.

The Burger Palace looked like something out of *The Jetsons*. The drive-in, presently being painted in a perfect fifties palette of pink and aqua, was topped with a celestial crown of silvery orbs. On the other side of the stage was a structure that looked like a bandstand. Crepe paper streamers, likewise aqua and pink, ran from its floor to the structural beams that formed the bandstand's sides and back. It was hard to tell what the final effect would be, though the sight brought to mind the overeager decorations committee of an underfunded prom.

I was touched by how hard all the kids were working, and without any apparent supervision. Granted, time was short—there would be a final dress rehearsal in the morning, followed by the performance at four o'clock—but to see fifteen or twenty kids between the ages of twelve and seventeen cheerfully working together to realize their shared vision was . . .

Oops. Someone, a girl, *accidentally* pushed someone else, another girl, into a third someone, a boy. Shrieking followed, and the dabbing of aqua paint onto a bare arm, leading to a round of retaliation in pink, this time onto painters' clothes. Multiple paintbrushes were now brandished in a spirited free-for-all that had probably been simmering all week, just waiting to erupt into a rolling boil. A teacher in his twenties appeared, just in time to prevent a full-scale, good-natured, *Grease*-style showdown between anybody and everybody.

My cell phone rang, and I got up and walked toward the back of the theater.

"Hello?"

"Hey! It's Bert."

"How'd you get this number?"

"You gave it to me."

"I did?"

"Actually, you entered it into my phone."

"I was kidding."

"Oh."

This seemed to throw him off stride, as he immediately got very businesslike. "I just had a call from Mark McGill."

I had stepped outside, and a gust of wind prevented me from catching the name.

"Who?"

"Mark McGill, the police chief. They have a match."

"What do you mean?"

"On the bottles. The lamp oil matched the accelerant they found at the barn."

"You're kidding."

"Nope. He's got a car on the way over to the Lawlor place."

"To arrest the girl and guy?"

"Well, to bring them in for questioning, anyway. They lifted some prints from the containers."

"What about the car?"

"I guess they'll impound it. See if there's any residue."

"Wow!" I said. "That's incredible."

"Yeah. Where are you?"

"Picking up Henry."

"At the school?"

"Yeah."

"Want a lift?"

Oh, he was *so* transparent. Did I want a lift? I could practically see the Grand View from where I was standing.

"Absolutely," I said.

⸻

"There's Vivi!" Henry shouted as the truck bumped along the road by the lighthouse.

"Where?"

Henry pointed. "Right there!"

And so she was. Her hair was flying as she dashed and darted, just barely eluding little Jamey, who stumbled along behind her. She would almost let him catch her, then dip away just as he reached out to grab her arm or her dress. Far from upsetting him, the game seemed to fill him with delight, judging from the happy shrieking in the air.

They were playing not far from where Baden was trying to plead our case with what had to be a couple of dozen ghosts. He and two other phantoms, whom I took to be the ringleaders of the scheme, were up on the porch of the lighthouse cottage. The rest of the spirits were clustered in groups on the grass and the rocks, close enough to be disturbed by the children's hooting and laughing. When I saw Baden glance angrily in Vivi's direction, I made a quick decision.

"Bert?"

He looked over.

"Could I ask you a huge favor?"

His eyes barely left the road.

"Could you pull over for a minute?"

He didn't ask why. He just steered the truck onto the soft, sandy shoulder.

"Remember the other day? That little boy we almost—the boy we saw?"

"*You* saw."

"Right. He's—his sister is—" *driving Baden completely up the wall,* I thought. "I really hate to ask you this, but could you take Henry back to Lauren's and ask her to keep an eye on him for an hour or so? Tell her it has to do with Mark's uncle. She'll understand."

"I can keep an eye on him." Bert looked a little hurt, as though I were impugning his babysitting abilities.

"That'd be great. I won't be long."

"I want to play with Vivi," Henry interjected.

"Who's Vivi?" Bert asked.

"I'll explain that, too," I told him. "Maybe I'll bring her back with me," I lied, intending to do no such thing. Even if I had been telling the truth, this was a little like promising to get water to run uphill.

"Okay," Henry said.

"I owe you," I told Bert.

"That you do."

"Give a little thought to how I can pay you back."

"Will do," he said dryly, but I thought I saw the beginning of a grin.

—

I hadn't noticed her at first, and now I couldn't imagine why. The ghost of Emilia, or at least the ghost I took to be Emilia, was right there in plain sight, pacing along the edge of the bluff on which the Southeast Lighthouse stood. Vivi and Jamey were playing on the damp lawn that ran from the building toward the sea, giving way to a sudden, steep, and sandy decline. Waves crashed fiercely on the rocks at the bottom of the slope, and it seemed pitifully apparent that Emilia was trying to keep Vivi and Jamey from tumbling off the bluff and onto the rocks.

But Vivi and Jamey were dead. No further harm could come to either one of them on the rocks or in the sea. Any sane ghost would know this. In her flowing beige dressing gown, Emilia paced restlessly along the rim of the drop, her gaze darting left and right, following the movements of the children.

Knowing Vivi, and how she had to feel about the woman who had kidnapped her baby brother, I suspected that games like this went on quite often, games in which Vivi, a sane little ghost, tormented the poor, confused Emilia by leading Jamey into situations that would terrify the parent of any live child.

I walked across the lawn. "Vivi!" I called, trying to sound cheerful and glad to see her. "Is that your brother?"

Vivi stopped short, but the toddler kept going, straight toward the spot where Emilia stood guard. Vivi regarded me with haughty suspicion. Or maybe outright contempt; it was a little hard to tell.

I continued toward her. "I'm sorry I got mad."

"You are not!" she shot back. "You're mean. I hate you!"

I couldn't suppress a smile. I feel this way every time I see a two-year-old throwing a rip-roaring tantrum in a store or on the street. The outraged, thwarted fury, the angry red cheeks: the whole thing just slays me.

I looked toward the sea. Emilia had picked up Jamey, and he was squirming theatrically to be set down. The ghost regarded me with ashen calm, another sign that she was not quite right. She clearly hadn't registered the fact that I was a live human being, talking to a ghost.

"Henry could have been killed," I went on.

"Good!"

This I found a tad less hilarious. "I'm sure you don't mean that," I said.

"Yes I do!"

I sighed. There wasn't going to be any reasoning with her, at least not now.

I crossed my legs and sat down on the grass. I immediately felt the wetness of the sod seep into the seat of my jeans. Vivi eyed me warily.

"I was scared to death," I said honestly. "That's why I turned into—Monster Mommy."

I thought I saw her expression soften.

"I'm sorry, honey. I really and truly am. I shouldn't have screamed at you like that. You were just playing a game, but it went too far. It was *Henry* I was really mad at. He promised to stay on the porch."

"Then you should've spanked him!"

"I did!"

"You *did*?" Now here was something Vivi could get behind.

She folded herself down opposite me, hungry for details. "How hard?"

I hadn't spanked Henry. I don't spank. Very often. All right, I'm not above giving him a little crack on the bottom, but this time, I hadn't so much as raised my voice. He'd been so shaken that I hadn't had to. But I wasn't going to sacrifice my precarious toehold by admitting this now.

"I'd better let *him* tell you," I said confidentially. "Because you wouldn't believe it if it came from me."

"Yes I would!" she assured me. Out of the corner of my eye, I saw Emilia advancing slowly in our direction. Vivi caught sight of her, too.

"I'm going to get Jamey back for you," I said.

"She thinks he's *her* baby."

"I know. But he's not."

"He's Mama's. And Papa's."

"And *yours!* Did you have any other brothers or sisters?"

She shook her head.

"I'm going to try to help," I said. "I'll do everything I can, okay?"

She nodded almost imperceptibly.

"I need *your* help with something, too. If I help you, will you help me?"

She appeared noncommittal. "What?"

"I'll tell you later. And no more Monster Mommy. I promise."

"Monster Mommy," she echoed, then she vanished into thin air.

"Hello, Emilia."

"Have you come about the slipcovers?" she asked vaguely. Her voice was wan, like everything else about her.

"No," I said quietly. "I've come to—" I broke off. I had to put some serious thought into how I was going to go about this. "My name is Anza. Anza O'Malley."

"O'Malley. We know the O'Malleys, Eileen and Colm and the twins, Peter and—" She faltered. "What's the other boy's name? Patrick? No. Peter and—"

She look so befuddled that I took a stab in the dark. "Paul?" That was kind of twinlike: Peter and Paul.

"Paul? Yes. Paul." She didn't seem convinced. She looked up searchingly. "Are you related?"

"Oh, probably somehow!" I chirped. "Your baby's beautiful. What's his name?"

"Leopold. Leo. My little *lion*."

In response, Jamey surprised us with a spontaneous growl. Someone must have taught him that that was the sound lions made. He was adorable, chubby and spirited. It was hard to believe he was a ghost.

"Right!" I said. "That's what the lion says! Rrrrr!"

"Rrrrrrrrr," replied Jamey.

"What does the doggie say? Doggie . . . ?" I asked.

"Uff-uff!" he barked, eyes beaming.

"The kitty?" Emilia prompted.

Jamey looked stumped for a moment.

"Meow!" I said quietly.

Instead of answering, he flung his body forcefully backward, trying to slip out of Emilia's grasp. She set him down and he immediately raced away. Emila turned and followed him.

"Nora will let you in," the ghost called over her shoulder. "The fabric is in the sitting room."

Fabric? Sitting room?

"We chose the beige damask. You can work on the dining table. Nora covered it with oilcloth, so you needn't worry about scratches."

I watched her wave and then follow the chubby little spirit toward the road. I fought my urge to go after them or call her back. For what would I do, right now, if I was to take up my subject this very minute? Confront her with a story she would never believe, even if she had the mental capacity to understand it, which it didn't appear she did?

What would I say? *You're dead? You're a ghost! And so is the baby you've cherished for a hundred years. And by the way, your little lion? He's not yours. You've kidnapped the child of a dead stranger.*

I had learned something vital in my few minutes with Emilia. I now knew that I would never obtain her cooperation if I had to rely on the truth. To do the kindest thing for everyone involved—to reunite Emilia, Jamey, and Vivi with the much-missed members of their own families—I was going to have to tell a little white lie. Or maybe a very big one.

Chapter Twenty-one

Most of the spirits had their backs to me, which was fortunate; as a group, they'd remained curiously oblivious to my conversation with Emilia.

I turned and made my way slowly toward the assembly. Daylight was fading, bathing the building and the lawn and the rocks in an eerie greenish glow, the kind that usually presages the approach of a tornado. Suddenly, the spotlight in the tower came on, sweeping the seascape and all the creatures in it with a harsh, almost fluorescent band of luminescence. There was a murmur and a rustling among the gathered phantoms, but the circulating beam was silent.

I wanted to be anywhere but here. It's one thing to deal with earthbound spirits one at a time; I've been doing that all my life. But to have so many ghosts assembled in one place filled me with an unaccustomed sense of dread.

What was I afraid of? I knew they couldn't hurt me, even if they were furious and turned on me all together, flying at me in alarming waves of impotent rage. I consciously tried to slow my accelerating heartbeat. They might not like my ideas, but if so, they'd just refuse to cooperate and carry on with their

plans to descend en masse upon the Grand View. Two or three
of the spirits glanced around at my approach, their woebegone
looks briefly leavened by curiosity. One, the ghost of a young
man about twenty-five, continued to stare at me as I came
closer.

I paused but did not make eye contact. Obviously concluding
that I, like every other live human being he'd ever encountered,
was unable to see him, he turned his gaze back to Baden, who
was speaking from the steps. I suddenly understood the foundation of my grave unease. I wasn't afraid of the assembled spirits;
I was burdened by the enormous sadness of the whole situation,
and by the fact that I had it in my power to end the suffering of
each and every one of these ghosts. Well, any one of them that
wanted my help, at least.

All my life, I'd kept my eyes down, picking and choosing
which spirits I would help, and declining to reveal myself to so
many more—thousands upon thousands of wandering phantoms that had crossed my path over the years. I'd made an
uneasy peace with this, primarily by trying not to think about
it too much.

That's how people got by, wasn't it? By changing the TV
channel when implored to "adopt" a suffering child for the
daily sacrifice of pocket change. By walking past the homeless
men and women shaking cups full of coins on the street. By
skimming through the reports on Google News of floods and
famines and suicide bombings in crowded marketplaces, instead scrolling down to the breathless dispatches that consti-
tuted the Entertainment section. Because there was just too
much pain in the world, so much sadness and suffering that it
hurt even to look. So much need that if you really took it upon
yourself to try to respond every time you could, you wouldn't

be able to get through the day, much less life. That kind of selflessness, I'd always assured myself, was not for ordinary people, even those with extraordinary gifts. It was for saints. And martyrs.

I wasn't looking away now, though. I couldn't, because now that I was close enough to see clearly, the ghost on the steps to the right of Baden looked so much like my dad that I honestly felt my hands begin to tremble. Every one of the phantoms assembled here had once been somebody's father or mother, or somebody's son or daughter. This time, I couldn't pretend not to see them, even if it meant taking on more needs and expectations than I'd ever attempted to manage before.

I walked toward the lighthouse, beginning to pick up snippets of the conversation. With any luck, Baden had simply told them that I could see and speak with ghosts, not that I actually had the power to help them cross over to what came next. If they didn't yet know that, we'd be able to remain focused on the question of the memorial, leaving the subject of the white light and all that it might mean for them to be unpacked at a later time, when I had a clue about how I might handle things.

I was struck by the irony: I'd been so annoyed by Baden's reticence, by his skepticism, by the way he kept his cards so close to the vest. Now I was immensely relieved that his temperament tended toward the secretive. This had probably spared me a lot of drama, for I seriously doubted that Baden, ever the cautious and strategic businessman, had told the ghosts anything but the facts that were relevant to the issue at hand: the wind farm, their watery graves, and the possibility of our erecting a more permanent memorial.

As I reached the back of the crowd, Baden turned away

from the ghosts he was speaking with, whom I took to be the spirits he had mentioned by name, Colonel Hannah and Mr. Duffield. Though dressed, like all the others, in the clothes they were sleeping in when the *Larchmont* was struck, they still projected confidence and authority. They had probably been leaders in life, and now they were leaders in death.

Baden gave me a questioning look, turning his hands palms up in a gesture I read as meaning, *So, what do you want me to do here?*

A number of the ghosts were now looking in my direction. I took a deep breath, fixing my gaze on the ghost who looked like Dad, and stunned myself by deciding at that very moment that I had no choice but to come out of hiding.

"I'm Anza O'Malley," I said. "And yes, I can see you."

There was a flurry of breezes and some shrieking, and a few of the ghosts began to rush toward me. Frankly, irrationally, I was scared to death, so I shouted, "No! Keep away!" I glared directly at them, and they stopped in their tracks. But a lot of them were talking excitedly now, and a couple appeared close to tears. The air seemed to hum with massive waves of released electricity, and it was 100 percent clear to me that I had to take control of this entire situation. Immediately.

I stood up straight and said, "I will walk away right now if any one of you comes near me. I mean it. I will. I *want* to help you and I *can* help you, but we're going to do this *my* way."

I looked around. The ghosts who had rushed me—a woman in her forties wearing a tattered silk dressing gown, a man in his sixties attired in a midshipman's uniform, and a teenaged girl with braids encircling her head, looking like an angel in a Florentine painting—retreated a few steps. The girl sank down onto the ground, and the man rejoined a clump of other spirits at the edge of the pack. He glared at me suspiciously.

I advanced nervously toward Baden. The phantoms stepped aside as I passed, like Moses through the Red Sea, and I pretended not to notice that many of them reached out and touched my arms and my clothes. I ascended the steps, turned, and faced them. Baden willingly relinquished the spotlight.

"Okay," I said quietly. I didn't really feel like going into the whole spiel—me, Nona, Vinny, Lola—but I didn't see any way around it, so I launched into the highly abbreviated version, which takes less than a minute. It's a lot easier to explain all this to ghosts than it is to people. Ghosts *know* you're for real, because you're probably the only live adult they've encountered since they died who's been able to have a conversation with them. Kids can talk to them, sure, but nobody believes that kids have been talking to ghosts. Live people, as opposed to earthbound spirits, have to take a lot on faith; since *they* can't see or speak with phantoms, there's no way for them to check the facts.

In my audience tonight, I didn't have any doubters. I had people who wanted to ask question after question, most aimed at determining whether I could be of any help to them, personally. And breaking the promise I had just made to myself, I told them everything, even that I could create the white light for them and help them cross over.

The crowd reacted noisily, almost violently, to this admission, and for a moment, I felt they might rush up onto the porch and overwhelm me. I took a step back, and the ghost who looked like Dad stepped to the front of the porch and shouted, "Silence!"

He had to be the colonel. From his tone of voice, I could

tell he was used to asserting authority over unruly subordinates, and he stopped them all in their tracks. This gave me time to close the circle of my idea: I would bribe them! If they helped me turn the attention of the ghost detectives away from the Grand View and abandoned their plans to block construction of the wind farm, not only would I create another memorial for them, I would open the white doorway for each and every one of them and help them cross over.

"It's true," I said, when the noise had died down. "I have the ability to open that white doorway again. You remember the doorway, the one you saw that first day or two after the *Larchmont* went down? The one that closed and stranded you here?" The crowd was nearly silent. All I could hear was the crashing of the waves and, now that I was so near to the lighthouse, some squeaking from the revolving of the internal works.

"You're here because something was left unfinished in your life. I know that, but I can't solve those problems. I just can't. I have a child, and I—"

I broke off. It wasn't like me to be rattled in the presence of earthbound phantoms, but I was, and I had to stay strong. "You're going to have to make a decision. Do you want to cross over, through the light? Or do you want to forfeit *this* chance, too, and stay here—forever?"

"Is it heaven?" someone asked. "Is it heaven's doorway?"

"I don't know. I honestly don't. I can't see through the light or past it. All I *can* say is that spirits like you seem really, really happy when *they* can see through. They call out to their parents, their husbands and wives, the people they loved most in the world."

There was someone pushing his way through the crowd,

and as he came nearer, I recognized him as the young man who had been eyeing me. He was fair and tall and reminded me of a self-portrait I came across one day at the Gardner Museum. The picture had struck me as impossibly sad, not just because its subject had aged and died, but because the very colors of the paint were dead, having lost all glimmer of life. The resemblance to the young man before me ended there, though. He seemed possessed of almost fearsome energy.

"I'll go," he said. "Use me! Show the others."

He came right to the foot of the steps and stood there, shoulders thrown back in a gesture of exaggerated bravery that revealed how he actually felt: scared to death.

I walked down the steps as all the ghosts gathered around.

"What's your name?" I asked.

"Redmond Mullins."

Redmond Mullins! I'd read his letter! He'd written to reserve the *Larchmont*'s private library, to ask his girlfriend to marry him! I'd imagined a much older man, but no, here he was, young and passionate and utterly bereft. I even recalled the name of the woman he loved: Evelyn Brosman.

"Why didn't you leave before? Right after the ship went down."

"I kept hoping—" He broke off.

"You'd find Evelyn. Evelyn Brosman."

A strangled cry escaped his throat and he began to sob. "Yes! Yes!" He buried his face in his hands. The crowd became noisy, some spirits shouting, a few running away, some crowding in close and reaching out to touch me.

"Are you ready to go?" I asked.

"Yes!"

"You're absolutely sure."

He clearly wanted to get this over with as quickly as possible, before he had a chance to back out. I closed my eyes and summoned the light. I imagined the pinpoint shining on the near wall of the cottage attached to the lighthouse. I opened my eyes and willed it to grow to the size of a sweet pea, then a grape, then an orange. I willed it into the width and height that would accommodate a grown man, and as I watched, the light grew brighter and whiter and cleaner, so bright that I had to look away.

Cries of astonishment swept through the crowd as Redmond turned and began to walk toward the light. Unlike most spirits about to take those decisive steps, he needed no urging at all, no reassurances, no whispers of encouragement. He said no good-byes to the assembled multitudes, but as he paused before the doorway, an ecstatic smile spread across his features, and I heard him whisper, "Darling! My darling girl!" Then the light consumed him.

At this point, there was a mad rush. I would never have predicted this, but before my astonished eyes, five or six spirits raced over and followed Redmond right through the doorway! If I had been able to think on my feet, I would have kept the doorway open until every last spirit had filed through. That would have solved the problem right then and there—no ghosts to haunt the Grand View! But I panicked. I summoned my power and shut it down. Several of the spirits cried out in protest. I had to think quickly.

I surveyed the crowd. Several phantoms were hurrying away, either in anger or to broadcast the news of my feat far and wide.

"Sunday morning!" I shouted. "I'll do this again on Sunday morning for all who want to cross over. I promise! But if a single one of you arrives at the Grand View tomorrow night, the deal is off! For everyone!"

I couldn't believe I had said these words! This wasn't me talking, it was Donald Trump issuing an ultimatum on *Celebrity Apprentice*!

"But the park!" one ghost said mournfully. "The book! Will we have a monument, too?"

"You have my word," I said.

Chapter Twenty-two

Darkness had gathered as the spirits slipped away, leaving Baden and me with Colonel Hannah and Mr. Duffield.

"Most extraordinary," the colonel pronounced.

Duffield eyed me suspiciously. He was tall and broad and looked like someone given to saying, "Preposterous!" whenever possible. Now, though, he said, "This changes nothing!" His handlebar mustache quivered with his intensity.

"My good man," began the colonel. "Surely you—"

"Surely nothing!" Duffield bellowed before vanishing into the wind. The colonel disappeared with him, and I could only hope that it was in order to try to bring him around to our thinking.

Duffield was the real leader of the scheme, Baden explained as we took to the road. A minor civic official—Baden thought he had worked as an assessor for the Providence tax board—Duffield had achieved in death the prominence and influence that had eluded him in life, chiefly by teaming up with the well-liked Colonel Hannah.

"He won't relinquish it easily," Baden said.

"Relinquish what?"

"The spotlight. The authority."

"Because they're all he has?"

"Perhaps," answered Baden.

I paused. This was sad. Was there no one Duffield wanted to see again waiting on the other side? It was possible. Maybe his parents had been cruel and cold. Maybe he'd been an only child, with personal qualities that kept him friendless. Maybe he'd never been in love. Maybe the companionship of the other waylaid spirits, here on the island, offered the most connection he'd ever had. If they crossed over and were reunited with all their loved ones, Duffield wouldn't even have them. Once again, he'd be all alone—this time forever.

Heartbreaking as this scenario was, I couldn't think about it right now. I had Lauren and Mark to worry about. As Baden and I made our way along the shore road, we drew up a tentative plan. When the ghost detectives arrived at the Grand View tomorrow, Baden would make himself scarce, hiding out in the barn so as not to trip any alarms or energy sensors inside the inn. It would be up to me to get the ghost detectives to the lighthouse. I had no idea how I'd do this, but I had until tomorrow to figure it out.

When the time came, Baden would make a circuit of the island and alert any of the spirits who were willing to cooperate. They didn't actually reside at the Southeast Lighthouse, but in sheltered groves, empty attics, and peaceful barns all over the island. He would let them know that we were on our way and that they ought to gear up for a grand, if not positively operatic, performance. With any luck, we could short-circuit the ghost detectives' interest in the Grand View by giving them more than their money's worth at the lighthouse.

We walked in silence for several moments, and then Baden spoke.

"You did a wonderful thing for that boy. You have no idea."

"I'd do it for anyone. I'll do it for you."

He drew in a deep breath and let it out slowly. "Would that I were as ready as Redmond."

"He wasn't ready," I said. "He was scared to death. But he did it anyway. It can be awfully hard to leave, even if it's the right thing to do."

"Yes. In my case—"

He paused. I looked over.

"In your case . . . ," I prodded. When he gave no indication that he intended to go on, I decided that the time had come for me to storm the gates. I was going to be leaving the island in a day and a half, and I'd really come to like the old guy. I knew he wouldn't appreciate my elbowing my way into matters he considered private, and possibly quite shameful, but I hated the idea of leaving him here, stranded on his own desert island when I went home.

"In your case," I said gently, "there isn't just one woman waiting for you there. There are two."

"But you forget, my dear. I don't believe there *is* a 'there.'"

"You think there's the light, and the door, and then nothing?"

"Precisely."

I nodded politely.

"Tell me about her," I said. "Your wife."

"Lise and I were married for fourteen years."

"Were you happy?"

"Completely."

I gave him a look. From my experience, people whose marriages are completely happy don't usually find themselves in the arms of lovers. Then again, how would I know? Maybe they do. And besides, how many marriages are "completely" happy?

"I know it does not sound possible," Baden went on, "but this is true. I had no complaints—she was a fine girl, lovely to behold, kind and honest."

"Did you have children?"

"No. This was not possible. As a child, Lise had rheumatic fever and her heart was badly scarred."

Aha! A clue?

"Did you want children?"

"No. Not at all. I have asked myself all these questions, searching for the roots of my behavior, and I still do not understand what led me to betray my wife. It all comes down to a very simple fact: I truly loved two women."

"That's not so terrible."

"But it is!"

"A person can't help what they feel!" I insisted.

"No, but a person *can* help what he does. If I had not acted upon these feelings, perhaps in time they might have faded."

"Maybe. Maybe not." I stopped and looked him in the eyes. "It doesn't really matter, though, does it? What happened, happened; you can't undo it now. You could stay here for a thousand years, for ten thousand years, and that fact will never change."

"I know this."

I sighed. I wasn't getting very far. I decided to try another angle. "I know you're not religious, but in my church—I was brought up Catholic—we believe that it's enough to own up to something and be truly sorry for it and determined not to do it again."

"That's the easy part," he quipped, and when I gave him a puzzled look, he said, "Not doing it again. She's dead and gone."

"And you're dead. And here."

I was determined to press on. "And then we do penance."

"Ah, yes," he said dismissively. "Sackcloth and ashes."

I felt a flash of annoyance. "Nowadays they try to keep it positive: do something good for someone else. Maybe helping Mark and Lauren can be your penance. Because after a person does penance, the chapter's closed."

"And your *God* forgives you?" Baden said with an ironic sneer.

I noticed a pair of headlights coming toward us.

"No," I said. "You forgive yourself."

The car was traveling fast. Way too fast. Baden was in no danger, of course, but the moon hadn't risen yet, there were no streetlights on this part of the island, and I was dressed in dark colors from head to toe. Just to be on the safe side, I stepped off the road as the headlights bore down on us and the car roared by. It was the Subaru! With the girl from Rawlings's party at the wheel!

"Good Lord," Baden said. The car's tailwind had blown him off his feet, though that's not really a problem for ghosts. They just float.

"That's her!" I said.

"Who?"

"The girl from the party. The girl who set the fire! Follow her!"

"What?" Baden stared at the car's taillights, which were receding around a curve.

"*Please*! I'll explain later. Go after her!"

"And what?"

"See what she's doing!"

I could tell he thought I'd gotten pretty bossy all of a sudden, which, admittedly, I had. But he also seemed to be enjoying the turbulence, almost in spite of himself, after the deadly calm of his last hundred years. He looked at least a decade younger than when we first met.

"I don't spy," he said proudly.

"Then start!" I commanded.

"I most certainly will not."

"Come on, Baden! This is the girl who helped set fire to the barn!"

"How do you know that?"

"Bert went through their trash."

"He *what*?"

"Look, I'd follow her myself, but the last time I was over there I practically got eaten by a dog."

"I know."

I took a deep breath and launched back in. "The police want her for questioning!"

"Then let *them* handle it."

"Do you see any police cars around here? No. Neither do I. Look, something fishy's going on. She was at the senator's party! Doesn't *that* strike you as a little weird?"

"You believe the senator is involved? Anza, dear, that's not true."

"No? Are you sure? He doesn't want the wind farm. Wouldn't want to obstruct those million-dollar views."

"Your cynicism stuns me."

I paused. Maybe I *was* a cynic.

"I'd be thrilled to be proven wrong," I said.

I thought he was going to continue arguing with me, but he shook his head and smiled. And then he went after the car.

I would have loved to follow him, but I had to get back to Henry. I didn't know whether Bert had taken Henry to his house or back to the Grand View, not that that presented me with a choice, for I had no idea where Bert lived. I walked for a while toward the lights of town, grateful to be alone for more than five seconds. It was turning out to be a beautiful night. Stars were just beginning to appear, and the sea air was sharp and cool on my face.

As I rounded the corner where Water Street straightened out, I saw Bert's truck heading toward me. I waved and he pulled over.

"Where's Henry?" I asked.

"Down for the count." Bert smiled.

"He fell asleep?"

"In the rocker by the woodstove."

"Oh!"

"Lauren put him to bed."

"She did? And he didn't wake up?"

Bert shook his head. "She's in for the night. She said she'd keep an eye on him, so . . ."

"So . . . ?" I smiled.

"You're sprung."

"I'm sprung?"

Bert nodded.

"Well, how about that!" I opened the door and got in.

"Where to?" Bert asked.

"What are the choices?" I couldn't imagine that there were many, at this time of year.

"Have you eaten?"

"Uh-uh. Have you?"

"Nope."

"We could go out somewhere," I suggested.

"Or . . . we could stay *in* somewhere." Bert didn't look at me when he said this.

The proposal sent a nervous charge through my body. Was he suggesting going to his house? Alone? Without any pressure to get back to the inn anytime soon?

He must have sensed my brief hesitation because he said, "I'm not half bad with a skillet. And I've got a ton of food in the back. I just went to the store."

"Oh!" I said. "Great!"

He'd planned this! Henry was taken care of, and Bert assumed I hadn't eaten and had gone to the store before coming to find me.

Nice.

He looked over. "Okay," he replied. He put the truck in gear and off we went.

I barely had time to start imagining the delicious offerings that might come my way in Bert's kitchen—or elsewhere in the house—when I saw Baden hurrying in our direction. Flying, actually, which is not his customary means of ambulation; he usually prefers to walk.

"Stop!" I said to Bert.

He hit the brake. "What? Why?"

"There's something wrong!"

He quickly pulled over to the side of the road. "Another ghost," I explained. And then, because I thought he might be getting a little fed up with all my supernatural distractions, I leaned over and gave him a kiss. And not just a chaste little peck. Then I threw the door open and got out of the truck.

"Baden!" I called out.

He immediately stopped and flew back to where I was standing.

"The old woman," he said. "She's in trouble."

"Mavis?" I asked. "The one with the dog?"

"She's ill," Baden explained. "She needs help."

"What about Mavis?" said Bert, who had gotten out of the truck and come around to where Baden and I were standing.

"She's sick!" I said.

"What?" He gave me a dubious look, as though I were hallucinating.

"She is!" I insisted, remembering suddenly that from Bert's point of view, it was just the two of us standing here.

"I'll explain everything later. I promise. Do you have your cell phone?"

Bert dug his phone out of his pocket and held it up.

"Does she need an ambulance?" I asked Baden.

"Yes."

"Who?" asked Bert. "Mavis?"

"Call 911," I said.

"You're sure about this," he said.

"I'm positive."

So Bert put in the call, and then we got back in the truck and raced over to Ballard's Way. It wasn't very far, so we were there in a couple of minutes. Baden met us at the edge of her property, and I instantly recognized one big problem: the dog. He was standing guard just outside Mavis's back door, and as soon as we got out of the truck, he rose to his feet with a menacing growl. Nobody, but nobody, was getting through that door. Not if he could help it. And now his behavior made sense: with his owner sick inside, he'd been taking his guard duty very, very seriously.

"I thought you didn't spy," I said to Baden.

"You are correct."

"Then how did you know she was sick?"

"The dog. He is starving, but he won't leave that door. I entered the house through the other side."

I passed along the information to Bert. "Baden thinks the dog is starving," I said. "But he won't leave his post."

Bert thought for a minute and then said, "Yeah? We'll see about that." He walked back to the truck, rustled around in the grocery bags behind the seats, and reappeared a moment later with a T-bone steak.

"Our dinner," he said apologetically.

"That's okay. Good cause."

Bert had taken off his denim jacket and wrapped it around his hand, in case the dog lunged for the steak and got Bert's arm instead. I caught my breath as Bert slowly advanced on the growling canine, one step at a time, holding the steak in front of him as he moved forward.

You could practically see the poor dog struggling: *Guard Mommy—Food—Guard Mommy—Food!* Bert talked quietly all this time, soothing words intended to lure the poor frantic animal away from the door. Then, finally, it happened. Just as we heard the distant sound of a siren, the dog stopped snarling, dropped his aggressive mien, and trotted over to where Bert was standing.

He sniffed the meat. He licked it. Bert then led him over to the truck and tossed the meat into the back. The dog jumped right up after it, and Bert slammed the tailgate. Bert got into the truck and turned it on. I had to hand it to the guy. It was a brilliant maneuver. Getting the dog away from the door so the paramedics could get inside.

"Back in a while," he called, steering the truck out onto the boulevard as the ambulance turned the corner and pulled up to the house.

———

Baden saved Mavis's life. It was only a case of severe dehydration, brought on by a stomach flu, but if Baden hadn't happened by, or happened in, who knows how things would have turned out. Mavis hadn't been out of bed in days. No wonder the dog had been fierce.

I still didn't know what Baden had discovered about Elsa Corbett, if anything. He'd disappeared as soon as the ambulance arrived, and I wasn't about to go looking for him. I'd had more than enough of ghosts for one day.

Bert made a pretty great dinner, given the fact that our main course had been sacrificed to the greater good. We still had the fixings for a very nice pasta, and I made a salad while he chopped tomatoes and sautéed shallots and grated cheese. By the time the fettuccine was done, we'd gone through almost a whole bottle of Zinfandel. I can barely remember the dinner itself. I just recall the sight of him across the table, all warm and flushed from cooking, goofily holding up another bottle of wine and then proceeding to uncork it. Oh, and I remember us laughing at Mavis's dog snoring. He turned out to be perfectly friendly, now that the hunger and anxiety associated with guarding his sick mistress had been assuaged.

"I'm going to regret this," I said, holding out my wineglass.

"You'll be fine. These are small glasses."

"What does *that* have to do with anything?"

He poured me an inch or two, and we left the dishes right where they were and settled in on a couch so soft and downy that I could have gone right to sleep. Bert built a fire in the fireplace while I cruised around on cable, lucking out with the opening frames of an old black-and-white mystery on Turner Classic Movies. And that was that; the evening was sealed, all the way to the moment when the good guy confronted the bad guy at the top of the Statue of Liberty.

All in all, it was probably just as well that despite a goodly number of truly memorable kisses, we didn't find our way upstairs or onto the floor or even into horizontal positions on the world's comfiest couch. I would have loved that, and I'm pretty sure he would have, too, but the facts were the facts: I was leaving in a day and a half.

Chapter Twenty-three

SATURDAY

Henry was awake at the crack of dawn. This shouldn't have surprised me, given that he was asleep at seven and didn't have supper. It was barely light outside when he crawled into my bed.

"I want to call Daddy," he said.

"It's too early." I glanced at the clock on the bedside table. It read 6:35.

"He's up," Henry said.

Declan probably *was* up, but still.

"Let's wait a little while," I whispered. "Come here." I pulled him close and attempted to adjust the blankets around him.

"No!" He squirmed away. "You said we could and we didn't. I have to talk to Daddy!"

I opened my eyes fully. "Why?" I asked.

"I had a dream."

"What kind of dream?"

"A bad guy got him. At work."

"Oh." I sat up. Recently, Henry's concept of what his dad did for a living had undergone an adjustment. For a long time, he seemed to imagine that the work of a Boston police detective resembled that of Michael, the friendly cop in *Make Way for Ducklings.* Michael lined up police protection so Mrs. Mallard could lead her babies across Beacon Street to meet the ducklings' father in the Public Garden. About a year ago, there appeared to be a brief transition in Henry's imagination, chiefly having to do with police on horseback and police on motorcycles, but lately, he had somehow come to understand that guns and knives and "bad guys" in speeding cars are often in play.

We'd tried to tackle his fears head-on, joking about Daddy's spending all day long at the computer or drinking coffee from Dunkin' Donuts, but at a certain point, this was insulting. Declan *did* have a dangerous job. Not as dangerous as under-cover drug work, maybe, but he still spent a fair share of his time in rough neighborhoods, where routine encounters could turn dangerous, if not fatal, on a dime.

I had never gotten used to this, not really, so I could hardly expect Henry not to worry. Dec wouldn't want him to be anxious, either, so I decided to give in to Henry's plea. I threw back the covers, located my purse on the floor, and pulled out my cell phone. Luckily, I had a little power left. I dialed Declan's number and handed the phone to Henry.

This was what Henry said.

"Hi, Daddy."

"Yup."

"Nope."

"No."

Now he smiled and looked over at me.

"Yeah."

"Today. We got the car done."

"Greased Lightnin'."

"Red, with, like, fire."

"I think tomorrow."

"Okay."

"Bye."

Henry handed me the phone.

"Hey there," I said. "Sorry to call so early. He had a bad dream."

"I was up," Dec said.

"And I think he misses you," I added, aware as I said it that this would embarrass both Henry and Declan. Normally, Henry would be at Dec and Kelly's right now. He's almost never gone this long without seeing his dad.

"He'll be home soon enough," Dec said, a little gruffly, just to demonstrate that he wasn't going to encourage this namby-pamby missing Daddy business.

"How are you?" I asked.

"Oh, fine, yeah. You?"

"Good. Quite the week."

"Yeah?"

"There was a fire where we're staying. Well, out in the barn, I mean." I glanced over at Henry and covered the phone with my hand. "It was set," I whispered.

Dec's professional skepticism kicked right in. "How do you know *that*?"

"Fire marshall," I said, hoping that if I spoke elliptically, Henry wouldn't tune in and start asking questions. I watched him as he got up, padded over to the bathroom, and closed the door behind him.

"No kidding," Dec said, and I suddenly wanted to tell him the whole story, right then and there.

"I wish you were here," I blurted out, now embarrassing myself.

Dec was silent. We always steer a very wide berth around the subject of our feelings for each other. What we'd had had been great, but in the end, he'd gone back to Kelly, and now, in addition to Henry, there were Delia and Nell in our odd little ensemble. This was never going to change, I told myself. Unless Kelly died, which was a horrible, terrible, unthinkable thought that I sometimes still had.

"Because we need a real detective," I hastily added. "There's something weird going on."

I imagined Dec perking up.

"What?" he asked, anxious to establish that I wished he were here not because *I wished he were here,* but because a professional detective might be able to make sense of some suspicious goings-on.

While Henry dawdled in the bathroom, I told Dec all about Rawlings and the wind farm and the speeding Subaru, about the accelerants in the bottles' matching the samples from the barn, and about the girl at the party who bought her clothes at the Salvation Army store in Back Bay.

"You get a name?" he asked.

"Elsa Corbett."

"License plate on the car?"

"No, but I might be able to."

"Do," he said. "Call me and I'll run both the name and the number."

"Okay. Thanks."

"What do *you* think it's all about?" he went on.

"I don't know."

"Got a gut feeling?"

Dec was big on gut feelings. Far from considering them to be insubstantial intuitions, he believed they were a form of superior knowledge and far more likely to be proven correct than many a rational hypothesis.

"I think it's all got to do with the wind farm," I ventured. "Lots of people oppose it for all kinds of reasons. The controversy's made for some pretty strange bedfellows."

He didn't say anything, so I asked, "What do *you* think?"

"You're probably right," he said.

We chatted for a few more moments. I promised to call him later with the license plate number of the Subaru, if I could get it, and then we hung up. Henry was running a bath for himself, and after peeking in and concluding that he had matters under control, I decided to crawl back under the covers. Not to sleep, but to think.

I thought about Dec. And Bert. I always did this, sooner or later, and there had never been a contest: Dec was always smarter, kinder, better looking, braver, nicer to waitresses and small animals, and in every significant way superior to the lunkhead or poseur with whom I had recently taken up. I used to do the side-by-side after the first real date, until my friend Nat convinced me that I had to give the poor helpless fellow a fighting chance. Now I try to wait. Three dates, four. But even before then, I start to imagine what it would be like to introduce Dec to my new flame, the fancy-schmancy lawyer or the post-post-post doc in cultural anthropology. I always imagine Dec's expression betraying his reaction, which is somewhere along the spectrum between "You've got to be kidding me" and "Huh?"

I hadn't really been on a date with Bert, but we'd had several meals together, I trusted him implicitly with Henry, and I'd seen plenty of evidence that he was a real guy's guy—my type. It had to have been hell losing his wife, so he wasn't a stranger to grief and tragedy, yet he didn't trot it out the minute you met him, or even a week after you met him. He was funny and self-deprecating and not at all the victim. He liked his sister. He wasn't weirded out by my traffic with ghosts; in fact, he didn't even ask for explanations. He was close to Mark and Lauren. He brought people fish. He showed Mavis's dog who was in charge, with a steak and not a harpoon. And he was gorgeous. *And* he didn't seem to know it.

I cautiously conjured up an image of Dec. I nervously imagined Bert. Then what happened was a first for me.

Dec turned to Bert, extended his hand, and said, "Grab a beer?"

The ferry carrying Mark and the ghost detectives was due to arrive in an hour. I had deposited Henry—well rested, excited, and full of peach-pecan pancakes—at the school at five minutes of ten. The final dress rehearsal was scheduled to run until one o'clock, after which there was going to be a pizza party in the cafeteria. After a little fine-tuning based on the morning's run-through, the curtain would go up on *Grease* at four o'clock.

I hurried back to the Grand View and dashed up the stairs. I wanted to be sure that neither Vivi nor Baden was on the premises, and I had to look at the novel that had first saddled the inn with the reputation of being haunted. I'd been trying to get to it all week, but every time I picked it up, I got interrupted.

According to Lauren, Wicklow had written about a ghost who looked like Abraham Lincoln, and another with her hands pressed to her ears. I hadn't come across them in the week since

I'd arrived, but I wanted to read what the author had actually said, in case I was missing a detail that could prove to be important. Thankfully, no one was around; Lauren had left me a note explaining that she had a couple of errands to run and then would pick up Mark and the ghost detectives when the boat came in at 11:10. They'd be back here by eleven thirty at the latest. I didn't have a minute to lose.

I flopped down on the bed and examined the book. The cover illustration could have been done by Edward Gorey. It showed a night sky filled with ominous storm clouds above the roofline and upper story of a building, presumably the Grand View. The windows glowed with a sickly yellow light. At one, the silhouette of a man wearing a black top hat and a formal jacket faced into the room. From out of the other window hung the tortured form of the female phantom, her hands stuck firmly to her ears. Spindly, leafless trees hugged the building, and the typeface of the title looked like antique comic book print. I opened the novel and inhaled that old-book scent that I love, equal parts dust and mildew.

I skimmed it as fast as I could. I couldn't comprehend the plot, flying along at this speed, but I did find descriptions of the ghosts, and Lauren had been right. They had allegedly appeared at the foot of the bed that used to occupy the room where I had first met Baden, the room with the evergreen wallpaper. I got up and crossed the hall. I opened the door to that room. It was deserted.

I decided to see if Baden was in the barn, where we had agreed he would wait for me. As I came down the steps to the first floor and headed down the hall and into the kitchen, I encountered not Baden, but Vivi. She was sitting in the rocking chair by the woodstove, apparently in a perfectly fine mood. Nearby, Frances was asleep on her massive cat bed, round and peaceful and purring quietly. I was surprised to find myself feeling very warmly toward the ample feline, seeing how calm Vivi was in her presence. I've never been much of a cat person, but then again, I've never had a cat. I wasn't much of a kid person until I had Henry.

"Hi!" I said to Vivi.

"Hi. Where is he?"

"Henry? He's at school. They're getting ready to do their play."

"What's that?" she asked, indicating the book.

I smiled. "A story about ghosts."

"Me?" she asked.

I paused. Was she asking if it was about her or if she was a ghost?

"Well," I said. "A writer came to stay here one time and he wrote a book about two ghosts he said were here."

"Who?"

"A tall man in a top hat."

"Mr. Nivens," Vivi announced matter-of-factly.

"Who?"

"*Mr. Nivens,*" she said, showing a flash of her customary impatience. "He used to be here. But now he isn't."

"Where is he?"

"I don't know. Any others?"

"A woman in her nightgown. She had her hands like this." I demonstrated, bringing my palms up to my ears.

"Amy," Vivi explained. "They froze like that."

"What did?"

"Her *hands.* They froze like that. In the boat."

I thought back to the horrific accounts I had read of the

hands, feet, ears, and noses of the doomed *Larchmont* passengers freezing in the lifeboats. The woman had obviously died with her hands covering her ears, perhaps frozen in place by the sleet and ice.

"Where is she now?"

"I don't know," Vivi said.

"Have you seen her around?"

"No!" she said freshly, obviously tiring of my questions.

I pulled out a kitchen chair and sat down. The wall clock read 10:45. This might be my only chance to enlist Vivi's help, and I didn't have a minute to waste.

"Vivi, I'm going to ask you something."

"What?" She was sounding now like her usual volatile self.

"Can I talk to you like a grown-up?"

"What do you mean?"

"I mean, can I ask you to listen very carefully to what I have to say?"

In response, she got the chair rocking hard, awakening Frances, who looked up, sleepy and baffled. Vivi didn't look at me, but I could tell she was listening.

"Can I? Can I talk to you like a friend?"

At the word *friend*, the rocking ceased briefly. *"Yes,"* she said, peering up at me and then back down at her lap. She got the chair moving again.

"You're a very smart girl. Henry really likes you, and so do I."

"No you don't." She looked up with a hurt expression.

"I do. I really do. But you know what? Sometimes people who are very much alike kind of get on each other's nerves. They are so similar that they—" I rubbed my hands together. "I think you and I are a lot alike."

"You do?"

I nodded. "We're both . . ." I paused. "Bossy. We think fast. We have a lot of energy."

"Crazy," she added.

"Definitely crazy," I conceded, and I saw her smile.

The minute hand clicked toward eleven. I had to get on with this.

"We don't have much time," I said. "There are some people coming here in a few minutes. I don't know if they can see ghosts or not, but they *say* they can. They want to prove there are ghosts here at the Grand View. But if they do, people won't come here to stay."

"Why?"

"Because people are afraid of ghosts."

"But why?"

"Because they don't understand. Most people can't see ghosts—"

She interrupted. "I *know*."

"Of course you know! They think ghosts might want to hurt them. They think ghosts can do all kind of things that you and I know they can't. And if people are too afraid to come here to the inn, Lauren and Mark will have to leave. Go somewhere else."

"Where?" she said, with alarm in her voice.

"I don't know."

"But who would be here? Would Frances have to go?"

"*Yes*! But there's something we can do," I said. "Something we can *try*, at least. And if you help me, I'll help you. I'll get Jamey back for you, and I'll get you both back to your mommy and daddy."

"You can't."

"I can. You're going to have to trust me a little bit, which I know will be hard to do. But it's the only way we can do this. Okay?"

She looked me straight in the eyes for a few minutes, then got up, came over, and crawled into my lap, just as she had that first night. I wrapped my arms around her, as much as you can wrap your arms around a skinny little spirit. What she said brought a tightness to my throat.

"I like you."

Chapter Twenty-four

CALEB WAS PEDALING into the driveway when I stepped out onto the back porch. He paused, and without getting off his bike, reached into his leather bag and pulled out an envelope. He held it up in the air. Puzzled, I walked over. He handed it to me.

"What's this?"

"Nice of you not to bug me, but I do have to pay you."

"I wasn't worried. I know where you live."

He rebuckled his bag. "See you at the play?"

"You bet."

He waved and pedaled off.

I glanced at the envelope. My name was typed on the front with what looked like an old-fashioned typewriter; traces of the inked ribbon blurred the edges of the letters, which caused faint indentations in the rich, creamy vellum. The envelope wasn't sealed, so I extracted my check. I was happy to see that nice, solid number, but the pleasure ended there. In stately type in the top left corner were the words *The Lenox Consortium.*

I was flooded with confusion and remorse. *These* were the people who were paying my salary—the very same parties who were trying to sandbag the wind farm? The folks who funded Rawlings's questionable environmental impact study?

In a sickening moment it all made sense: to bring alive the tragic story of the *Larchmont*'s dead at the very moment that the wind farm debate was heating up! What a coincidence of timing! Oh, they were sly! The cunning was positively breathtaking.

And I had played right into their hands. In fact, I'd raised them one! Not only would the new book rescue the story from oblivion, but I'd also talked Caleb into exhibiting Honor Morton's photographs! And I'd talked him into the idea of display cases, too, assuming the money to build them could be found and the upstairs space refurbished. No wonder Rawlings had pushed me for answers about what all this would cost. What better way could there be to elicit sympathy for the poor souls whose bones would be smashed and scattered by the gargantuan windmills than to let everyone gaze at the tattered relics of their lives, thrown up by an indifferent sea?

Strike another blow to the wind farm.

Well, I wouldn't take their money! I sank down into a chair and thought of my checkbook balance. I had to take their money! No, I didn't—I hadn't done much of the work yet; I could just pull out of the whole project and tell Caleb why. I wouldn't let them use me like this!

But what about the *Larchmont*'s dead? Didn't they deserve to have their stories told, regardless of what effect this might or might not have on a debate raging a century later? After all, I had personally made promises to them. I stood up, marched into the kitchen, and threw the check into the wastebasket. Then I pulled it out and wiped off a little dab of jelly. My head was spinning, and I had to make it stop. I folded the check, tucked it into my pocket, and went out to the barn, looking for Baden.

He was resting in one of the chairs I'd rescued during the fire.

"How's it going?" I asked. I thought about getting into the dilemma swirling around in my head, but I knew we didn't have time.

"I quite like it out here," he responded.

"Good thing." I smiled. "Lauren's gone to pick up Mark and the TV guys. They should be back anytime. I think Vivi's going to help us."

"I wouldn't count on it."

"No, I really do."

"Perhaps. Have you had any news on the woman?"

"Mavis? She's going to be fine. You saved her life, you know."

"For the moment."

"Very funny."

"How old is she?" Baden pressed.

"Ninety-one. She shouldn't be living alone."

"She should be living any way she likes."

"But how do we know she likes it? Maybe she doesn't have any family."

He was about to answer me when I heard the crunch of tires on gravel. I hurried over to the window.

"They're here! Oh my gosh!"

"Calm down, dear."

"I've got to get Vivi."

I raced back into the house and found her on the kitchen floor, sparring with Frances.

"It's time!" I said, trying to sound really excited. "Come on!"

Vivi hopped to her feet and accompanied me out to the

barn. When she glimpsed Baden, she became uncharacteristically shy, hiding behind me like a much younger child.

"Vivi," I said, "You know your great-uncle."

"Hello, Viveka," said Baden. To his credit, he kept the judgmental tone out of his voice.

She didn't answer.

"Say hello, Vivi," I said. "There's no need to be shy."

"Hi," I heard her whimper.

I stepped aside and she was revealed.

"Mr. Riegler has a story to tell you."

Baden regarded me with a look that said, *I do?*

"About the lake in Austria?" I suggested. "What you used to do there when you were young, in the summers?"

He blinked a few times, as though trying to recall if he had ever mentioned anything about this. He hadn't. I was just trying to give him a hint; he didn't seem like the kind of person who would have a clue about what to do to amuse a kid.

"I'll be back in a little while," I said, ducking away before either of them could protest.

Mark's green pickup was in the driveway, and two men, presumably the "ghost detectives" themselves, were unloading bulky black boxes from the back of the car. I walked over.

"Hi, Mark!"

"Anza, hi! How are you?" I thought he was giving me a significant look, but I wasn't sure. And if he was, I definitely didn't know what it meant.

"Anza, this is Dayne White and Gavin Robinson. You've probably seen their show, *The Ghost Detectives.*"

"I have! It's terrific. Great to meet you."

One of the men, who appeared to be dressed for swampy encounters, gave me an indifferent glance. The other, attired in cowboy boots, ironed jeans, and a starched white shirt, extended his hand.

"Gavin. Playsed to meet yih."

"I'm Anza," I said, and we shook hands. "I've heard a lot about you." I couldn't bring myself to say that I loved their show, so I added, lamely, "You must be here to film the lighthouse."

"Lighthouse?" Gavin said.

The other man stood up and scowled, as though a foul odor had just reached his nostrils. "No. Why?"

"The Southeast Lighthouse?"

Gavin shook his head. I definitely had their attention now.

"Well, I just assumed—because everyone on the island *knows* it's haunted. Isn't it, Mark?"

I tried to make my eyes communicate the message: *Say yes!* I had no idea if Lauren had told him about my paranormal abilities, but I was sure she'd kept her promise not to tell anyone else.

"Uh, yeah," Mark said, unconvincingly. "Yeah, it is. Absolutely!" He had a dazed look on his face. He obviously didn't know where this was going, but he was doing his best.

"I could take you there if you like," I offered.

Gavin looked at Dayne, who shrugged.

"Maybe tomorrow," Dayne said. "Depending on what we get tonight. But thanks."

"Is it open on Sundays?" I asked Mark, stalling for time.

"It's not open for tours until after sometime this summer," he answered. "But we could probably get Chief McGill to unlock it."

"Could you?" I asked. "Because it would be a shame for them to miss it, don't you think?"

Gavin and Dayne had gone back to their unloading, so I nodded furiously at Mark, hoping to clue him in.

"It would, yeah. Oh yeah, absolutely!"

I watched with some amazement the assortment of boxes being unloaded. If I wasn't going to get Gavin and Dayne to the lighthouse immediately, I wished they'd go indoors as soon as possible. For all I knew, the renegade spirits had a sentry keeping watch, letting them know when the television team arrived.

"Can I help you carry something?" I asked.

"No, we're fine."

"Let me help," I said, grabbing two boxes before anyone could protest. "I'm going in anyway."

A half hour later, the equipment was all cabled up and spread out in the room where Henry had watched the Three Stooges. This room had been designated the duo's base of operations. In the adjoining living area, I was the one playing sentry. I couldn't allow a ghost near their equipment, even if it meant revealing myself to any spirit that came snooping. I was also trying to figure out what to do, having failed completely in my effort to interest them in a visit to the lighthouse.

Outside, in the space of two hours, the weather had gone from cool and overcast to cold and misty, and from the look of the funnel clouds on the horizon, a storm was heading our way. Churning whitecaps were visible across the boulevard, and seeing them, I stepped over the line separating feeling on edge from being wildly anxious. How in the name of heaven was I going to pull this off?

At any moment, Duffield or any of the ghosts planning tonight's invasion might arrive on the scene and set off the heat and infrared sensors. To maximize the show's spooky appeal,

Gavin and Dayne usually waited for darkness to fall before beginning their movements about a building, but I didn't have the luxury of waiting for tonight.

Long before that, any ghost still determined to bring down Mark and Lauren could be here. They could show up at any minute, and the machines in the next room would go off, alerting the Australians. I didn't even want to imagine it. And to make the situation even more unmanageable, Henry would soon be back underfoot.

Henry! How was I going to get to the play, with all that was going on? It didn't start until four, so I still had a little time, but I had to get Dayne and Gavin to the lighthouse soon, because no matter what, I couldn't not show up for Henry's play! He'd be crushed! He'd never forgive me, and I'd never forgive myself. Since I might not be taking any money for the work I was doing—I couldn't, in good conscience, not if my efforts would help defeat the wind farm—the play might end up being the only good thing that came out of this week. Oh, and meeting Bert.

My anxiety moved toward alarm. I was practically hyperventilating as I imagined myself in the thick of things at the lighthouse as the minute hand clicked around a clock face, heading toward twelve, and four o'clock. *What* would I do? I had to do something to get this show on the road. Now!

Then I had my brainstorm. Vivi!

My original plan had been to keep her out of the way until Sunday morning, when I hoped to convince Emilia to take both children into the white light. *How* I was going to do this—Emilia was stark raving mad, after all—had yet to be determined. Like much of what I was up to right now, crossing my fingers and making everything up on the fly, this was nothing but a half-baked scheme waiting for a stroke of inspiration. One that might never come.

But this one had! I looked out the front window to be sure there wasn't a squadron of phantoms marching right up the front sidewalk. Then I hurried out to the barn. Vivi was sitting on Baden's lap, and he was in the middle of explaining how the children in his family used to take turns cranking homemade ice cream. Vivi was entranced. They both looked remarkably happy, and given how seldom this could be said of either of them, I hated to break things up. But I had to pull Vivi away. I also gave Baden the nod. It was time to get the ghosts to the lighthouse!

The first raindrops were falling as Vivi and I walked back to the house. To her credit, she listened carefully as I outlined my idea. I noticed that Lauren and Mark's car was gone from the driveway, and I hadn't seen Lauren when I passed through the kitchen. This was probably just as well. I certainly didn't want them at the lighthouse when everything was happening, and the fewer people I had to explain my actions to, the better.

Vivi and I entered the living room. I pointed into the adjoining room, where Gavin and Dayne were messing around with their equipment, and Vivi stepped into the space. I immediately heard something that sounded like a Geiger counter start to click, and there was a whining whir. I couldn't hear what the two of them were saying, but chairs scraped and something fell over and I heard the clicking intensify. It sounded like a frantic scramble in there. Vivi peeked out, and I gestured for her to move slowly, very slowly, into the living room. She approached me one step at a time.

Right behind her were Dayne and Gavin, struggling to get their equipment in place. Dayne was holding a video camera on his shoulder and attempting to put on headphones. Gavin was waving two devices around in the air; beeps and clicks and whirs were more and less audible, depending on how close the equipment was to Vivi.

I looked up from the magazine I had just grabbed from the chair into which I had just plopped.

"What's going on?" I asked innocently.

Gavin didn't respond. Instead, he looked right into the camera and said, "We've just arrived on historic Block Island, off the coast of Rhode Island. And we've just been surprised by our very first ghost."

Probably is *your first ghost,* I thought meanly.

I stood up and pretended to be startled as they moved through the living room, then I followed them out the front door. Vivi was walking slowly, as I had instructed, so the instruments would track her progress, and I whispered a quick prayer that she had both the focus and the will to pull this off and lead them all the way to the lighthouse.

Had there been any traffic to speak of, they would have made for a curious sight, hurrying along the street in the increasingly heavy rain, Gavin aiming his equipment at the air and Dayne attempting to capture everything on video. Vivi was skipping merrily, moving fast—almost too fast. But she did understand what she had to do: stay close enough to all of us that her presence kept the needles and sensors activated. When she noticed that Gavin and Dayne had paused and were looking around in bafflement, she would circle back around and get the sensors dancing again. The role was tailor-made for her and must have fulfilled her deepest fantasy: to be the one with all the power, leading live human adults around by their noses.

Gavin and Dayne paid no attention to me, so I grabbed an umbrella from the stand beside the door and slipped along behind them quietly, just watching the scene unfold. After a few minutes, the lighthouse came into view, just as Vivi seemed to be tiring of the parade. Then I saw Baden, approaching us as swiftly as a wave. He took Vivi's hand, and they stood there in the middle of the street, giving Gavin and Dayne plenty of time to locate them. The detectors went into overdrive when they met the force field surrounding the two spirits, just as I had seen the equipment do on the television show when I could see no ghosts at all. Clearly, Gavin and Dayne knew how to trip these devices for manufactured thrills, but the gizmos also worked in the presence of real ghosts.

I stumbled on a pothole. The rain was coming down hard now, and I wondered if the camera might actually pick up a ghostly image. It was fairly unlikely, but it sometimes did happen: blurs of white on the edges of the frame, cloudy presences of which the live people in the photograph or film were unaware.

Soon I found myself wishing that the video *could* record images, because what awaited us not a hundred yards ahead was a scene, I was sure, unlike any that had ever been broadcast on the series. Even I felt the hairs on the back of my neck begin to prickle. My heart rate picked up at just about the same time that the equipment in Gavin's hands started to go crazy. I was drenched now and freezing; an icy wind was whipping the waves into froth, and the rain was coming down in sheets.

The scene before us was like something out of Dante. Everywhere I looked were grim and doleful phantoms, and few were animated, as some had been at the meeting last night. There were nearly two dozen, I guessed, and their dress and general appearance reflected the tortured manner in which each one had died, frozen in the lifeboats, trapped in the berth of a swiftly sinking vessel, cast into the frigid sea, all in the grip of overwhelming terror. Here, this afternoon, as the storm waves crashed against the rocks, sending sprays of mist skyward, they presented themselves silently and stoically as Baden and Vivi led Gavin, Dayne, and me into their very midst.

First one, then a few, then a number moved toward us, and soon they encircled our little group. I heard a low moan escape from one of the older spirits, a man in a top hat at the back of the group, and it registered on one of the sensors. Dayne had been keeping up a running commentary, pretty much since we'd left the Grand View, but he suddenly went silent as the spirits drew tighter and tighter around us, enclosing us in a little circle about ten feet across.

"Did you see that?" I said to Gavin, pointing to the sensor that was picking up the sound. I looked up and caught the gazes of a number of the spirits, who were staring at me, just waiting for some kind of cue. "The sensor picked up a sound!"

Well, that was the cue they needed. They instantly broke out into clamorous wailing and moaning, shrieking and screaming like nobody's business. Dayne stared at his equipment, unable to believe what the gauges were doing, as the other box he was carrying began to emit a piercing wail and the clicking kicked into what sounded like machine-gun patter. The boxes were practically jumping in his hands, and Gavin looked so pale and was suddenly so motionless that I thought he might be having a stroke.

"Gavin?"

He didn't answer.

Gavin had squatted down in the mud and was fiddling

around with one of the pieces of equipment. Dayne kept the lens focused on the dials and needles while Gavin attempted to describe what was happening. Then, suddenly, Dayne trained his lens on something else. I don't know if the camera had picked up a shadow or a glow, but he began to walk slowly toward the edge of the breakwater, staring through the lens the whole time.

"Be careful!" I said when his foot slipped on a slimy rock. I didn't like what was happening. Some of the spirits were leading Gavin toward the edge where the land dropped off abruptly, and he was now within a few feet of that drop. In three or four more steps, if he didn't pay attention to where he was walking rather than to the shot he was getting, he would go tumbling onto the craggy boulders below, a drop of at least fifty feet.

"Stop!" I called. "Stop!"

The camera had to have picked up the image of a ghost, for Dayne was so mesmerized by the image in the frame that he had absolutely no idea of the imminent danger he was in.

I flew to my feet and raced toward him, reaching the parapet just as he stepped off with his right foot and began to tumble obliquely. I caught hold of his left arm as he tumbled, half sideways and half forward, and I was able to keep him from slipping down onto the rocks.

Not so the camera. It flew off his shoulder and bumped heavily down from rock to rock, landing, finally, in the churning black sea.

I wish I could share with you the rich, imaginative, and eye-opening string of Australian curses and universally cherished invectives that followed, involving mothers, Australian mammals, personal hygiene habits, and psychiatric diagnoses. The ghosts cheered wildly, inaudible to everyone but me.

Chapter Twenty-five

WE WERE BARELY through the opening number of *Grease* when my cell phone started to vibrate. I felt hugely guilty squeezing past the knees of the performers' families and friends, but a peek at my phone had told me that it was Dec calling, and I knew that if I didn't talk to him now, it might be late tonight if not tomorrow before I could. Once he was at work, he often couldn't return a call for hours. Besides, according to the program, Henry wouldn't be onstage for a while.

I caught the call just before it went to voice mail.

"Dec!"

"Hey."

"How are you?"

"Fine. Yeah, so—looks like the girl has some history."

"What kind of history?"

"Arson, breaking and entering, destruction of private property. Given the locations and nature of the crimes, she's probably got some connection with the Oceanic Liberation Front."

"What the heck is that?" I asked.

"You got a computer handy?"

"No! I'm at Henry's play! Who are they?"

"Eco-terrorists. They commit acts of violence against property. Usually arson, but sometimes they sabotage equipment in buildings that are unstaffed. They don't harm people or animals."

"Why?" I asked.

"For political reasons. To stand up for the environment."

"They want to burn buildings down?"

"No, no, it's . . . symbolic. They're trying to make a point. The target represents something that's a threat to the health of the oceans. Like companies that dump chemicals into streams and rivers, chemicals that eventually wind up in the sea basin."

"That doesn't make sense."

"Why not?" Dec asked.

"If she wanted to protect the oceans from harm, she'd be in favor of the wind farm."

I heard Dec sigh. "Anza, I'm on the clock here—I've got a meeting in ten minutes. These are the facts; what they add up to is a different question."

"I know, I know. Thanks!"

"Did you get that license number?"

"No, sorry. Just one question—should I tell this to the cops down here?"

"I'll give them a heads-up."

"You will?"

"Yeah."

"Thanks, Dec. I really appreciate it."

"No problem. See you soon."

We hung up. I didn't feel like crawling back across the aisle to where I'd been sitting, so I took a seat way in the back.

The sight of Henry in costume gave me a shock. It was not just that his hair was slicked back and the sleeves of his T-shirt were rolled up (that had better not be a *real* cigarette pack in there!), or that he'd been made to look like a miniature teenager. It was that he had . . . attitude: hip-swinging, eye-winking attitude. He was a diminutive version of the slick, sly teenager I hoped he would never become.

Fortunately, this sneering facade dissolved as soon as Henry began to dance. And there was the Ellen I'd heard so much about, in all her shorn and six-year-old insouciance. I had to hand it to them. They might not have followed the beat of the music, and they sure weren't in sync with all the other dancers, but their performance was breathtakingly fearless and full of confident bravado. The audience seemed to hold its collective breath; where could this zealous combination of ineptitude and pluck end up, but in disaster?

It ended in triumph, at least from Henry and Ellen's point of view. For three or four minutes, for better or worse, they literally stole the show.

Gavin and Dayne spent the rest of the evening trying to repair their camera, which they were finally able to recover from the lighthouse rocks. They took hair dryers to the innards of some of the other equipment, which, in their zeal not to miss the moment unfolding when Vivi led them out of the house, they'd neglected to protect properly against the rain. They opened all the cases and partially disassembled the internal works, and it was a good thing they did, because we were visited just after seven o'clock by the dogged Mr. Duffield and a ragtag gang of his followers. Had any of the equipment been working and on, our worst fears might have been realized.

I was sitting in the dining room with the inn's first actual guests, two retired couples from Ontario who had been on the ferry with Mark, Gavin, and Dayne. As they had originally planned to visit Nantucket and had made an impulsive decision to take in Block Island first, they hadn't made a room reservation when they fell into conversation with Mark on the boat. That was how they ended up here. And that was why Lauren had been absent when everything was happening with Vivi and the ghost detectives; she'd run out to shop for welcome, but unexpected, guests.

Duffield, thwarted in his effort to rouse any reaction at all from the distracted Australians, had stormed right into the dining room and bellowed at me. I wasn't actually eating dinner—Bert and Aitana were coming over later and I was planning to eat with them and our hosts—but one of the guests had gone to Harvard and was anxious to chat with me about Cambridge. I'd agreed to join them for a glass of wine when in marched Duffield.

I ignored him. I didn't have any choice. What was I supposed to do, with all the others sitting right there? If he'd shown a shred of sensitivity to my situation, I might have found a way to excuse myself for a moment and lead all six of them to an empty room upstairs, but the ruder and louder he got, and the harder they all tried to disrupt the conversation I was having, the more determined I became to act like every other live human being, blind and deaf to their urgent entreaties.

I took no pleasure in this. It made me enormously nervous, and then—as they retreated one by one, followed, in the end, by the dejected Duffield, his posture slumped in defeat—just as enormously sad. I hoped I would see them tomorrow. I hoped I could help them, in the end. But I hoped just as hard that I wouldn't see them again tonight.

Henry, who had been wired beyond belief and stuffed to the gills with cake and cookies from the after party in the school cafeteria, had fallen asleep at six thirty and was still asleep upstairs. We were all around the kitchen table, about to tuck into a first course of lobster bisque that Aitana had contributed. Mark was fairly bursting with news he had saved until we had all sat down for our dinner. As Lauren ladled the soup into bowls and Aitana handed them around, Mark could hold out no longer.

"Okay," he said. "So I called up this buddy of mine who lives in Cambridge. He works at a think tank at MIT, but before he did that, he used to write for the *Globe* and the *Times*, mainly about energy issues."

"Oh my gosh!" I said excitedly. "I forgot to tell you guys something! But go on—you go first."

Mark nodded and resumed. "So I ask him about Rawlings. I mean, I know where the senator stands on all the big issues, but I have to tell you, this fierce opposition to the wind farm just doesn't make sense to me."

"It makes perfect sense to me," I said. "He doesn't want the view from his beach house ruined."

"I don't think it's that," Mark said. "I really don't. Anyway, I ask Andy—my friend, Andy Fuller—what he knows about Rawlings's background, if anything. He tells me he'll do some checking around, call a few people and get back to me."

"And?" Bert said as Lauren hopped up to check on the potatoes.

"And," Mark continued, "he calls me back last night. Turns

out Rawlings is the son of *Hiram* Rawlings, who founded Rawlings Enterprises in the early fifties."

"What's that?" asked Aitana.

"The R of RMI Partners: Rawlings, McKeene, Itzkoff—three huge companies in the energy sector that merged into a multinational conglomerate in the early seventies, at the time of the first energy crisis. They all brought different things to the table, but now they've got a hand in everything to do with fossil fuels: oil refining, coal, petroleum coke, composite pipe manufacturing. And . . ."

Mark drew this out, increasing the suspense. "They haven't announced it yet, not officially, but they're getting into the business of wind power. They've been hiring guys from European universities—ETH Zürich, TU Munich—because like all the companies that make their money from fossil fuels, they see the writing on the wall. Maybe not this year, maybe not in ten years, but one of these days, the party is going to be over. If they don't get on top of the new energy wave while they can, it's going to wash right over them."

"So you think he's blocking the wind farm," Bert said, "hoping that one day, his family's company can get the gig?"

"I don't know," Mark replied. "Possibly. He had to sell off his shares a long time ago, to avoid a conflict of interest. He just got out of the business. But his brother and sister are still on the board, and you know darn well that he's got some kind of arrangement in place so that in the end, he'll get his share of the family fortune. These guys didn't get rich by being Pollyannas. They know how to take care of business."

Lauren appeared with the first of the dinner plates, and I stood up to give her a hand. She'd produced yet another remarkable meal—a beef daube with buttered fingerling potatoes and whipped butternut squash. I set down a plate in front of Aitana, and when I put Bert's down in front of him, he placed his hand on mine and held it there briefly.

"You really think it's that?" Lauren asked, sitting down to her own dinner and picking her napkin up from the floor.

"No way of knowing, really. But the strategy makes a certain amount of sense: defeat the little start-ups who've gotten the ball rolling, practically force them into bankruptcy by throwing obstacle after obstacle in their paths, and then when they drop out of the fight, because they just don't have the resources to keep fighting any longer, swoop in and get the contract."

Bert whistled. We all traded glances and sat silently for several moments, partaking of the dishes before us.

"And that's not all. Rawlings has had a lot of dealings with a nonprofit based in New York. They're basically a group of lobbyists with an environmental agenda, and they do a lot of good work, no question. They sponsor a couple of events a year, one in the Hamptons in the summer and another on Lake Placid—a ski weekend fund-raiser that attracts a handful of movie stars and many, well, ladies who lunch. And look good in ski outfits. They raise a lot of money. And to give them their due, they do some good things with it."

"But . . . ," Lauren prompted.

"But . . . you look a little closer, and who's involved in all this 'green' crusading?"

Mark held up his hand and ticked off fingers as he listed names. "Manya Itzkoff and her husband, Sam; Hillary McKeene; Helena McKeene; Billy McKeene; Susie Dean-Itzkoff, wife of Ben."

"The children of RMI's founders?" I asked.

"Grandchildren," Mark clarified. "Their houses in New York and in the Hamptons were all bought with money made in the oil business, but for all the world to see, these people are champions of the environment."

"Wait!" I said. "Before I forget again, I have to tell you what *I* found out!"

"From whom?" Bert asked.

"I have my sources. No, it's Henry's dad. He's a Boston cop—well, actually, he's a detective. He turned up a history on the couple in the car. He's calling Chief McGill."

"That's fantastic!" Aitana said.

Bert looked a little subdued, but maybe I was imagining things. Had I popped the bubble by mentioning the other man in my life? He wasn't my boyfriend, after all—he was someone else's husband. And it wasn't as though Bert was without his own complicated history.

We ate quietly for several moments.

"Everything's great, Lauren," I said. "It really is."

"Beyond great," Aitana echoed, sipping her wine.

"What was the name of the nonprofit?" Lauren asked casually. "Berkshire something?"

"The Lenox Consortium," Mark replied.

I felt a little drop in my stomach, realizing anew how I had been played. I wasn't just an innocent bystander in this whole convoluted campaign to topple the wind farm initiative, I was right in the middle of it. There wasn't a single angle they hadn't exploited. They'd probably planned it all that weekend, while eating Aitana's meals.

If the islanders didn't yet know that the wind farm would be built among the bones of the tragic dead, they'd know it soon. Rawlings and his crew would make sure of that when the Block Island Historical Society celebrated the unveiling of the *Larchmont* Collection.

Bert seemed to notice the change in my mood, but here I drew the line. I couldn't tell any of them that I had a check upstairs from this very organization, that I was on the payroll of the bad guys. I had to figure out what I was going to do, and I honestly hadn't a clue.

Chapter Twenty-six

"So here's my problem," I said.

It was almost eleven on Saturday night. Henry and I were leaving tomorrow, and I wanted nothing more than to spend every remaining minute with Bert, who at the moment was sitting next to me on the living room couch. Aitana had gone home to Peter, who was nursing a cold and had decided to stay home; the dishes were done; and Mark and Lauren had turned in for the night. Dayne and Gavin had gone off to a bar called the Pier, the only game in town. None of their equipment was working, and they were giving it until tomorrow to dry out before they declared the weekend a complete and unmitigated disaster. Henry had been asleep for close to two hours, until Vivi made an appearance at about ten thirty, and now he was wide awake again. They were upstairs in our bedroom.

"I know," Bert said. "It's okay."

He didn't really know. It wasn't because of Henry that I couldn't spend the rest of the evening with him. Well, it was, but not for the reasons he imagined. We had a long night ahead of us, Henry and Vivi and I. Tonight, if all went well, I was going to explain the white light to Henry for the very first time and try to persuade Emilia to accompany both Jamey and Vivi to the other side. Tomorrow, I'd open the door for the rest of the spirits.

"I'll probably go out for a beer or two."

"Where?" I asked. I was immediately determined to make this work, if there was any way I could do what I had to do, get Henry back here and into bed, and get to where Bert was going before he decided to call it a night.

"The Pier. Same place I sent your pals."

"They're not my pals. Where is it?"

"Down on the water—out past Rawlings's house, a mile or two down that road."

"How late are they open?"

"Another hour or two. Depends."

"I wish I could come."

"Maybe you will," he said, getting up. "Call me, if it works out. I'll come get you."

"You will?"

"Course I will! Where's your cell phone? I'll put the number in."

"You already did."

"Did I?" he teased.

"I'll try to make it work," I said.

He nodded. "But if it doesn't, no problem. I'll see you tomorrow. Okeydoke?"

"Okeydoke," I said, and then he kissed me. Not like someone who says okeydoke, either, like someone in a country where the air smells sweetly of jasmine and other flowers I have never even seen.

Emilia and Jamey resided in an old carriage house, on a rolling piece of land at the center of the island. Vivi led us directly there, moving so fast that Henry and I could barely keep up, but tonight I was happy for her momentum. Anything that would move this along quickly was all right with me.

The carriage house was locked. Triple locked, actually. The house on the property had been closed up for the winter, and it appeared that the owner had not yet been down to the island to open everything up.

"Can you go in and get her?" I asked Vivi. "Tell her we're out here?"

Vivi now shook her head. "She doesn't like me."

"She doesn't *have* to like you. Just tell her that someone else is here to see her."

"No. You."

I sighed. I'd been hoping for a few moments alone with Henry, to prepare him a little for what was about to happen: he was going to have to say good-bye to Vivi. At least I hoped he was, for both their sakes. He was going to experience a real crossing over, and it might not be an unalloyed pleasure. I'd been terrified the first time I witnessed it, and Nona had been preparing me for a long, long time. She hadn't just thrown me in at the deep end, which was exactly what I was doing to Henry.

If I'd had a plan at all, it had been to divide and conquer, sweeping Vivi up in the excitement of taking Jamey to their parents, while not upsetting Henry any more than I had to. But things weren't going according to plan. There was a very good chance that I might not be successful at what I hoped to do for Vivi, and it wasn't in my power to change that. If she wouldn't cooperate, or if Emilia refused to surrender herself and the child she believed to be hers to something she probably couldn't even understand, well, there wasn't a whole lot I could do.

I had to do some straight talking here, right now. It was the only chance I had to make something happen.

"Okay, you two. Sit down here for a sec."

They ignored me. Henry had picked up a stick and was turning over some rocks with it, exposing creepy crawlies in the damp black dirt.

"Come on, guys. Come over here with me."

I sat down on a log that ran the length of the carriage house, separating where the summer grass was cut from plants and weeds allowed to grow wild. Henry plopped down on one side of me, and Vivi sat on the other.

"I want you to listen to me, okay?"

"Okay," Henry said. Vivi didn't speak, but she also didn't move.

"It's time for Vivi to go and see her mommy and daddy."

"No!" she protested.

"Calm down. You're not going all alone; you're going to take your little brother."

"I don't want to," she said.

"I don't want her to!" Henry chimed in, pouting.

I turned to Vivi. "You don't? You don't want to see your mother and father? They've been waiting a long, long time for you. They would be so, so happy to see you."

I so, so hoped this was true.

She shook her head, but not as vehemently, and her gaze found my eyes. She was lost, and scared, and little, and all but completely alone in a very big universe. I hated to say what I had to say next.

"Vivi, if you don't let me get you—and Jamey—back to your parents tonight, you may not get another chance."

"Ever?" she whispered, eyes wide.

"I don't know. In my whole life, I have only known one other person who could do what I can do, and that is my grandmother. There probably *are* other people out there—I'm sure there have to be—but I have never met one single one of them. And if they live in China or Russia or England—"

"Or on the moon," Henry offered helpfully.

"Right, on the moon, what good is that to you? They won't know you're here. So I know it's really hard and scary, but you're going to have to decide right now, tonight, if you want me to help you. Henry and I are going back to Boston tomorrow. There's not going to be another chance."

Tears were forming in her eyes.

I turned to Henry. "What do you think you'd do, bear?" I asked him. "Would you want to try to go find me and Daddy?"

"Yeah!" he said, without hesitation.

"Even if you were scared?" I pressed. "Would you make a run for it?"

He nodded. He was absolutely sure. Now my own eyes were filling with tears.

Vivi remained silent.

"How about we try to talk to Emilia? If you don't want to go in and get her, I'll just knock on the door and tell her we're out here and that we want to talk to her."

"Okay," I heard Vivi whisper.

"Okay," I said. I stood up, walked over to the door, and knocked.

"Emilia?" I called. "I'm sorry it's so late, but I need to talk to you. Can you come to the door?"

There was no response.

"Emilia?"

I was listening hard, and then I remembered: I wasn't going to be hearing any footsteps.

"Emilia, *please*?"

Almost in unison, Henry and Vivi shouted, "Emilia!" Vivi followed this up with, "Jamey! Jamey! It's me!"

Jamey appeared first, and I had a cruel thought, one I instantly suppressed—get him and Vivi out of here, and through the doorway of white light, before Emilia had a chance to object. But I couldn't do that to the poor, deluded phantom. It would be like someone's kidnapping Henry, a nightmare I've had on a number of occasions. Jamey might not actually *be* Emilia's child, but she *believed* that he was and *loved* him as though he was. I couldn't do that to another mother.

While we were waiting, though, I decided to bring up the white light.

"Henry," I said, intending to draw his attention to what I was about to do.

But he and Vivi had gotten Jamey interested in the worms crawling around underneath the rock. I'd answer his questions later, if he had any.

I closed my eyes and concentrated on an image of the carriage house. I felt that moment, which is like a pilot light suddenly igniting into flames, and when I opened my eyes, there was a small, bright circle on the weathered wood, near where the foundation of fieldstones met the weathered shingles of the structure. The building was old, very old; it had seen hard use. Probably as a result of the fire the other night, I had an irrational fear that the light would set fire to the ancient shingles.

Emilia still hadn't appeared, so I made the light brighter,

and whiter, and the entrance wider and taller. Vivi looked up, but for Henry, the worms were far more interesting. Jamey stared and blinked, but they all seemed to accept this sudden manifestation as just one of those things that happened in life, something a benevolent adult would explain in due time, like icicles, thunderstorms, and scabs.

Emilia suddenly appeared.

"Hello," I said.

"Hello." She looked a little confused. Seeing Jamey happily occupied poking at bugs with Henry—Vivi had stepped out of sight, back behind the carriage house, where I could see her but Emilia could not—she turned her attention to me.

"Yes?" she said.

"Emilia," I said.

"Was there a problem with the fabric?"

"I didn't come about that, Emilia."

"Because I can order more. Mr. Sampson's very good. It wouldn't take more than a week or ten days."

"I had plenty of fabric," I said, biding my time. Because out of the corner of my eye, I saw that Vivi had emerged from the shadows and had taken Jamey by the hand. Slowly, ever so slowly, she was leading him toward the doorway of light. Henry barely noticed. He had dug a long worm out of the ground, and it now hung like a strand of spaghetti over the stick in his hand.

"It's lovely fabric," I said, trying to keep my voice level.

"It is, yes. I thought about a pattern, but one tires of patterns, doesn't one? A pure, solid color is so much nicer."

"Especially in summer," I said, my heart in my throat. "It feels cooler." In my peripheral vision, I could see the figures of the two little spirits hovering at the edge of the light. I couldn't look directly at them. I couldn't alert Emilia to what was happening, no matter how much pain I might cause her. Those children deserved to be with their parents! If Vivi was ready to go, and to take Jamey with her, I wasn't going to get in the way.

Then Henry shouted, "Mama!" He flew to his feet and pointed at Vivi and Jamey.

"Go!" I shouted at Vivi. "Now!" Vivi appeared to hesitate for just a moment, then she swept Jamey up in her arms and carried him right through the doorway. In a matter of seconds, they were gone.

Henry looked over, baffled and scared.

"It's okay, honey," I said. "Don't be afraid."

His outburst had drawn Emilia's attention. She turned around quickly, confusion and a trace of panic in her eyes.

"He's fine!" I said. "Don't worry. He's just gone over there." I pointed to the light. "I can see him."

She visibly relaxed. "He's like quicksilver! Always getting away."

I watched as she hurried over to the light and looked right through the gleaming doorway.

It wasn't just relief that appeared on her face, it was something akin to rapture. A cry escaped from somewhere deep and primal in her being, but she hesitated hardly a moment. She looked back at me with surprise and joy, and then she disappeared.

Chapter Twenty-seven

Henry began to wail, and when I picked him up, he was shaking.

"It's okay, honey."

I carried him over to the steps that led up to the house, and he clung to me like paper to a wall. We sat down together and he scrambled up onto my lap. He seemed to want as much surface-to-surface contact as he could get, and I had the impression that if he could have crawled inside me, he would have. I'd felt just the same way at his age, the first time I watched someone leave this life, and I'd already been clued in to what was going to happen.

Sitting there in the dark, I held him tight while he cried. It wasn't the moment to ask questions. He was probably sad, scared, angry, and surprised—everything all at once. I'm not proud to admit it, but these days I welcome the moments when Henry seems to need me as much as he did when he was a helpless infant. I took a deep breath of the cool sea air and waited for the crying to subside.

Finally, it did. From his position on my lap, he pulled back and looked at me. I didn't say anything.

"Vivi went away," he said.

"I know."

He hiccupped an errant sob. "Why?"

"Why? Well, because it was time for them to go. They seemed kind of happy, didn't you think?"

"But they weren't *old*."

"No," I said quietly, "but sometimes young people die, honey. They get sick, they have accidents."

"I *know*," he said, apparently beginning to feel a little better.

"You do?"

"Chloe's *sister*," he said insistently.

The eight-year-old sister of one of his nursery school classmates, Chloe Barsamian, had drowned in a freak accident, while on vacation in Maine with her family. As Madeline had also attended the school, several years earlier, the kids, parents, and teachers had all been rocked by the tragedy.

Suddenly, I felt a wave of unease. All week long, I'd been rolling around in my mind the consequences of Henry's sharing my gifts. But what if our abilities *weren't* the same? What if he could see and do things that I couldn't? What if he could see *into* the white light and *beyond* it, capabilities I absolutely did not have. What if he had been frightened not by the sudden departure of his pal, but by something else, something terrifying and soul-shattering?

What if there was *nothing* on the other side? What if Henry had watched the three of them step into the light and then— evaporate? Or float off into the endless darkness that was the universe, met by no one and nothing, no mother, no father, no God, no—eternal anything? I felt a growing sense of dread. I wanted to ask him, but now *I* was the one who was beginning to tremble. Did I really want to know? What if this *was* all there was? What if what really lay on the other side of the light was not a joyous reunion with those we loved, and those who loved us, but simple and final oblivion?

And what if Henry had seen that and would have to go through life, alone among the human race, with absolute personal knowledge that the soul did not live on, but flickered out like a candle in a breeze. Plenty of people believed that, of course, but no one really knew. How would that singular knowledge affect Henry's life?

If this was the ball game, I didn't really *want* to know. On the other hand, if this was the ball game, and Henry knew it, then I really *had* to know, because my main job in life is to be his mom, and I had to be able to help him, if there was any way I could.

I took a deep breath. "What did you see?" I asked. "In the light."

He had gotten up from my lap and was walking toward the road. He seemed to have pulled himself together in the last couple of moments, and the barking of a dog rang out in the stillness.

"A lady and a man," he answered.

A lady and a man?

"You mean Emilia?" I asked.

"No! Another lady."

"And a man?" I asked, but this time he didn't answer. The barking of the dog was getting closer, and it was a happy bark, the bark of a cheerful pet being taken out for a late-night walk.

Henry astonished me by skipping toward the street. Hadn't he just been disconsolate not a minute and a half ago?

I took in one of the deepest breaths of my life. We could

take this up again at another time. He would let me know when he was ready, and until then, the nugget of information he had imparted was quite enough for me—*someone* seemed to have been there for Vivi and Jamey.

I quickly got up and followed Henry out onto the main road, the one that encircles the island. There wasn't a car in sight. I dug in my pocket and found my cell phone. I pulled up my contacts, located Bert's number, and hit Send.

The dog came into sight just as Bert picked up the phone. It was a gangly puppy, all legs, a retriever of some kind, maybe a year old. It loped toward Henry with all the abandon of a twin recognizing its twin, from whom it was separated at birth.

"Hi," I said, when Bert picked up. I hurried toward the road, where the puppy was now jumping up on Henry. "Can you pick me up in forty-five minutes?"

I didn't hear his answer, because the wildly friendly dog had knocked Henry onto the ground and was now on top of him.

"Henry!" I shouted, dropping the phone as I raced over to help. "No!" I yelled sharply, watching the nipping and barking grow increasingly aggressive. The dog had gained dominance and he knew it. He was really giving Henry the business. Where was this bad boy's owner?

"No!" I screamed again. The dog nipped at my foot as I tried to kick him away, and then I remembered advice I'd gotten from a surgeon once, while he was stitching up my hand after I'd tried to help a friend's puppy that was caught up in a nasty fight. "Pull the dog's tail," the doctor had said.

I grabbed the dog's tail and pulled it as hard as I could.

He yelped in pain and let go. Henry scrambled backward into a thicket of brambles as two men, one of them presumably the owner of the dog, hurried in our direction. Out of the corner of my eye, I saw the taller of the men snap a leash onto the puppy's collar. Henry was crying again, so I picked him up, trying to discern if he had been hurt or was just scared and scraped up.

"Did he bite you?" I asked.

Henry needed all his lung power to produce the volume of sound that was shattering the calm; he didn't have any air with which to answer my question. I set him down on the grass and began to inspect his arms and legs.

The man with the dog hurried over, and I instinctively shouted, "Get away! Get that dog away!"

I was shocked at the ferocity of my own voice. Fortunately, I wasn't finding any puncture wounds; no streams of blood were trickling down Henry's limbs.

"He's all right," the man said.

He's all right? How did this stranger know that? And even if it were true, despite the owner's clear lack of caution, was *that* all he had to say after *his* dog had knocked the daylights out of *my* child?

I stood up and glared at him. It was Senator Rawlings, out for a midnight stroll with another man, who seemed to be in his twenties. I remembered seeing him at the party. I wondered now if he might be the senator's son.

I was brought up to respect people in authority. My father would have been horrified at how I behaved next, but my protective parent's switch had been thrown, and I couldn't control the effects of the adrenaline.

"I think the proper thing to say," I snapped, "would be 'I'm very sorry.' "

The senator made a face, taken aback by my lack of bowing and scraping in his presence.

"He seems fine, dear. I think you're overreacting."

Dear? Had he just called me *dear?*

I took a deep breath, struggling to rein in my impulse to haul off and deck the guy. But I had other weapons at my disposal, and the urge to use them gathered force like a rogue wave. I wanted to hurt this smug, sneaky, selfish stuffed shirt, even at the risk of getting myself into trouble. I wished I didn't have Henry right here, but I swept him up in my arms, ready to walk proudly off as soon as I dropped my bombshells. Besides, a senator wouldn't *dare* threaten a woman with a small child.

"I've got a couple of things to say to you, *Senator.*"

"Oh? Well, *please*," he answered condescendingly.

I fired my first volley. "I know what you're up to."

"Up to?" The two men exchanged a bemused glance, which was like pouring lighter fluid onto my coals.

"I don't appreciate being used like this."

"Used? In what way, might I ask?" The senator's companion, a lanky cowboy type in jeans and a faded barn jacket, stepped forward protectively. It occurred to me for the first time that he might be more of a bodyguard than a friend. I didn't care.

I shifted Henry's weight and took a deep breath. "Yes, *used*, in your sneaky effort to block something that's really, really important not only to this island, but also to the planet. And the future."

"I have no idea what you're talking about. I don't know where you're getting your information, but—"

I interrupted him. "I know all about the Lenox Consortium. I know about the Itzkoffs and the McKeenes and their connection to you and all your nearest and dearest at RMI. I know about Elsa Corbett and the OLF, and so does Chief

McGill, courtesy of a friend of mine in the Boston Police Department."

At this mention, Henry perked up. "Daddy?"

"The police would be interested to know that Elsa was at your party."

I saw some headlights coming toward us, fast, and I was glad, because having said my piece, I was now ready to stomp away. I felt a little relieved to see someone else on the road, because I now understood that this had been a pretty bad idea, spouting off like this on a dark, deserted road, where no one would come to my aid if I needed it.

The cowboy grabbed me by the arm and tried to whirl me around.

"Who the hell do you think you are?" he growled. "You don't know who you're threatening here."

"Ow!" I said. "Let go! You're hurting me!"

The dog began to bark as the vehicle disappeared around a bend and then came back into sight. It was almost upon us, racing toward the other side of the island, when I realized it wasn't a car, but a truck; and not just any old truck, a truck with Bert at the wheel.

"Bert!" I screamed, and he screeched on the brakes. He reached into the space behind his seat, and when he stepped out of the truck and onto the road, leaving the engine running, I saw what he had in his hand: the harpoon.

The man let go of my arm. I put Henry down, shouting, "Get in the truck."

Holding the harpoon in front of him, Bert swept his gaze across the scene, taking in our faces one by one.

"Everything okay here?" he asked. I hurried to his side and turned to face Rawlings and his companion.

"Fine," Rawlings said evenly. "We're just out for a breath of fresh air."

"You know Senator Rawlings, don't you, Bert?" I asked.

"I don't think I've had the pleasure," said Bert flatly.

We drove right to the house of Chief McGill, and for the next hour, over a pot of coffee, with Henry dozing on the rec room couch, we filled him in on everything that had happened in the previous half hour, everything Mark had dug up on Rawlings, and everything Dec had told me earlier in the day. McGill had had a message that Declan had called, but the two men hadn't yet connected.

How much of this was criminally actionable, McGill didn't yet know. It wasn't a crime for a nonprofit foundation to commission an environmental impact study, even if the results were less than objective. Nor was it a crime for Rawlings to invite someone to a cocktail party, even if that someone was later shown to have committed criminal acts. Elsa Corbett had been detained and brought to Providence for questioning, but she might or might not be convicted, depending on whether they could get a fingerprint match. It was one thing to smell the smoke, the chief admitted, and another to find the fire.

"What about Elsa's boyfriend?" I asked. "Did you ever find him?"

McGill shook his head.

"You think he's still on the island?" Bert asked.

"I think he probably is. But he's not staying in that house. He's got to be bunking with somebody else."

"Do you know what his name is?"

"Alfred McKeene. Goes by Freddy."

"Do you know what he looks like?" I asked.

"Tall, fair, late twenties. There's no one by that name who owns property on the island, so he's got to be staying with a friend. We've been watching the ferries. Course he could just sail across, if he had access to the right boat."

"Does Rawlings have any kids?" I asked the chief.

"Two daughters from his first marriage. They'd be, oh, in their thirties by now. I haven't seen them around."

"Does he have any security?"

McGill shook his head.

A moment later, he said, "You think that Rawlings is involved in this? *Personally* involved?"

"Depends what you mean by 'personally,'" I said. "But you might want to pay him a visit. He had a young guy with him tonight. It might have been Freddy McKeene."

We found my cell phone back by the side of the road. Bert had heard it drop, heard me screeching for the dog to get off Henry, heard the dog barking while Henry screamed. The call had never disconnected and Bert had hurried to try to help us.

The line was still open when I fished the phone out of the brambles.

"I doubt I'll be able to sleep," I said after Bert carried Henry upstairs and we put him to bed. "I never should have drunk all that coffee."

Bert smiled. "Plan B?"

"What's that?"

"Lie in the back of the truck and stare up at the stars? Watch the sun come up?"

I could hardly think of anything nicer. "Think Lauren would mind if I borrowed some blankets?"

"I've got blankets," Bert said.

Which was how we came to be lying on the beach just opposite the Grand View at four thirty on Sunday morning. The truck bed was uncomfortable, so we dragged the blankets over to the sand and put one beneath us and one on top. We had been fooling around and talking and laughing and fooling around for quite a long time when, in the quiet broken only by the gentle lapping of the waves, I felt tears gathering in my eyes.

"What's wrong?" Bert asked.

I shook my head, and the tears spilled over. "I like you," I whispered.

"What's wrong with that? I like you, too."

"No, I mean, I *really* like you."

"I *really* like you, too."

I looked over at him. He grinned and nodded.

"So what are we going to do?" I whined.

"About liking each other?"

I nodded and sniffed.

"Keep doing it?" he suggested.

Chapter Twenty-eight

SUNDAY

I NEVER COULD CONVINCE Baden to leave.

He stood by my side as nearly three dozen earthbound spirits filed, one by one, through the shining doorway to the other side, which I had called up for them on the tower of the Southeast Lighthouse.

As I watched them go, I tried to connect them to the nightmarish stories I had read earlier in the week. Which of the spirits had died in the lifeboats, and which in their berths? Could the little girl holding the hand of a ghost I assumed to be her mother possibly be the child for whom the birthday cake had been ordered? And there, I assumed, was the man who had slit his throat in the lifeboat, driven mad by the effects of wind and ice. Off to the side, taking the arm of each spirit as he or she approached the brilliant doorway, was certainly one of the ship's officials. He seemed to have assumed a supervisory role, standing respectfully at attention beside the person next in line to enter the doorway. It was as though having failed to shepherd his passengers safely to New York on that night more than a hundred years ago, he was now determined to escort them graciously from this life.

It was a strange experience. A heavy fog all but obscured the individual phantoms; they seemed in their ghostly grayness to be part and parcel of the early-morning mists enshrouding the whole of the island, and I suppose, in some dreary and ephemeral way, they were.

Perhaps it was my lack of sleep, or the feeling of being suspended in time and space that fog on an island induces, but the ghosts seemed not to be crossing over in the way I am accustomed to spirits crossing over. They seemed to be entering the lighthouse tower, and when the last of the phantoms had disappeared, and I had shut down the light and was walking back to the Grand View with Baden, I couldn't shake the feeling that all of them were trapped in the tower, rather than joyfully experiencing the first, long-awaited moments of their liberation.

"But I don't understand," I said to Baden.

"Am I the first to refuse your help?" he asked.

"Well, actually, you are."

"Ah! I see."

"What's that supposed to mean?"

"It's a new experience for you. To have your assistance refused."

"It's not that," I insisted.

"No? Then what is it?"

I shook my head. "Is it—since you don't believe in God, or in the possibility of anything being over there, on the other side—"

"What happened today gave me pause, I must admit," Baden conceded. "There were certain—indications I could not ignore."

"It does make sense, though," I said. "If you don't believe

there's water down below, why would you want to jump off the cliff?"

"I love *life*," Baden finally explained. "I'd like to be *with* life and *around* life for as long as I possibly can."

"And," I teased, "you know I'm coming back sometime this summer."

"I do," he said.

***

The fog had all burned off by noon, revealing placid seas under a sky the blue of a robin's egg. It actually smelled like spring, so we all took our coffee out to the front porch and left the brunch dishes spread out in the dining room. Lauren and I took the chairs in the corner, where I could keep an eye on Henry, who was playing in the side yard.

"I don't know how to thank you," said Lauren.

"Thank me for what?"

"I don't know how you did it, but—"

"Did what?" I gave her an evasive little grin. The less said, the better.

She tilted her head toward Dayne and Gavin, on the other side of the porch. They were leaving on the same boat we were taking. Only one of their sensors had been restored to working order, and while the camera turned on, its lens was cracked. There wasn't much point to their remaining on the island.

"Thank you for having us," I said, determined to steer the conversation away from all things ghostly. I hadn't allowed myself really to think about our leaving, and I'd been so busy, I'd hardly had time. Now, suddenly, I felt like crying.

I have one good girlfriend, Nat, but nothing like what I'd experienced this week: friends eating dinner together all the time, in and out of each other's lives many times a week. Lauren was great. So was Mark. I wished we lived near each other, so I could help them when the baby came along and sit having tea with her at her kitchen table.

"You're coming back this summer, right?" she said, as though reading my thoughts.

"Yeah."

"You'll be amazed at the difference. It's like another place."

"I like it like this."

"So do I," she said moodily. "I never thought I'd say that." She turned and reached out for my hand.

"So don't say good-bye." She gave my hand a squeeze.

I squeezed back. "I won't."

Bert drove us down to the ferry and piled all our bags and boxes by the side of the boat. They were immediately taken up by a member of the crew and stowed somewhere inside. Bert knew the ferry's captain and asked the weathered old seaman if Henry could sit up front with the crew.

"Can I trust him?" the captain teased, in a heavy Scottish brogue.

"You bet you can," Bert replied. "He's a good sailor."

"Can he swim?" the captain asked, and Henry glanced nervously at me.

"He won't need to swim if you do *your* job," Bert shot back.

I leaned down and whispered, "He's only kidding, honey."

The captain took Henry by the hand and led him away, leaving Bert and me to be awkward with each other.

"Safe trip," Bert said formally.

"Thanks. Thanks for everything."

He nodded and glanced out at the horizon. "Should be a smooth crossing."

"You'd know."

"Not always, but I think you'll be fine today. How will you get home from the boat?"

"Grab a cab."

"Good, yeah."

Bert raised his eyes and then waved to a member of the crew. I turned around and saw that final preparations for departure were under way: the gangplank connecting the dock and the boat was about to be slid aboard.

"Take care," I said, longing to say something witty and charming and full of just the right kind of feeling, the kind that wouldn't embarrass him and yet would communicate the fact that I was crazy about him and couldn't wait to see him again.

I wasn't able to think of anything.

Nor was he, apparently.

He leaned over and gave me a swift kiss on the cheek.

I searched his eyes. They were warm and kind, but firm and resolved.

I could have made this harder, by getting all mushy and saying all the wrong things, but I could tell he didn't want that, and neither did I.

"See you soon," I said brightly, and then I turned and walked away.

"The sooner the better," I heard him call.

And that did it. I turned and saw the grin on his face, then raced back and threw my arms around him one last time, breathing in the scent of his coat and his hair and the sea and the hint of aftershave that reminded me of my dad's. The crew blew the whistle. I had to get on. I gave him one last kiss on the side of his neck and pulled myself away.

Chapter Twenty-nine

❦

JULY

THE LARCHMONT COLLECTION was opened to the public in the middle of July. The celebration went on all weekend. There were two lectures: one on the historical uses of Long Island Sound, from commercial fishing to travel and recreation, and a second on the tragedy itself, a gripping and dramatic account of the fateful few days by a maritime hobbyist, a retired navy admiral now living in Little Compton.

On Sunday afternoon, a professor of art history from Brown, a specialist in photography, gave a talk called "The Brownie: Into the Hands of Everyman (and -woman)." After her lecture, we all walked upstairs to the cramped but freshly painted rooms displaying the photographs of Honor Morton. There hadn't been enough money to frame them all, but I'd personally cut sixty-four window mats from stiff, cream-colored stock, and we'd set the matted photographs on pushpins encircling the two upstairs rooms. Over the course of the three-day celebration, 179 people signed the guest book, trudged up the stairs, and filed past the images that had never been seen before, except by our eyes and the artist's.

On Sunday night, there was a dance in the ballroom of the Ashmont Hotel. The music, played by a seven-piece orchestra called the Mill Stream Boys, was all waltzes and show tunes from a hundred years ago, and Bert and I shared a table with Lauren and Mark and Aitana and Peter. As usual, in my rush to get Henry packed and off for the weekend with Declan and Kelly, I hadn't given enough thought to the clothes I would need, so Lauren loaned me a green chiffon dress and Aitana talked me into wearing a pair of her heels, heels so high that after a couple of dances, I had no choice but to spend the rest of the evening barefoot. You can't just start wearing high, high heels when you're almost thirty years old. You need toes that have grown to meet in a point.

Conspicuously absent from the weekend's festivities was the senior senator from Rhode Island. According to the aide who had phoned Caleb on Thursday afternoon, the senator had been called to Washington on urgent committee business, but in my opinion, shared by everyone around the table, the crisis was more personal than legislative.

The previous Wednesday, a piece had appeared on the front page of the *Boston Globe*, written by none other than Mark's friend and confidant Andrew Fuller. According to the article, the Project on Government Oversight, an independent non-profit that investigates charges of political corruption and misconduct, had called for a probe into the links between RMI Partners, the Lenox Consortium, and Senator Rawlings, particularly relating to issues of alternative energy. The piece suggested that Rawlings might be guilty of conflict of interest, and further referenced RMI Partners' recent forays into wind and solar power technology.

The article had been picked up by the Associated Press and

had garnered national attention. No mention had been made of links to the Oceanic Liberation Front, but Andrew had been apprised of our suspicions. He was looking into all that now.

This probably should have been the highlight of the weekend for me, but it came in a distant third.

Second place was occupied by a conversation I had with an elderly farmer who came dressed in his work clothes to the lectures and the art opening. He was Honor Morton's second cousin. His grandfather Lawrence Ames had been ten years younger than Honor's mother, Phyllida, who had married a man named Marcus Morton. Honor had not ended her own life, I was awfully happy to hear. She had died of tuberculosis in a sanitarium in Massachusetts.

As excited as I was to learn more about the elusive photographer, I was even happier with the latter part of our conversation. Hugo explained that as he was getting on in years and no longer interested in working eighteen hours a day, he had decided to divest himself of some property he owned on the island. The parcel in question consisted of a small barn built entirely of fieldstones, and an open meadow giving onto an unobstructed view of the sea. Over the course of the weekend, Hugo had come to feel that the *Larchmont* Collection deserved a place of its own on the island. Did I think that the Historical Society might welcome a gift of the barn and the land, so as to create a permanent home for the photographs, books, and mementoes?

Did I ever! Not only would his cousin's photographs, my very favorite part of the exhibit, receive the permanent display they so clearly deserved, but this might be the solution to the problem of my promise to the ghosts! I began to envision a serene and glorious garden, with wooden benches and paths of crushed seashells and a breathtaking view of the sea. I walked Hugo over to Caleb and made the introduction. And then I went looking for Bert.

In my ranking of the things that had happened on Block Island, my time with him occupied place number one. All my efforts to tie the experience up in a neat little package have completely failed. It's a series of happy images and memories, pieces I take out and arrange and rearrange, like a toddler on the floor with colorful blocks. Being out on his boat as the sun is setting. Cooking lobsters. Seeing shooting stars—some in the sky and some behind my eyelids. The hike that took four hours. The breakfast that took three.

I could go on and on, for there was literally nothing I saw, ate, drank, heard, or felt in my three days on the island that didn't rest somewhere on the spectrum between pretty fantastic and absolutely great. We have plans for another weekend in August, and our phone calls and e-mails are getting more frequent.

Only one thing made me sad that weekend: I never caught sight of Baden again. He was obviously avoiding me, and I finally understood why.

The why had weighed nearly nine pounds and was twenty-one and a half inches long at birth. The name bestowed upon him by his very proud mother and father was Christopher Baden Riegler.

As for that check, I tore it up. Caleb paid all the suppliers directly, and I did the work for the balance in my spiritual checkbook. There was no point in telling Caleb this, so I didn't. It was a little tight at the end of April, but I've been there before and I'm sure I'll be there again. There are worse things in life than having to eat a little more pasta.

In the grand scheme of things, my refusal to cash the check probably didn't make a bit of difference. But you do what you can do. It mattered to me.

Jay's probably right: I should get a real job.

I'll have to give that some thought.

ACKNOWLEDGMENTS

My husband, Ted, for his love and encouragement in all areas of my life. Our daughters, Amber and Tara, for keeping me young at heart.

Jennifer Gates, my literary agent, for doing your job so well; you are incredible. The support from Lane Zachary and the staff at Zachary Schuster Harmsworth.

Maureen Foley, your amazing skill; you have gotten better and better. It is a privilege to work with you.

Thanks to Three Rivers Press and our editor, Heather Lazare, for being so available and supportive.

Scott Schwimmer, for all of your legal guidance done with such love and humor.

All of my relatives and friends. Thank you for all of your love and support.

Thank you to every earthbound spirit I have met or will meet. You all have a story to tell.

Thank you, God, for my abilities. I know that they are Your gift to me.

——MARY ANN WINKOWSKI

I offer warm thanks to Lane Zachary, Mary Ann Winkowski, Jennifer Gates, Heather Lazare, Dyana Messina, Sibylle Kazeroid, and Cindy Berman. For their generous provision of a quiet place in which to write, I am most grateful to Sarah Baker and Tim Albright. For insights about Block Island, I am indebted to Susan Kenyon, Rick Abrams, and Justin Abrams. And I extend my deepest gratitude to my beloved children and husband: Charlie, Grace, and Rob Laubacher.

——MAUREEN FOLEY

ABOUT THE AUTHORS

MARY ANN WINKOWSKI is the author of *When Ghosts Speak*. She is a paranormal investigator who has collaborated closely with several federal agencies and is the high-profile consultant for the CBS series *Ghost Whisperer*. Visit her online at www.maryannwinkowski.com.

MAUREEN FOLEY is the acclaimed writer, producer, and director of the films *American Wake* and the award-winning *Home Before Dark*. Visit her online at www.hazelwoodfilms.com.

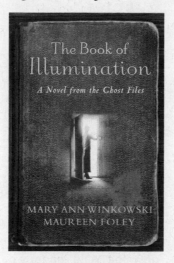